"She's definitely not dead," he added, pushing to his full six foot plus height. His rich chocolate gaze locked with mine. "Not yet anyway."

"You're not making me feel any better." Talk about the wrong thing to say to a sexual demon. His gaze brightened, gleaming a brilliant gold. Heat rolled off his sexy body, curling around me and luring me closer.

He had short, dark hair that looked as if he'd just rolled out of bed and shoved a hand through it. He wore a brown Henley that hugged his broad shoulders and accented a narrow waist. Faded jeans clung to his long, muscular legs. He had bed-room eyes and perfect white teeth and more sex appeal than Eric Bana, Brad Pitt and my favorite clerk at the Starbucks all rolled into one.

Talk about some serious temptation.

"I'm in a relationship," I blurted. "A happy, committed, monogamous relationship. With Ty," I added on the off chance that guys didn't talk about these things. Ash and Ty crossed paths on occasion, but I couldn't really see them having a heart-to-heart. Especially since demon Ash didn't actually have a heart and Ty's ticker had been dead for quite some time now.

Also by Kimberly Raye
published by Ballantine Books

DEAD END DATING
DEAD AND DATELESS
YOUR COFFIN OR MINE?
JUST ONE BITE

A Dead-End Dating Novel

Sucker for Love

Kimberly Raye

BALLANTINE BOOKS • NEW YORK

Sucker for Love is a work of fiction. Names, characters, places, and incidents are the products of the author's imagination or are used fictitiously. Any resemblance to actual events, locales, or persons, living or dead, is entirely coincidental.

A Ballantine Books Mass Market Original

Copyright © 2009 by Kimberly Raye Groff
Excerpt from *Here Comes the Vampire* copyright © 2009 by Kimberly Raye Groff

Published in the United States by Ballantine Books, an imprint of The Random House Publishing Group, a division of Random House, Inc., New York.

BALLANTINE and colophon are registered trademarks of Random House, Inc.

This book contains an excerpt from the forthcoming book *Here Comes the Vampire* by Kimberly Raye. This excerpt has been set for this edition only and may not reflect the final content of the forthcoming edition.

ISBN 978-0-345-50366-4

Cover illustration: Kathleen Lynch, based on photographs © andrearan/ Shutterstock (woman), Serhio Grey/ Shutterstock (lollipop)

Printed in the United States of America

www.ballantinebooks.com

OPM   9 8 7 6 5 4 3 2 1

For my ultra-fab editor, Kate Collins,
for your encouragement, support, and enthusiasm.
I feel truly blessed to have you!

Acknowledgments

Writing is a tough business. Sometimes I want to pull out my hair. Sometimes I want to scream. And sometimes I even want to whip out the Classifieds, put an end to my misery, and get a real job. The thing is, I love writing and, really, it's just too cool!

So to those key people who keep me plotting my life away (instead of banging out burgers at the local McDonald's), I want to say THANK YOU, THANK YOU, *THANK YOU*.

My agent, Natasha Kern—what would I do without you?

My writing BFFs Nina Bangs and Gerry Bartlett—you guys rock.

My own megalicious hottie, Curt Groff—you give good reality check.

The wonderful staff at Ballantine Books—I owe you guys big-time.

And to all of the readers who've fallen in love with Lil as much as I have—I truly couldn't do this without you!

One

❤ ❤ ❤

Are you tired of nursing down that bottle of O+ all by your lonesome? Did you spend the last full moon drinking Cosmos and lusting over the American Kennel Club finals? Do you spend every evening scarfing a Hungry Man (or woman) and watching TiVo?

If your first reaction was Uh-oh or How'd she know that? to any of the above, then you are cordially invited to a meet and greet dinner party, hosted by Dead End Dating, Manhattan's number one matchmaking service for vampires, humans and Others. Join fantabulous host (and incredibly well-dressed vampire) Lil Marchette for a night of dinner and dancing and romance in the penthouse of the Waldorf Astoria.

Disclaimer—DED is an equal opportunity dating

*service that does not discriminate based on race,
sex, looks (or lack of) or appetite. Net worth, however, is an entirely different matter—i.e., don't forget the checkbook, debit card and/or Visa Gold.*

I propped up the framed copy of the engraved
vellum invitation I'd mailed out to every appropri-
ate single in Manhattan and tried to calm the but-
terflies in my stomach.

I'm the Countess Lilliana Arrabella Guinevere du
Marchette (Lil for short), a five-hundred-year-old
(and holding) born vampire. I've got super-fab taste
in clothes, a to-die-for collection of MAC cosmetics
and a hot, hunky, bounty-hunting boyfriend. I *so*
had it going on.

Ix-nay the nerves, right?

Wrong.

I'm also the owner of Dead End Dating, Manhattan's primo matchmaking service for vampires,
weres, Others and even the occasional human. As of
five minutes ago, I had exactly one week to match up
over a dozen paid-in-full clients, otherwise I failed
to make good on my Find-your-one-and-only-in-six-
months-or-get-your-money-back! guarantee.

Since I didn't do refunds (not unless I wanted to
return half my wardrobe and say *bye-bye* to my
new iPhone), I had to pick up the pace. Pronto.

Hence, my latest super-fantabulous brainstorm—

the meet and greet dinner party about to happen right here. Right now.

I drew a deep breath (not because I had to, but, hey, when in Rome . . .), straightened my green Roberto Cavalli dress (a floor-length, strappy chiffon number à la Rihanna) and finished setting up the hostess table. I added DED business cards, name tags, promotional pens, koozies and calendars, even a few pics and testimonials from previous clients. I sprinkled some rose petals and debated whether or not to hand out the Viagra samples in my bag or just spike the drinks when no one was looking.

I knew none of the born vamps in attendance would need a little penis pick-me-up (our entire existence revolved around sex—we were conceived via the nasty, we stopped aging when we lost our virginity, we chose an eternity mate based on orgasm quotients and fertility ratings), but what about the dozens of Others out there? FYI: While I'd been spreading the love to the wealthy and weird for several months now, I'd led a very pampered, sheltered, elitist existence in all the 499 plus years before then (emphasis on *elitist*). In other words, I wasn't exactly Dr. Drew when it came to mating habits of the various species.

The only thing I did know for sure? The hornier the clients, the lower the standards, the sooner everyone paired up.

I eyeballed the bag a split second before stashing

it, complete with samples, under the table. What? So I'm a romantic. I freely admit it (to anyone except my ma, that is).

"Help!"

The frantic voice drew my attention and I turned just as a frustrated blonde rushed up to me.

Evie Dalton could man the phones, key in profiles, text multiple clients and suck down a steaming latte—all without smudging her lip gloss. She was the best assistant a vampire could ask for. She was also human, and completely unaware of my fanged and fabulous status.

The 411 on tonight?

She thought it was just another movie theme party. Like the toga fever spawned by *Animal House* and the fifties sock hops à la *Grease*. Tonight's brain candy? Contemporary monster mania courtesy of the barrage of recent horror movies such as *30 Days of Night* and *The Mist*.

In honor of the occasion, she'd donned a silver jacket with eight sparkly "legs," a sequined mini–smock dress and three-inch glitter sandals. She looked like Spidey's wet dream. So good in fact that, with the exception of a fading bruise on her neck and some seriously rank breath, it was impossible to tell that just two short weeks ago she'd been possessed by a demon. *And* that she'd come this close to heading downtown (way, *way* down) to become Satan's own personal bee-yotch.

I'd been so busy hiding her from the long arm of

the Prince brothers (a hot, hunky trio of demon hunters who just so happened to be demons themselves) that I'd sort of let the rest of my work pile up.

The demon was now back in hell, the Prince brothers were back to making women drool and rounding up hell's Most Wanted, Evie was back in the office (and munching Tic Tacs) and I was making up for lost time.

"Say cheese." She snapped several pics with her digital camera before handing me a clipboard and a copy of the invitation. "I need you to take these and brief Nina while I get them to relocate the flambé table ASAP. The fangs on the ice sculpture are melting. Thankfully I got a picture for our brochure before they completely dissolved."

Evie had decided that free donuts and coffee weren't enough. We needed a high quality, full color brochure to pimp our services. She'd found a rock-bottom price (courtesy of her computer savvy/sexual deviant cousin—think small furry animals) and I'd jumped at the idea.

"Now," she declared, turning and glancing around the crowded foyer. "Where the hell is that catering manager?"

"Why not just hike the air-conditioning down?" I suggested.

"Won't the guests be cold?"

"They'll be more inclined to pair up and snuggle."

She grinned. "I knew there was a reason you were the boss." She handed me a small box with a corsage.

"Make sure Nina puts this on, too. *If* you can find her. One minute she was at the bar sucking down a Bloody Mary and the next—*poof*—gone. Vanished into thin air."

Or the nearest storage closet.

"I knew it," I declared when I threw open a nearby door to find the MIA Nina.

Nina Lancaster—aka Nina One, the blond half of The Ninas, who'd been my best friends since birth— was the daughter of filthy rich hotelier Victor Lancaster, who owned the Waldorf along with several five star establishments throughout New York and Paris. Nina was rich, beautiful (big surprise, right?) and living with my middle brother, Rob. They'd been seeing each other since I'd hooked them up a few months ago. Judging by the spaghetti straps that sagged near her elbows and my brother's untucked button-down shirt, they'd been about to see a lot more of each other in the next five minutes.

I glanced at Rob. His eyes were glazed and hooded. His fangs gleamed. A hungry growl vibrated the air.

Okay, make that the next five *seconds*.

Anxiety rushed through me. "Can you please boff my brother on your own time?"

"I'm not boffing him." She grinned and tugged her straps back into place. "Not yet." She touched a hand to her mussed hair. "Besides, this isn't your time. I donated the ballroom, so that makes it *my* time."

She had a point.

I traded in pissed-off client for desperately needy

friend. "But I need you to screen guests at the entrance."

"Get Evie to do it," she said as Rob leaned in to nibble at her neck.

"I'm sending her back to the office on a 'dating emergency.' I want her out of here before the party's in full swing." Which was why I'd purposely scheduled a new client this evening. My plan? To pretend I'd forgotten the newbie. I would then beg Evie to handle the profile meeting while I stayed and captured pics for the infamous brochure. "She's the best assistant in the world. I can't have her wind up as some vampire's sex slave, or the midnight snack for a hungry werewolf."

Or worse, realize that the fangs I was sporting were the real deal. I wasn't ready to break the born vamp's number one commandment—Thou Shalt Keep a Low Profile—and come out of the closet to Evie. My mother would kill me. Even worse, I wasn't sure if Evie was ready to work for a vamp. So far, she'd been wonderful. But it was a lot to swallow and I just wasn't sure whether she'd take me out for chocolate martinis to celebrate or call in the rowdy villagers. I hadn't gone into mega credit card debt decorating my office to have the whole thing wind up torched.

Rob kept nibbling and Nina all but swooned.

"Hello? Did you hear a word I said? I've got a no-human policy happening here."

"You're talking," Rob murmured, "but there's nothing coming out."

I leaned in and pinched my brother. He paused to glare and I appealed to Nina again. "Evie won't be here. She *can't* be. You have to do it."

"Who says?" she asked as Rob resumed his nibbling.

"Your best friend in the entire universe." I gave her a knowing smile. "We're practically sisters. You know you'd do anything to help me."

"Which is why I loaned you the ballroom for free."

"And I totally appreciate it, but I still need this one teensy, tiny favor."

"Tonight's my night off." In addition to being Daddy's Little Vamp, Nina was also the hotel's chief hostess. "I just showed up to tell you to make sure that nobody gets blood on the white settees. Daddy will kill me."

"I'm willing to beg."

"I'm a born vampire. We're not genetically wired for sympathy."

"Are we genetically wired for greed? Because I'm willing to pay."

She grinned and shooed away Rob's hands. "What'd you have in mind?"

I did a mental of my most recent purchases, singling out the key items that I knew would melt her hard-ass resolve. "Ferragamo sunglasses?"

"I've got three pairs."

"Michael Kors bangle bracelets?"

"Got 'em."

"Hermès lipstick compact."

She shook her head. "There's no such thing."

"If you think so." I shrugged a shoulder. "But I just happen to have one from the insanely small, limited edition collection purchased by a select few clients who have the right connections." In this case, a bisexual sales assistant at Barneys who I'd glammed ages ago. I'd been scamming primo purchases ever since. "But if you're not interested—"

"Okay, okay. I'm going." She gave Rob an apologetic smile. "Sorry, babe. What can I say? I'm shallow."

He grinned and dropped a quick kiss on her lips. "Just one of the many things I love about you."

Awwww . . .

My heart swelled for about an eighth of a second before I remembered who was actually in the closet with Nina.

My very own flesh-and-blood *brother*.

Middle-born son of Countess Jacqueline and Count Pierre Gustavo Marchette of the French Dourdou Valley.

Descendant of one of the first (and snottiest) born vamp families in existence.

Propagator of the species and all-around playa playa.

And he'd just used the *L word*.

Shut. *Up*.

Before I could find my voice, Nina grabbed my hand and hauled me off toward the entrance to the ballroom. "What color?"

Rob. Nina. Love? "What color what?"

"The lipstick case." She nudged me, shattering my thoughts. "What color is it?"

I shook away my sudden excitement and focused on the here and now. "Hot pink with rhinestones and Swarovski crystals."

"No way."

"And there's even a tiny diamond inlay on the inside mirror near the Hermès logo."

She squealed and snatched the corsage from my hands. A few seconds later, she had a single red rose pinned on the bodice of her Carolina Herrera original and the clipboard in hand. "I'm armed and ready. What do you want me to do?"

"Just greet everyone and check invitations. No one gets inside without one."

"What if he's cute?"

"It doesn't matter. No invitation, no party."

"Well dressed?"

"Hand him a business card, talk us up and send him on his way."

"Rich?"

"Stick a name tag on him and send him in." What can I say? This vamp had her priorities.

After a few more instructions (pass out an extra pack of DED promotional mints to all weres, hand over cologne samples to every demon, ask blood type preference for vamps), I left Nina at the entrance and headed inside to see the end result of eight days of wicked stress and frantic planning.

The room was huge, with ornate frieze work and gleaming black marble. A large dance floor had been set up in the very center, the circular area surrounded by clusters of round tables covered in crisp white linens. A polished silver candelabra dominated the center of each table. A black napkin tied with gold filigree rope adorned every place setting. Candlelight flickered, making the china and crystal sparkle. Moonlight filtered through the wall of glass windows behind the small (I'm on a budget, all right?) but tasteful band I'd booked for tonight.

The place oozed romantic ambience, and for the first time since I'd started planning the event, I actually believed that it might work. Up to that point I'd been running on sheer desperation and crazy hope.

My gaze shifted to the far corner of the room and the huge silver fountain flowing with champagne. Next to that sat a Bloody Mary bar. Mary herself wasn't in attendance (not yet anyway—my mother *had* sent her an invitation on my behalf), but there was plenty of AB–, vodka and Tabasco sauce to keep the vamps happy. Next to that sat a meat lover's buffet sporting everything from roast beef to lamb chops. The food was barely cooked (we're talking *rare*) and plentiful for the weres. For the demons? Several gleaming silver tureens filled with split pea soup. Add a dessert bar with everything from fudge overboard to raspberry cheesecake for the few fairies who'd been invited, and there was a little something for everyone.

In fact, the entire room reminded me of the "It's a Small World" ride at Disneyland. I had the sudden urge to sing "Kumbaya."

Or, in this case, "Monster Mash."

Everything looked absolutely perfect.

Which should have been my first clue of the coming disaster. I mean, really. A roomful of vamps, d-men, weres and fairies? Talk about a massacre just waiting to happen.

The first to draw blood? A hot-looking brother from down under. At least, I *thought* he was a demon since I couldn't smell him (nix vamp), nor could I read his thoughts (forget human) and he didn't look ready to howl at the moon (so *not* a were).

His name was Justin Something-or-other and he was über hot. I wasn't sure where he'd come from (he wasn't on my guest list), but I wasn't about to argue with the whopping cash retainer he presented to Nina when he showed up at the door. Or the Visa Gold Card he flashed for incidentals. He was desperate to find a plus-sized made vampire and I just so happened to have the perfect woman for him.

Esther Crutch was a nice, sweet, stylishly chic made vampire I'd met while getting a spray tan at my favorite salon. Unfortunately, the stylishly chic packaged a size 14 body and so Esther didn't get as much nooky as the rest of her kind.

Made male vamps were so shallow.

Ahem.

Okay, so were born male vamps, but enough with the details.

Esther and Justin. Talk about a perfect match. I introduced them and stepped back to let Cupid do his thing.

One minute they were doing a hot salsa number and eyeballing each other and the next, they'd traded the ballroom for the sitting area. Go Cupid!

I wasn't sure what happened after that. I just knew, judging by the bloodstained sofa, that it wasn't good.

My heart pushed up into my throat as I stared at the crimson mess.

"I knew someone was going to spill a drink," Nina said as she came up behind me. "Daddy's going to take it out of my allowance for sure."

"I don't think this is a spilled drink," I finally managed, my voice small and tight. I picked at a torn piece of Esther's dress that had caught on the edge of a mirrored coffee table. The fabric was soaked with red, the edges jagged where it had ripped on the table. Or where someone had ripped it.

An image flashed and I remembered Esther, a strange expression on her face as Justin had led her from the ballroom.

I'd been five steps behind them because I'd wanted a pic for the brochure. I'd paused to calm down an overly excited were who'd been upset because we'd run out of au jus for the roast beef.

By the time I'd reached the sitting area—my

camera poised and ready to capture an eternally-ever-after in the making—they were gone.

"Holy shit," Nina gasped as the reality of the situation seemed to hit her. Her nostrils flared and her eyes brightened. "That really isn't wine, is it?"

"No." My throat tightened around the word. "It's Esther." I forced a swallow. "I think she's been kidnapped." The ripe smell of fresh blood flooded my senses. Goose bumps crawled up and down my arms and a strange sense of doom settled in the pit of my stomach. "Or worse."

Two

♥ ♥ ♥

"This isn't so bad." That's what Ash Prince told me when he and a handful of men I didn't recognize showed up a half hour later to examine the crime scene.

I'd called Ty first, but he was off chasing one of New York's Most Wanted vampires who'd skipped out on bail (not that Ty discussed his cases with me, but we were mentally linked thanks to some mutual bloodsucking and so I picked up on a few details every now and then when he let his guard down).

With Ty going straight to voice mail, I'd had no choice but to call the only other name in my iPhone who hunted bad guys for a living.

Make that bad *demons.*

Ash and his brothers worked for the Big D himself

(that's Devil not Daddy). They hunted condemned souls on the lamb from hell. Rapists, murderers, IRS auditors. They had expertise when it came to dissecting a crime scene.

Or so I hoped.

"No headless corpse." Ash typed in notes on his BlackBerry and walked the small sitting area outside the ballroom. Inside, his men had spread out to question the few remaining guests. "No smoldering ashes. No brain matter splattering the walls." He hunkered down and looked under the sofa. "No scattered body parts."

Ugh. Can we tone down the details?

"She's definitely not dead," he added, pushing to his full six foot plus height. His rich chocolate gaze locked with mine. "Not yet anyway."

"You're not making me feel any better." Talk about the wrong thing to say to a sexual demon. His gaze brightened, gleaming a brilliant gold. Heat rolled off his sexy body, curling around me and luring me closer.

He had short, dark hair that looked as if he'd just rolled out of bed and shoved a hand through it. He wore a brown Henley that hugged his broad shoulders and accented a narrow waist. Faded jeans clung to his long, muscular legs. He had bedroom eyes and perfect white teeth and more sex appeal than Eric Bana, Brad Pitt and my favorite clerk at the Starbucks all rolled into one.

Talk about some serious temptation.

"I'm in a relationship," I blurted. "A happy, committed, monogamous relationship. With Ty," I added on the off chance that guys didn't talk about these things. Ash and Ty crossed paths on occasion, but I couldn't really see them having a heart-to-heart. Especially since demon Ash didn't actually have a heart and Ty's ticker had been dead for quite some time now.

"So you two are together now, huh?"

"That's right."

He arched an eyebrow. "Are we talking *together* as in getting wild and naked on the weekends, or *together* as in picking out his and hers coffins?"

"Definitely coffins." He arched an eyebrow and I shrugged. "All right, so we haven't actually gotten that far, but we're on the way." Sort of.

I know, I know. Where was the *most definitely*? The thing was, while I was head over heels for Ty, he'd never come out and actually said the L word.

He couldn't.

Long story short, Ty's maker—a ruthless born vamp by the name of Logan Drake—was on a personal mission to see that Ty suffered for the rest of his afterlife. Logan wanted Ty miserable, and so he wasn't too fond of yours truly because, let's face it, I was the sunshine in Ty's otherwise doom and gloom existence.

Ty was hesitant to get close, fearful that Logan might target me. But I'd faced off with Vindictive Vamp once before when he'd kidnapped Ty for a

little reality check in the form of torture and muti-
lation. I'd also saved the day—i.e., Ty's ass.

Logan Drake didn't scare me.

Okay, so maybe he scared me a little (torture, mu-
tilation, nuff said). But I was willing to take the risk
because I loved Ty. And he loved me.

Really. I so didn't need to hear it. His actions spoke
volumes.

He'd helped me prove my innocence when I was
wanted for murder. He'd bit me and sucked out a
nasty demon when Evie's exorcism had gone south.
He'd given up women and started bottling it when
it came to his dinner. He'd left a toothbrush in my
bathroom and he'd sent me flowers. He'd bailed on
me several days ago and all my calls were now going to his voice mail—

Wait a second. Wrong exit. I hopped back on the
road toward commitment bliss.

"It's just a matter of time before we do the happily-
ever-after thing," I added, more to convince myself
than Ash.

"So you already took him home to meet your
mother?"

"We haven't actually gotten around to that part,
but we will." Just as soon as I worked up my nerve.
Ash shook his head and I added, "What? I'm waiting
for the right moment."

"There is no right moment. Ty is a made vampire,
which leaves him out of the running for son-in-law
of the year."

"And you're an expert because . . . ?"

"I'm not. But it doesn't take a genius to figure things out. You're a born vampire which means your mother is a born vampire, which means Ty is going to be about as welcome in her house as the local SOB."

"For your information, she and my father have a very amicable relationship with Vinnie Balducci." Aka the local representative for the Snipers of Otherworldly Beings—SOBs for short—an organized group responsible for hunting and annihilating any and all Others. "They give him free toner cartridges." Because, of course, even dangerous, bloodthirsty snipers had to do paperwork. "And he doesn't drive a stake through their hearts. It's a win/win."

"I bet your ma doesn't have him over for dinner."

"She might." If he were the right blood type. "Listen, I know it's not likely that my mother will fall all over Ty at the first meeting, but she'll come around."

"Yeah."

"Stranger things *have* happened."

"Name one."

"I'll name three. The mighty T-Rex has gone the way of crocheted ponchos, the Olsen twins have turned from sitcom sweethearts to drug-addicted divas and my orgy-loving brother, Jack, has given up his womanizing ways to marry a human. All seemed impossible at one time, then bam, it happened. Instant miracle."

He gave me a strange look and shook his head.

"What? Vampires can't be optimistic?" He opened his mouth to answer a big, fat *No* and I cut him off, "So what do you think happened to Esther?"

He shrugged. "There are several possibilities. You say this guy wasn't a vampire, right?"

BVs gave off a sweet, succulent unique scent that only other BVs could smell. "The only thing tickling my nose was Giorgio."

"A made vamp?"

"Maybe." I couldn't actually smell an MV, which was why Ty and I had hit it off so well. He didn't reek of crème brûlé or bread pudding or chocolate ganache, and so he didn't clash with my eau de cotton candy.

"Maybe he was something else. A were. A demon." Ash's gaze locked with mine. "What did his profile say?"

"He didn't actually fill one out. He just showed up tonight with lots of cash and this." I handed over the business card with *Justin Barrett Findlay* in black script and an address. "And a Visa Gold card."

"We'll run a trace on the Visa number and see if it matches the name and address on the business card. But I wouldn't hold my breath. If something bad did go down here, I'd be willing to bet this guy didn't use his real name." He examined the couch for a few seconds before leaning in and taking a huge whiff. "It doesn't smell like vamp blood."

"Meaning?"

"The most likely scenario is that you're overreacting. She probably bit him and he turned out to be a bleeder."

I shook my head. "She didn't bite him."

"How do you know?"

"Esther is extremely weight conscious. She would never pig out in front of—or on—a potential eternity mate."

He shrugged. "We'll gather some info and see what we can find out about this guy." He walked to the open ballroom door and signaled two of his men who stood near the buffet table. I figured they were both werewolves, on account of they were practically drooling over the roast beef tray. "Get this scene processed and analyzed," he told them when they reached us. "Then we'll know what we're really dealing with." He turned to me. "I'll call you if anything comes up."

"An hour, right?" I asked hopefully.

"More like twenty-four. We'll have to bag and tag all the samples, do some testing. That takes time."

"What do I do in the meantime?"

"You don't do anything. I'll handle it from here."

"You're going to find her, right?"

He nodded. "If she's even missing. I'm betting the two of them snuck off somewhere and are having a good time as we speak." He gave my shoulder a reassuring squeeze and his voice softened. "You should stop worrying and head home. It'll be daylight soon."

"If?" My brain was still stuck on the first word. "What do you mean *if*?"

"There are a ton of possibilities as to what happened here."

Sneaking off. Humping like bunnies. Sucking like leeches. I could so relate to that. But this was different. It felt different.

It felt . . . *wrong*.

"She wouldn't just up and leave without saying good-bye. She's too nice for that."

"Maybe she wasn't thinking too clearly. Desperate women do desperate things."

Amen.

My mind went blank, giving way to a very vivid image of me minus my clothes. Ash was there, touching and stroking and . . .

My breasts grew heavy and my tummy tingled.

Bad tummy.

"When's the last time you had a date?" I blurted, desperate to ignore the lewd and lascivious thoughts that suddenly rushed through my head. "Because if you need one, I would be more than happy to help." He grinned and reality zapped me. "That is, I could find you someone," I rushed on. "A nice female demon. Someone you could take home to Papa."

"I seriously doubt he'd go for that." His cell phone chose that moment to beep and he shifted his attention to the display. "I've got to go. Mo and I are working a case in the Bronx and he just spotted our subject." His gaze collided with mine and his eyes smoldered again for a split second. "Will you be all right?"

"Why wouldn't I be?" I shrugged. "You said yourself, it's probably nothing."

"I could drop you off at home on my way out."

And I'd sit next to him in the backseat of a cab? As it was, I had the crazy urge to strip naked and haul him into the nearest storage closet. A dark, cramped backseat would surely send me over the edge into nympho-land.

My legs shook and I felt the wetness between my thighs. I stiffened at the realization. I knew why I was having such an intense physical reaction to him (he was a sexual demon, after all), but it didn't make it any less startling.

Get thee behind me, slut.

I licked my lips and gathered my strength. "Thanks, but no thanks." I couldn't help lusting after him, but I could keep from acting on that lust.

Think Ty.

Think monogamy.

Think happily ever after.

Think.

"You go on," I told him. "I still need to pack up a few things here."

He stared at me long and hard, his eyes dark and hot and oh, so dreamy, but I held my ground.

"Suit yourself," he finally said.

I watched him disappear (thankyouthankyouthankyou) into the elevator. The doors whooshed shut, and just like that the strange sensations subsided.

I spent the next hour watching Ash's men bag and tag. Finally, they gave the go-ahead for Nina to have the sofa moved to a storage closet to await disposal. They spent a few more minutes questioning the waitstaff and then they left. Nina had a new sofa brought up from storage and soon the sitting area looked as picture perfect as when I'd first walked in that evening.

There wasn't a trace of Esther left behind.

The realization made my eyes water and I blinked frantically.

Ash was probably right. It was probably nothing. Just a great big misunderstanding.

That's what I told myself as I grabbed the last of my things and loaded them into a box.

The problem was, deep in my heart I didn't actually believe it.

Three

❤ ❤ ❤

I was not going to cry.

Because I'm, of course, a badass vampire and BAVs did *not* cry unless a) they were on the sharp, pointy end of a stake, b) they were being burned alive by overzealous villagers or c) they ruined a pair of high dollar Zac Posen booties while chasing an extra from *The Exorcist* (hey, confession is good for the soul, right?).

A missing client/friend didn't score waterworks.

Unless it was the client/friend who'd stuck with me through not one but twenty-nine failed dates (thirty if you count tonight's bloodbath). Despite Esther's long list of losers, she'd kept trying. Hoping. Believing.

In me and in her sucky social life.

I wiped at a big fat tear that squeezed past my

eyelashes, picked up my box and headed down the elevator. The concierge helped me outside and flagged down a cab. I loaded my stuff into the backseat and climbed in.

I know, I know. I was Super Vamp. I could leap tall buildings in a single bound. Listen in on every conversation for a three block radius. Sniff out a one-of-a-kind Donna Karan bag from a mile away. I should just do the pink fuzzy bat gig and save a few bucks, right?

Unfortunately, I had a bad habit of losing things during the metamorphosis and I was decked out in all my faves tonight. Besides, a bat toting a box of name tags and a credit card machine? How inconspicuous was that?

"Where to?" The female cabbie eyed me in the mirror. Her name was Evelyn and she lived in Brooklyn. She had four kids, ten dogs and twenty-two hamsters. She'd had twenty-three but just last night she'd had to flush one because one of her labs had tried to use it for a chew toy.

A mental picture hit me and my stomach pitched.

Sometimes being a highly sensitive Super V wasn't all it was cracked up to be.

"Take a left at the corner and head east." I gave her my address before settling back into the seat and pulling out my cell phone.

I had three texts and two voice mails. I punched in my mailbox code and waited for Ty's frantic *Are you all right?*

Instead, my mother's exasperated, "What's the point of having a cell phone if you don't answer it?" blared in my ear.

Before I could hit the DELETE button, she rushed on, "Then again, what's the point of having a premium fertility rating if you're just going to waste it on a human woman who has no hope in the universe of giving birth to an heir to carry on the sacred Marchette name."

O-kay.

"Obviously, said human has discovered that she can still give birth thanks to your brother's premium born vampire sperm, which can fertilize *any* egg. But without two vampire chromosomes to make it a pure blood, the child is obviously doomed to be inferior."

In layman's terms? *Human.*

"I swear," she added, "I would slit both my wrists if I thought it would put me out of my misery. But the last time I did that, your father thought I was trying to seduce him with a snack. We ended up having sex on my imported Belgian rug."

I *so* didn't need to know that.

"Needless to say, I couldn't find a dry cleaner in Connecticut who would touch it. I ended up shipping it to a filthy expensive preservatory." She heaved a sigh. "*Never* again. If your brother thinks I'm ruining another rug just because he has this crazy idea that he's going to give me a human grandchild, then he's sorely mistaken. I'm not going to stand by and let him sully our family's name. I mean, really. What will everyone say?"

Everyone meaning the card-carrying members of the Connecticut Huntress Club. Also known as the local 101 for snotty, pretentious, born female vampires.

My mother had been the refreshments chairwoman for the past three decades. She passed out glasses of AB– and O+ along with a primo sales pitch to hook me up with available sons, nephews, grandsons, great nephews, great grandsons, uncles, cousins, friends of cousins, friends of friends of cousins—namely any born male vamp with a penis, a fertility rating and a bank account.

Gee, thanks Ma.

"I simply won't let it happen," she declared. "We've never ever had an actual human in our family tree until now."

Three words—Great-uncle Peter.

"Oh, wait. There is Peter. Last I heard, he was still shacking up with that cocktail waitress from Vegas. But we all know he hasn't been right in the head since he bit that priest back during the Crusades. And as crazy as he is, he still hasn't gone so far as to marry the woman. Last I'd heard they were barely sharing an email account. It's that Mandy, I tell you. She's bewitching your poor brother until he can't even think for himself . . ." *Beep*.

The message timed out and my mom's tirade ended. I sent up a silent *Thank you* to the CEV (Chief

Executive Vampire) of Upstairs, Inc., for sparing me more misery.

I checked the phone number on the second message—so much for mercy—and hit the DELETE key before moving on to the texts.

The first was from Nina Two about five minutes before I'd discovered the bloody couch. *Knock em dead 2nite.*

My chest tightened and I blinked frantically. If only she knew.

I pulled up the second message, which had come through thirty seconds later.

OMG.

What can I say? Good news travels fast with my BFFs.

Number three? *Miss u. Want to lick u all ovr.*

Uh, yeah. She'd obviously mistaken me for Wilson, her significant other. At least I was hoping as much. While some BVs buttered their bread on both sides, I'd never been one of them. I'd take Brad over Ang any day.

My hands flew over the keypad. *No lickng 2-night. How bout shopping 2-mrow?*

I hit SEND and stashed my phone just as the cab pulled up in front of my place.

The renovated duplex that housed my apartment wasn't anywhere close to the plush high-rise near Central Park that my parents kept for those last-minute city trips. No marbled foyer. No private elevator. No blood-slave/doorman named Maurice. Not even a porch light. Rather, my building had three concrete steps leading to a very narrow stoop and a single glow-in-the-dark door buzzer.

I handed the driver a ten, a DED card and a mental *You're desperately lonely and should call for a date ASAP.* What can I say? She was female and, therefore, unsusceptible to my BV charm, but I gave it a shot anyway. Sexual preference was such a gray area these days and I hated to miss a prime advertising op.

"Thanks," she murmured. Her gaze caught and held mine in the rearview mirror. Sure enough, I saw an image of the two of us playing a game of strip poker.

I was winning, of course.

I smiled and added a persuasive *Call me* before I climbed out of the cab and headed for the front door.

Entering the building, I power-walked five flights of stairs and headed down the long hallway that led to *mi casa*. Across the hall, my neighbor—an accountant who loved Thai food and cheap perfume—was just hitting the SNOOZE button. I slid my key into the lock and let myself in.

The apartment was just the way I'd left it—cat hair clinging to the rug, a pile of dirty clothes in one corner and a stack of shoe boxes I'd been meaning to organize in the other (FYI—in addition to being allergic to stakes and sunlight, I had a strong aversion to vacuums and cleaning products).

I made a few kissy-kiss sounds guaranteed to

bring the average, loyal, devoted pet running to the door to greet his master. Needless to say, Killer kept his fat, furry ass planted on my couch.

"What? No love?"

I'm weak from lack of food. He blinked. *I can barely lift my head.*

"I fed you before I left."

I'm even hallucinating, he went on. *I took a piss in the litter box and I swear the wet spot is the spitting image of Garfield. eBay, here I come.*

"You're not auctioning off your pee and you're not weak from lack of nutrition. I fed you Kitty Cuisine lamb and vegetables before I left."

Is that what I yacked up all over your shoes?

"You didn't."

He blinked. A wave of dread rolled through me even before I turned and spied the surprise near the sofa. I contemplated tossing him from the nearest window, but that totally went against the whole born vamp creed of keeping a low profile. The last thing I needed was to wind up getting cuffed on the Animal Planet equivalent of *COPS*.

I glared at him. "You're cleaning it up."

In your dreams, sistah. He rested his head on his paws and closed his eyes. *I don't do manual labor, and I don't eat lamb and vegetables. I already told you, I like the sardines. The imported ones that you brought home last week.*

"Last week was a special occasion." I'd been celebrating my first full week of coupledom with Ty.

He'd gotten stuck working a case and I'd ended up celebrating on my own. An imported bottle of AB– for me and Italian sardines for Killer. "Those things are expensive."

Yeah, well, so are designer shoes.

Maybe I could use a pair of pantyhose and disguise my face before I threw him out the window. I contemplated the idea as I went in search of rubber gloves and some antibacterial wipes.

I ended up with an old pair of gardening mittens left by the previous tenants and a few hand towels. I spent the next fifteen minutes cleaning up the mess and envisioning a street full of splattered feline. Talk about an upbeat way to end my otherwise depressing night.

At the same time, I kept picturing the bloody couch, which made me nauseous, which kept me from smearing Killer's sorry hide all over the pavement.

"You're lucky I had a stressful night."

And you're lucky I didn't yack into your handbag so it could match the shoes. He purred. *What can I say? I'm just a softy at heart.*

"I should spike your food."

You wouldn't.

I gave him an evil grin. "Oh, wouldn't I?"

Confession time—as much as I despise Killer at times, I've gotten used to having him around. Which is the only reason I didn't pour a bottle of Windex into his food bowl. Well, that and the fact that I didn't actually have a bottle of Windex—see the above reference to cleaning products.

Instead, I dished out the last can of sardines and then headed for the shower. My head hurt and my chest felt tight. I desperately needed to wash away the past few hours.

The water poured over me, blending in with the moisture that rolled down my face. When the hot water ran out, I toweled off and pulled on a worn red T-shirt that read *Santa, I can explain* and a pair of fuzzy white socks. Not the typical sex dominatrix ensemble one would expect from an all-powerful *vampere,* but I was going for warm and comfy rather than bitchy and ballsy.

I flipped the deadbolt on the front door, checked my cell phone for any messages from Ty—did I mention that he was still stuck on said case and I hadn't seen him in four days, five hours, and fifty-seven minutes?

Not that I was counting. Or feeling sorry for myself because my new boyfriend had pledged his devotion on Monday, only to disappear on Tuesday.

A sigh worked its way up my throat as I closed the heavy-duty blinds on my trio of windows. Climbing into bed, I burrowed under the covers and pulled the goose down over my head.

I closed my eyes, conjured my favorite fantasy and tried to forget that poor Esther might be in serious trouble.

And that it was all my fault.

*   *   *

It was the hottest fantasy I'd ever had.

And trust me, at five hundred (and holding) I've had more than my share.

I've had my toes licked by Hugh Jackman. My back massaged by Patrick Dempsey. My feet tantalized with a pair of one-of-a-kind python pumps with diamond-encrusted straps. (What? We're talking *Jimmy Choo*.)

My latest—and my most fave—involved me, a breezy beach cabana, a mesh bikini and a certain sexy bounty hunter.

Surprisingly, there wasn't a grain of sand or a palm frond in sight. Instead, I was completely naked, spread out on a pair of pale pink Egyptian cotton sheets.

Ty leaned over me, his body silhouetted against the flickering glow of a single lit candle. His naked body covering the length of mine, his muscles hard beneath my roaming hands. I felt my way up, over his toned ass, the dip at the base of his spine, the sinewy planes of his back, his broad shoulders. His dark silky hair brushed my skin and my eyes shot all the way open.

Everything went from fuzzy to focused and Ty's handsome face loomed over me.

You were dreaming about me. His lips didn't move, but his deep voice echoed in my head, reminding me of the fact that he'd drank my blood and I'd drank his.

We were connected now in a way that went be-yond his-and-hers hand towels. While this little bit of FYI had freaked me out at first, I'd actually started to like it.

At least when it came to sex.

We're talking better than a mood ring.

I smiled (all of five seconds) until I remembered that he'd bailed on me. No note. No phone call. No email.

"I sent you a text on Tuesday." He dipped his head and nuzzled my ear. He flicked his tongue and a lightning bolt zapped me.

"To say you were working late," I managed, de-spite the yummy heat seeping through me. His tongue grazed the side of my neck and electricity sizzled from the point of contact. It spread through my body, pausing in several interesting places. My armpits. My nipples. My belly button. Lower . . . "Late usually means a few hours," I said when I fi-nally found my voice again.

"Not in my line of work." Another flick of his tongue and a few nibbles and he pulled back to stare into my eyes. "I'm on a tough case that's still wide open. I shouldn't be here now, but when I got your message, you sounded so upset . . ." His voice trailed off and I didn't miss the brightening of his eyes. "I needed to see you."

I touched his face. Rough stubble rasped my fin-gertips, dispelling any lingering notion that I was dreaming.

I wasn't sure if it was the stress of the past few days spent worrying and wondering if he'd changed his mind about us or the stress of the past few hours, but I had the sudden urge to throw my arms around his neck and burst into tears. He was here now and while I knew I didn't need his comfort (I was the ultimate badass, independent, single and successful vampire), I still wanted it.

He kissed me then, effectively distracting me from the crazy realization. My brain zeroed in on his tongue and the way he stroked mine and, well, who could think with all that going on?

"I'm sorry about the frantic phone call," I told him when we finally came up for air and I had a twinge of conscience. "I was pretty stressed."

"I wish I could have helped."

"That's okay. Ash took care of things."

"I heard."

I didn't miss the flash of jealousy in his gaze and warmth spread through me. "He thinks Esther's off having a wild, passionate affair and that I'm freaking for nothing."

He nodded. "It's possible."

I shook my head. "She wouldn't just disappear like that."

"Maybe. Maybe not. But worrying over it won't help one way or the other. Wait and see what Ash turns up. Then you can freak."

"He said it would be at least twenty-four hours

before he knows more. I don't think I can wait that long."

He grinned. "I can think of a way to pass the time." His expression grew serious and his eyes blazed bright and fierce. "I really missed you."

A smiled played at my lips. "I missed you, too." I pressed my body against his. "And I missed this."

"Ditto." He pressed his thigh between my legs and rubbed against my slit. Sensation bolted through me and my entire body shook.

His lips captured mine again and his tongue plunged deep. His pulse beat echoed in my head, keeping time with the frantic *ba-bom-ba-bom-ba-bom* of my own.

I clutched at his shoulders and opened myself to him, but he held back. Instead, he teased and stirred until I just knew I was going to lose my mind.

I exerted a little BV strength, rolled him over and straddled him. My gaze locked with his as I slid down his hard, hot length. He throbbed deep inside me and pure ecstasy gripped me. Every nerve in my body started to buzz. To want. Suddenly I couldn't feel him deep enough. Fast enough. I rode him hard then. Taking and giving and . . . there. Right . . . *there*.

My orgasm was fierce, slamming over me, picking me up, shaking me around. Until I stopped thinking and worrying and I simply *felt*. Ty inside of me. Surrounding me.

My body bucked and my head fell back. He pulled me down to him then, his hips lifting as he caught my nipple with his mouth. He sank his teeth deep and started to drink, and I plunged over the edge.

I gripped his head and held him to me as the convulsions ripped through my body. One after the other. Each more fierce than the last. My body sucked at his cock the way his mouth drew on my nipple and it went beyond anything I'd ever felt.

My own hunger stirred then, gripping and twisting until I felt my fangs against my tongue. The urge hit me then and I couldn't help myself. I gripped his hair and pulled him up until we were face-to-face.

I kissed him then, tasting my blood on his tongue. It was warm and sweet and the hunger roared inside of me.

Now. The deep command echoed in my head and the next thing I knew, his head was tilted back and my mouth was on his neck. His blood pulsed past my lips, drenched my tongue and slid down my throat.

Sweet.

Succulent.

He gripped my hips and came then. His body shook and a growl vibrated in my ears.

I drank a few more seconds while he bucked and trembled. I released his neck, licked my lips and melted against him. He held me tight then, not moving or speaking. Just holding.

At that moment I stopped wondering if he loved me. I felt it. Deep in my heart. My soul.

Unfortunately, the feeling lasted all of an hour.

All too soon, Ty crawled out of bed, pulled on his clothes and left without one word (a kiss on the lips *does not* count).

Luckily, I was half-asleep and so relaxed that I didn't fly out of bed and open up a can of whoop ass on him. Or worse, morph into a blubbering idiot and blurt out how much I loved and adored and worshipped him.

Wait a sec. Did I just say worship?

Press rewind and forget that last one. I might be a sucker for love, but I *so* wasn't a sappy idiot.

Anyhow, back to blurting out my love and adoration.

Not happening. At least not until I was absolutely, positively sure that he felt the same way.

Of course, I wasn't worrying about any of that right now. Or whether or not the meet and greet party was going to pay off and save me from massive refunds. Or Esther and the bloody couch.

Especially Esther and the bloody couch.

Rather, I was basking in the glow of wicked hot sex.

I pulled Ty's pillow on top of my head, drank in his scent and pretended all was right with my world. In a matter of seconds, I was fast asleep.

Hey, sometimes it pays to be a vampilicious optimist.

Four

❤ ❤ ❤

When I cracked open an eye late that afternoon, I fully expected to find the bed beside me empty.

What I didn't expect was my mother, live and in color, looming over me.

"Ma? What are you—" The words stalled in my throat as I cast a frantic glance at the tangle of sheets next to me just to make sure I hadn't imagined Ty going AWOL again.

Sure enough, the bed was empty.

Thankfully.

Not that I wanted a one-sided relationship with a made vampire who couldn't commit. But we were still in the honeymoon phase, so I was willing to hang in there and see where things might lead. Just because, you know, I'm the curious sort who likes to experience afterlife and all that it has to offer.

All right, already. I'm the hopeless romantic sort with a weakness for happily-ever-afters, particularly my own.

I simply could not live with myself for the next trillion or so years if I didn't at least give him a chance. Even if I did have the unnerving feeling that I'd latched onto a bona fide commitment-phobe.

On top of that, I was born and he was made, and Ash was one hundred percent right. My mother was going to freakin' *freak*.

But not just yet.

While I wanted my mother in-the-know when it came to my relationship with Ty, finding out about the man your only daughter is boffing and actually catching them *en boff* were two very different things.

I gathered the sheet up under my arms, struggled to a sitting position and tried to look innocent.

My ma could sniff out the dreaded G faster than a werewolf could locate the nearest barbeque joint. I drew a deep breath (hey, it helps the average human) and tuned out the *Ack! She is so going to kill me!* I ignored the heat creeping up my neck and focused on the zillion questions inspired by my ma's sudden appearance.

Why?

What?

When?

Where?

Cartier?

My gaze snagged on the pearl and diamond

choker that encircled my mother's slim neck. I forgot my mental inquisition and drank in the vampire standing beside my bed.

Jacqueline Marchette was rocking it in a pair of gray Armani tailored pants, a black silk shell and a fitted red Marni jacket that accented her tall, svelte figure. Her long dark hair was swept back in a chic ponytail. Dark eyeliner rimmed rich brown eyes framed with perfectly arched eyebrows. High sculpted cheekbones, a delicate nose and flawless skin betrayed her pure bloodline. She smelled of cherries jubilee, Chanel No. 5 and determination.

Uh-oh.

"How'd you get in here?" I blurted.

"I'm a vampire, dear. I have ways."

My gaze ping-ponged toward the heavy-duty blinds to my left. "You levitated through the window?"

"Don't be silly. I don't levitate when I've got a perfectly comfortable pair of Jimmy Choos to walk in."

"You used your super-strength to break the lock on my front door?"

"And risk a three hundred dollar Belgian manicure? Darling, please."

"You morphed into a whiff of smoke and seeped through the cracks?"

"And risk smelling like the inside of your father's favorite pipe? Stop being overly dramatic, Lilliana. I slipped your building super a few fifties." She held up a key. "It's a capitalist society, dear. Money trumps vampire magic every time. Provided you have money, of course." She fingered the edge of my bedsheet and stared down her perfect nose. "Cotton poly blend?"

My defenses went on full alert. "These are Egyptian cotton. Sort of." She shook her head and I stiffened. "The good sheets are dirty. I haven't made it to the Laundromat yet."

"Well, that explains why you're naked."

"Maybe I was having hot, random sex with strangers," I heard myself say. Hey, a vamp's gotta have her pride and my mom was much too quick to buy the Laundromat excuse. "A really hot, handsome stranger."

"If only." My mother cast a glance around her. "You know, if you would just take your father up on his offer, you wouldn't have to live like this. Not only is the salary good at Moe's, but we just added dental."

"My fangs are fine, Ma."

"And maid service."

"I like cleaning. Really."

She didn't say anything. Instead, she gave a disdainful little sniff that made me feel like I should be starring in *The Biggest Loser*.

"Did you drive all the way from Connecticut just to criticize me?"

"Don't be silly, dear. I can do that over the phone." She shook her head. "Someone has to stop your brother from making a tragic mistake that he will regret for the rest of his afterlife. Your father and I are headed over to Park Avenue right now to talk some sense into him." She nailed me with a stare. "And you're coming with us."

My mom needed me. As terrifying as the thought was, it was also sort of sweet. In a weird, twisted, *Mommy Dearest* way. My ego perked. "I'm the moral support?"

"You're the distraction, dear." She flicked an invisible piece of lint from her sleeve. "First, we'll try to persuade him with a nice fat, juicy raise. If that doesn't work, we'll throw in a four-week, all-expense-paid trip to Hawaii. And if *that* doesn't work, I'm going to slip these into the human's drink." She held up a small silver packet of pills.

"Please tell me those are vitamins."

She shook her head and gave an evil grin. "Birth control pills, dear. I got them from Millicent Von Waldenburg, who got them from her son, Ivan. You remember Ivan?"

"Isn't he the one who slicks his hair back?"

"It's a classic look, dear. Think Frank Langella."

"Or the Fonz."

She gave me a pointed glare. "You're much too picky, Lilliana. You'll never find a decent eternity mate if you don't bend a little. Ivan is a fabulous prospect. His fertility rating is an eight and he's got several nice real estate investments that are paying off heavily."

"I'm not going out with Ivan."

"Of course you're not." She waved a hand at me. "You're going out with Remy."

Remy Tremaine was the chief of the Fairfield Police Department and the perfect born vampire. He had a fabulous fertility rating, a smoking body and a nice side business providing bodyguards for the rich and famous. We'd grown up together, terrorized each other and, more recently, had our very first official date.

And our last.

I'd explained about Ty and given the spiel about how I'd still like to be friends. While Remy hadn't bought it (made + born = not a chance in hell), I'd set aside the few feelings I had for him and moved on.

My mother obviously hadn't gotten the email on that.

"Remy and I are just friends," I told her for the bizillionth time.

"We'll see," she said in a voice that never failed to strike fear in the hearts of frightened villagers and send yours truly running online to MyTherapist.com.

"Ivan is feeding off this gynecologist from Queens," she went on. "When he heard what Jack was contemplating, he got them for me. Your father and I aren't the only ones up in arms over your brother's poor judgment. The entire born vamp community is outraged. They understand, of course, that it's not Jack's fault. He wouldn't willingly betray his species. He's just powerless against such strong magic."

"For the last time, Mandy is *not* a witch. She's a medical examiner."

"She comes from a long line of witches, and you know what they say."

"Live and let live?"

"The snake doesn't slither far from the egg."

What?

"She's mesmerizing him, all right," she went on. "But her powers are nothing compared to ours. Now get up and get dressed. Your father is waiting downstairs in the car."

I gave her my most apologetic smile. "Gee, I'd love to help save Jack and the pristine Marchette reputation,"—*not*—"but I've got a schedule full of clients." An even bigger *not*.

I wasn't spiking my sister-in-law's tea with Yaz. For one thing, Jack and Mandy's baby plans were none of my business. Two? I actually liked Mandy. And three, I wasn't climbing out of bed in my birthday suit even if my mother had seen it all before.

She hadn't seen it in a good 488 years. Nor had she seen the heart-shaped tattoo I'd had done the day before I'd lost my virginity and stopped aging. It wasn't the greatest tat (think small wagon, a vial full of henna and an ancient gypsy rather than a state-of-the-art shop, sterilized needles and an Ed Hardy wannabe), but it was mine and it summed up my romantic personality.

"Why don't you take Nina and Rob?" I suggested. When my mother didn't look the least bit excited over the prospect, I added, "Nina was just saying to me last night how anxious she is to get to know you."

"That's ridiculous. We've known each other for ages." My mother picked at another piece of nonexistent lint. "She grew up with you."

"You know her as the BFF of your one and only beautiful, vivacious, über hot daughter. You don't know her as the potential mother of your first grandchild. There's a huge difference."

That got her attention. She nailed me with a pointed stare. "What are you talking about?"

I shrugged, gathered the sheet tighter and wiggled my way toward the edge of the bed. "Just that she's a born vampire and Rob is a born vampire and things have been going pretty great between them. The next logical step is for them to move in together. Maybe open a joint bank account. And maybe, you know, possibly pledge their eternal commitment to each other."

Actually, the next logical step for Nina was to dump Rob, because her longest relationship to date was just under six weeks and she had a huge fear of waking up one evening and feeling as if her afterlife had passed her by while she'd been stuck having sex with the same vampire.

Likewise, Rob usually jumped ship just after seven weeks, or right before the Moe's Memorial Day Dinner Under the Stars, whichever came first.

What, you might ask, is the MMDDUS? Take one

lush Connecticut estate, add a fireworks display, an all-you-can-eat chicken wing buffet (for the humans) and at least three dozen Hooters girls (for the vampires), and you get the picture.

Rob had a thing for orange shorts, as did every other male vampire on the Moe's payroll. Hence his sudden need to be single and a total jerk-off when May rolled around.

Until then . . .

"They're definitely getting serious." I nodded. "Commitment vials, matching coffins, monogrammed blood bags—the works."

She looked like one of Satan's hounds who'd just caught a whiff of a runaway soul. "I suppose we could make a detour by Rob's." Before I could blink, I heard my apartment door open and close and, *poof,* she was gone.

I hurried to the door, threw the deadbolt and turned to glare at Killer, who sat curled up on the sofa.

"You could have warned me when she got here."

What do I look like? A watch dog? I don't do loyalty or protection or any of that crap. I'm a cat, i.e., snotty, selfish and hungry. He blinked. *Speaking of which, if I don't hear the can opener in the next five seconds, things are going to get ugly.*

"I'm trading you in for a cocker spaniel."

Yeah, yeah. And I'm the next Miss Congeniality. Get moving, sister.

I glared and then headed to the kitchen. I know, I know. I should let him starve. But I needed all the good luck I could get and I had a feeling animal cruelty wouldn't score me any brownie points with the CEV Upstairs. Unless I was sucking said animal dry.

I contemplated the notion all of five seconds before opening a can of Kittylicious and dumping it into Killer's bowl. Then I spent the next hour doing hair and makeup and trying not to think about Esther.

Ash was right. She was probably off with Mr. Visa having hot, wild sex and sucking each other dry. When she finally came up for air, she would call and explain the couch incident. He'd spilled a drink. She'd spilled a drink. They'd both been having an emo moment.

Something.

I had absolutely nothing to worry about.

My head knew that. Unfortunately, my gut wasn't buying it. It kept nagging at me, insisting that something was wrong.

A feeling that grew stronger as I left Killer parked near his scratching post with strict instructions not to pee or barf on *anything,* locked up my apartment and headed for the office.

Five
♥ ♥ ♥

Ash was waiting for me when I walked into Dead End Dating. He wore a gray button-down, faded jeans and scuffed brown biker boots. While there was nothing designer about his clothes, his buff bod was the stuff Calvin ads were made of.

Not that I noticed that sort of thing since I'm officially "involved" with Ty.

All right, already. So I noticed. I'm involved, not dead.

Okay, so I'm technically dead, too, but you get the point.

I ix-nayed the lustful thoughts that rolled through my brain, dropped my purse on the corner of my desk and sank down into my chair to brace myself for what I knew had to be bad news.

Ash paced the floor in front of my desk, his mouth stretched into a thin line, his brow furrowed.

"Something's wrong," he said.

What'd I tell ya?

My stomach hollowed out despite the three Rock-stars and extra-large glass of O+ I'd chugged before leaving my apartment. "She's dead, isn't she?"

"I'm afraid it's worse than that."

"What could be worse than dead?"

"Torture. Then death."

Yep, that would be worse.

"We did a background check on your guy," he went on, "and it turns out that his name isn't Justin. It's Mordred Lucius."

"Why does that sound familiar?"

"Mordred was the evil knight who fatally wounded King Arthur. This isn't any relation. At least, none that I can put my finger on. He isn't a demon either. He's a very powerful warlock."

"A male version of Glenda the Good Witch?"

"Only if Glenda traded in her Lollipop Guild membership and joined a satanic cult." Ash shook his head. "This guy is into black magic. I did some checking once I found out his name and it seems he can be traced back at least eight hundred years."

"He didn't look a day over twenty-five."

"That's the point. It turns out he was ousted from his coven for performing illegal rituals. I talked to the vice-president of the local AWW, who told me—"

"AWW?"

"Association of Witches and Warlocks. This Mordred was convicted of plotting to perform a human sacrifice to preserve his own youth. The AWW outlawed the ancient Mayan ritual over one hundred and fifty years ago when they decided to mainstream with the rest of society. They didn't want any of their members causing bad PR and so they banished him. Obviously mutilating and killing humans is much too high profile for their tastes."

"But Esther isn't human."

"Technically, no. But she's still a vital entity. One with enormous power and energy. If he kills her, he not only absorbs her youth, he soaks up her immortality, as well."

"Meaning?"

"She'll be the ultimate sacrifice"—his words were low and serious and my stomach flipped—"because she'll be his last."

"If he wants eternal youth, why not just find a born vampire to turn him?"

"Vampires have limitations."

Tell me about it.

"No sunlight," Ash went on. "No pigging out at Shoney's." Ash shook his head. "This guy is greedy. He wants the best of both worlds."

"And Esther is his ticket."

Ash nodded. "We went by his place. He punched in his security code a half hour after you called me last night. It looks as if he left the hotel and stopped by his apartment to pack up a few things."

"He's going somewhere."

Ash nodded. "The ritual requires that he make the sacrifice on his birthday which, according to my sources, isn't until next Friday."

My curiosity piqued and my mind started to race. While I knew Ash was a badass demon, I'd yet to realize the extent of his powers. I knew he could read minds because he was forever dipping into mine and I couldn't help but wonder what other tricks he had up his sleeve. "Scrying cup? Tarot cards? Magic 8 Ball?"

"Driver's license." He didn't miss my disappointment because he added, "I only use the Magic 8 Ball for special occasions."

"Very funny." I swallowed the sudden lump that had jumped into my throat. "So why kidnap her early?"

"Nabbing her in advance gives him time to prepare the sacrifice. He'll start by starving her first to cleanse her system and then he'll slice and dice slowly. A little skin here. A little skin there. She won't be able to heal if she isn't eating, which means she'll suffer appropriately—"

"I really don't want to hear this."

He gave me a strange look.

"Not that I can't take the blood and gore," I blurted. "I love blood and gore. It's just that I don't want to hear about what *might* happen. I'd rather live in the moment, and at the moment she's alive." At his pointed stare, I added, "Right?"

He nodded. "That's the assumption we're going on."

"Which means we have time to find her if we can figure out where he took her. Can we figure out where he took her?"

"The ritual requires that the sacrifice be made at a place of supreme power."

"Like an ancient burial ground?"

"No, this is more personalized. It has to be at a place of supreme power for the individual warlock. A place where *Mordred* has been. A place where he felt extremely powerful. Unfortunately, we don't know where that is at this time, but we're running a check on all outgoing flights at JFK and La-Guardia."

"Do you really think he checked a trussed-up vampire with baggage claim? Or worse, used her as a carry-on?"

Ash shrugged. "We're also contacting the local charter companies, train stations, local cabbies and rental car companies."

"Crawling into a cab with an unconscious vampire in tow? Wouldn't that be much too conspicuous?"

"For most. But he's a powerful warlock. He could easily work a spell to make her invisible or glamour any eyewitnesses."

"So why even bother asking around? He'll make sure no one remembers anything."

"Probably. But if there's one thing I've learned over the last two thousand years, it's that everyone slips up once in a while. Witch, warlock, vampire, were-wolf, demon—they all make mistakes. Not often, but it only takes one time. A chink in the armor, so to speak. What?" he added when I just stared at him as if he'd hauled his pants up to his armpits.

"You're two thousand years old?"

"Give or take a few hundred." Before I could ask any more questions, his cell phone rang. He took one look at the display and said, "It's Zee. I really have to go."

"Is it about Esther?"

He shook his head and pressed a few buttons before sliding the phone back into his pocket. "Another case I'm working on. Listen, I've been checking into this because you asked me to, but I have to bow out now. It involves sorcery and magic, which puts it out of my jurisdiction." He reached into his pocket, pulled out a white business card and handed it to me. "This is the name of the investigator who'll be heading up things. If you can think of anything else about last night, anything you might have forgotten, just give him a call."

"Merle N. Ambrose?" The name echoed through my head and the pieces started to click. "Merlin? *The* Merlin?"

He grinned. "He's a good guy. We go way back."

"How far?"

"First cousins."

My brain rifled through all the history lessons I'd endured at the hands of a strict tutor named Jacques. "But I thought Merlin was the son of the Devil?"

"Nephew," he replied as he reached for the door.

Which meant that Ash was a chip off the old Big D block.

"Later." He gave me a quick wink and disappeared before I could voice the thought out loud.

Merlin.

Mordred.

The Devil.

Esther.

Mayan sacrifice.

The info whirled in my brain and I had the sudden urge to heave. I was a sucker for happily-ever-afters, not death and destruction. Even more, I was nursing some major guilt for introducing Esther to this guy in the first place.

I drew a deep breath on the off chance that it might ease my panic and tried to calm the frantic beat of my heart.

Think positive.

Yes, the situation looked grim, but that didn't mean things couldn't turn out. There were a whole ten days before next Friday. Plenty of time for the good guys to find some valuable clues, pinpoint Esther's whereabouts and save the day. She was alive at this moment. Maybe, possibly, in severe pain, but still alive.

I held tight to the hope, tamped down on the sudden anxiety that churned in my stomach and focused on the four messages sitting on my desk.

Message number one? A born vampire by the name of Clarice Harlow Montgomery who was desperately searching for that perfect someone. Namely another born vampire with at least a ten fertility rating (she needed off the charts to balance out her less than impressive orgasm quotient which measured a measly three, which explained why she needed me in the first place). She'd attended last night's ball with high hopes of finding Count Right. Instead, she'd gotten drunk and ended up in bed with The Wolfman. She was now revolted and blaming yours truly because she'd gone from being a sophisticated, happening *vampere* to a lowly were ho (her words not mine).

O-kay.

Message number two came from Yolanda Jackson, a fashionable were panther and head of security for Barneys New York. "I slept with a demon and my mother's going to kill me."

I definitely shared her pain.

My gaze went to the third slip of paper and my stomach jumped. It was from another client, who'd left a cryptic *I want my money back now!*

Number four? Ditto on the refund.

I punched the intercom for Evie. "Did we have any positive phone calls about last night?"

"The band called to thank you for the tip."

"Any calls from clients?"

"No, but Word hit it off with a receptionist from Stern and Finley Investments. He told me all about it when I dropped off my camera so he could download the pics." Word was the cousin/sexual deviant who'd given us a rock-bottom price on the new ad brochure.

"We don't have anyone from Stern and Finley in our database."

"He met her at a club last week, asked her out and, *bam,* instant chemistry. Can you believe it? We hooked him up with fourteen girls and not one of them would go out with him again. His first time flying solo and, *bam,* he hits a home run."

"You're not making me feel better."

"Look on the bright side. At least you know that love is still alive and well in the Big Apple. That, and your outfit is totally fab."

Normally such a comment would have safely distracted me from my misery for at least a nanosecond (we're talking black Zac Posen mini-skirt, ivory shell and Oscar de la Renta pink python heels). Instead, my gut clenched and the backs of my eyes burned.

What can I say? I'm growing.

"And I love that eye shadow. What is that? MAC's glitter sunrise?"

I smiled. "Sephora." I haven't grown *that* much.

I disconnected from Evie and powered up my computer. I was just pulling up last night's guest list to cruise for possible matches when the phone rang. A few seconds later, Evie buzzed me.

"Don't tell me. It's Janice Tarrington calling to thank me for introducing her to Michael Branden-berg." Both were born vampires. High fertility rating for him. Impressive orgasm quotient for her. Both had a fondness for opera and the Mets. They'd danced all night and I'd even seen Michael licking Janice's neck during a soulful rendition of Marvin Gaye's "Let's Get It On."

Sure, they'd left in separate cabs after he'd tried to bite her and she'd told him to put his commitment vial where his mouth was, but what's love without a little tiff every now and then? Even one that involved bitch-slapping (boy, can Janice pack a punch) and crying (who knew a male vamp could wail in three different octaves?).

"It's your sister-in-law."

So much for optimism.

"She sounds worked up," Evie added.

"Thanks." I punched line one. "Mandy? Are you okay?"

"I'm fine. I'm better than fine. I'm ecstatic. Jack and I are going to have a baby and it's all because of your wonderful, supportive mother."

The words stumbled around in my brain for a split second. "Come again?"

"Your mother is the greatest."

"*My* mother?"

"The sweetest."

"Jaqueline Marchette?"

"The kindest."

"*The* Jaqueline Marchette, who lives in Fairfield, Connecticut?"

"The most compassionate."

"The one who takes up two parking spaces? And butts her nose into everyone's business? And gives away boxes of raisins at Halloween?"

"Raisins are healthy."

"Exactly." My mother was always thinking in selfish terms. Load up the kids with raisins. They grow to be healthy adults and a perfect food source should the blood bottlers go out of business. "Halloween is all about Hershey bars and Pixie Stix. Any self-respecting human knows that."

"All right, so she might need a little redirection when it comes to trick-or-treaters, but otherwise she's the most wonderful female vampire in the entire universe." Mandy drew an excited breath. "She's promised to do everything in her power to help us have a baby."

"That's too cool." Or it would have been if we weren't having a give and take that starred *my* mother. "I'm glad it all worked out." I licked my lips and chose my next words carefully. "But I was sort of under the impression that she was a little concerned about the whole situation. Not because she doesn't absolutely love you or because she thinks you guys never should have tied the knot, or anything crazy like that." I went for a laugh. "It's just that it's sort of an unusual situation and not very common. I mean, you are human."

"That's exactly what your mother said. But when I explained that I've been doing research and there's no reason that Jack and I can't have a normal, healthy human baby, she was fine with it."

"She was?"

I could practically hear Mandy nodding on the other end. "Thrilled, even. She and your dad even insisted on toasting us. They brought a bottle of champagne just for the occa—"

"Do not *drink the champagne!"*

"I wouldn't drink champagne, silly."

Relief rolled through me. Short-lived when she added, "I drank hot chocolate. Your mother brought it especially for me. She wouldn't let Nina have even a sip."

"Nina and Rob were there?"

"They didn't want to miss the happy occasion. Anyhow, Nina asked for hot chocolate, but your mother insisted it was something special just for me. Said it was her own secret recipe."

This news sparked a big *uh-oh* for two very important reasons: 1) my mother didn't have any special recipes, on account of she never cooked or whipped up stuff or did anything remotely domestic, and 2) she was a pretentious lunatic vampire who would sooner flay herself than do anything nice for a human.

Hence, upon hearing the news I was this close to having a coronary.

"You should have seen her," Mandy went on, upping my heartbeat until I was nearing a full-blown code blue. "She was fussing over me as if I were already pregnant. She made Nina move to the love seat so that I could sit in the recliner. She made me put my feet up while she rushed off to the kitchen to mix up a cup. She even left a canister of the stuff so that I could enjoy another cup later. Isn't that thoughtful?"

"She definitely did a lot of thinking." And plotting. And planning. "Listen, Mandy. Don't drink any more, okay?"

"But why? It's so delicious."

"Because . . ."

Because your night creeping mother-in-law doesn't want human grandchildren and will do anything to sabotage your chances.

Because she's a controlling, manipulative born bloodsucker who wants everything her own way.

"Because it's chocolate," I blurted, my mind racing for a plausible excuse that wouldn't hurt her feelings and start a major family feud. "Chocolate has caffeine and caffeine is bad for you."

"Not in such a small amount, silly." She paused as if remembering something. "Then again, I don't want to do anything that might inhibit my chances at conception. Maybe I should lay off the caffeine entirely."

Atta girl. "It's the only way to be totally safe."

"I'll give the rest to Jack. He loves hot chocolate."

"That might not be such a good idea."

"Why?"

Who knew what Yaz-tainted hot chocolate would do to a male BV's fertility rating. A quick mental of Jack's Mr. Happy withering up and falling off and I blurted, "If you have to give up your favorites, he should have to sacrifice a little, too. He *is* the father."

"True." She seemed to think. "It really isn't fair that my butt spreads and my ankles swell, while he sits around sucking down imported chocolate and getting massages."

"Massages? You mean . . ." I wasn't going to think it, much less say it.

"Hans is here."

Hans was six feet plus of beautiful, blond Swede. He had bulging muscles and awesome hands and I lusted after his hot oil massage the way a PMSing female lusts after a triple chunk brownie.

Unfortunately, my mother kept Hans to herself and so I'd only experienced the magic once, when she and my father had attended an Old World French Vampires reunion in Paris.

I'd been house-sitting and Hans had been bored and, well, *abracadabra*.

"She really left Hans with you?"

"She said a massage would relax Jack and up his chances of shooting a bull's-eye."

And give her a spy in the household to report back Jack and Mandy's every conception attempt.

Big Brother had nothing on Big Mama.

"You don't need a massage. What you need is some alone time with my brother."

"I do feel funny having a stranger in the apartment. I tend to get a little noisy when we're, you know, having intercourse."

Too much info. "It's settled, then. Send him over to my place and I'll see that he gets back to my mom."

"You'd do that for us?"

"What are sisters for?"

"You're the greatest. I swear, you and your mom are two peas in the same pod."

As if I weren't feeling crappy enough over Esther's disappearance, Mandy's comment stirred up a giant wave of *Ugh, my afterlife sucks.* I said good-bye, gave a last warning about the chocolate and hung up. And then I shifted my attention to the stack of bills sitting on the corner of my desk.

I was this close to staking myself as it was. Might as well go for broke.

Six

❤ ❤ ❤

When the whole world is going to Hades in a Hermès silk bag (we're talking a *major* stack of bills), there are certain strategies a girl must employ to get by: a double spritz of my favorite, Gucci Rush, an extra-large Starbucks House Blend with three shots of espresso and ten minutes of online lusting at Bloomingdales.com (that would be online *shopping* for anyone with a lucrative job who doesn't rely on the dating habits of the fanged and fickle).

"I'm heading out." Evie ducked her head in the doorway. "Don't forget to brainstorm some tag lines for the brochure. Personally, I'm leaning toward *Get Your Monogamy On*, but it's your call."

I hadn't told Evie about Esther's disappearance. I didn't want to worry her, much less raise a zillion questions regarding made vampires and ancient warlocks. Better to keep my trap shut and my fingers crossed.

Besides, Esther was going to be okay. No sense in drumming up a huge drama, when everything would turn out in the end.

At least, that's what I was telling myself.

"Speaking of calls," Evie went on, "Mia wants to set up a meeting for Monday."

Mia van Horowitz was a Jewish princess turned tattoo queen who'd come to DED searching for the perfect man—namely one who could keep it up and satisfy her nympho tastes. She was very human and very scary and she wanted a man who could do it at least three times in one night.

"She says that she might have to lower her standards since we haven't been able to hook her up," Evie added. "She sounded really depressed, so you might want to give her a buzz. Also, don't forget to touch base with Mary Weathers—she's the florist at the Waldorf. She claims one of our guests stole three dozen begonias and she's sending us a bill."

The news just kept getting better and better.

"It couldn't be one of our guests." I racked my brain for a mental of someone—anyone—absconding with several vases filled with flowers and came up with nada.

"Maybe it was someone from that tofu convention that was going on downstairs," Evie offered. "Heaven knows they'll eat anything green."

"Good point." I reached for the phone and Evie shook her head. "You might want to wait until after your seven o'clock."

"I have a seven? Since when?"

She glanced at her watch. "As of forty-five minutes ago. She called and said she needed a date this very minute, so I told her to come right over."

"I think I love you."

"That's what they all say." She winked. "Should I show her in?"

I nodded and pushed to my feet just as a tall, voluptuous redhead walked into my office. She was the quintessential party girl in a silver lamé mini-dress, knee-high silver boots and an excited expression.

"Miss Marchette?"

I smiled. "Call me Lil."

"Awesome." Her voice was as perky as the double Ds outlined by her fitted dress. Bright green eyes rimmed in silver liner bounced around my office. "Wow. This place is fan-frickin'-tastic."

"Thanks. And your name is?"

"Tabitha. Tabitha Gallows." She perched on the edge of a nearby chair. Her fingers twitched and her feet tapped. She looked ready to bounce back up at the first sign of a Katy Perry song.

I could practically feel the energy rolling off her.

Feel being the key word.

I couldn't read a damned thing. Her eyes sparkled so clear and glistening, yet I couldn't see one itty-bitty thing about her. Which meant she wasn't the bubbly, peppy human she appeared.

My nostrils flared, but other than a spritz of Very Sexy and the faint aroma of a recent manicure, I smelled nothing but my own eau de cotton candy.

Nix a born vampire.

She wasn't a made vampire either. I realized that when she didn't flash a pair of fangs and try to hump my leg in the first five seconds.

Or a werewolf (she didn't blink much less gaze longingly when I offered her a leftover burger Evie had left in the mini-fridge).

Or a demon (no cursing or vomiting when I accidentally spritzed her with holy water—I had oodles of the stuff left over from Evie's recent possession).

Which left me wondering *What the fuck?*

"A warlock," she said, as if reading my mind.

"You're a warlock?"

"No, silly." A brilliant smile parted her full lips. "I'm looking for a warlock."

"So you're a witch?"

"Hardly." Before I could question her further, she shifted the conversation back to finding the perfect Mr. Magic. "He has to be tall, dark and handsome. But not too handsome. He should have a few flaws. Eyebrows that are a little too bushy and a quarter-inch scar running across the left side of his chin. And one dimple cutting into his right cheek. And he has to have brown eyes. Dark brown with a hard gleam. No beard or mustache. Short hair. Six-two."

"Sounds like you have someone in particular in mind."

"No, not really." Laughter bubbled past her lips. "Just my own imagination at work. But I'm sure there's a real man out there who fits the bill." Expectancy lit her gaze. "Have you seen him?" Silence stretched between us for several long seconds as she eyed me and waited for a reply.

"Without a doubt," I finally said. "I have over two thousand eligible bachelors in my database." Give or take 1,488. "I'm sure one of them will fit the description to a T." I settled behind my desk and reached for a pen. "But before we get ahead of ourselves, the first thing we need to do is get to know the real Tabitha. Your likes and dislikes. Your hopes and dreams." I gave her my most convincing smile, along with a mental *You should take the ultra-deluxe package.*

I know, I know. She was obviously an Other and she was looking for a member of the opposite sex. But hey, it couldn't hurt to try.

"Why don't you get started filling out this questionnaire?" I pulled a form from my bottom desk drawer, attached it to a clipboard and handed it to her. "The best matches are tailored to each individual, so the more I know about you, the better."

"You don't need a form for that. I love dancing and parties and having fun. End of story."

"No hobbies?"

"I do like to shop."

I smiled and made a quick note. "Shopping's good."

"I like watching E! and I'm addicted to Oxygen's *Bad Girls Club* and I never miss Fashion Week."

"Just jot it all down and I'll see what I can find for you. Evie mentioned that you need a date fast. Is there a special event coming up?"

"Definitely."

"A wedding?"

"Not really."

"Engagement party?"

"No."

"Office get-together?"

"Something like that. If I don't have my warlock with me by midnight next Friday, I'm getting fired."

"That's urgent, all right. Don't worry, we'll find you someone," I said with the utmost confidence, despite the nagging voice that kept reminding me about Esther and last night's fiasco and the fact that I was this close to bankruptcy and a Moe's lime green polo shirt.

A wave of anxiety rushed through me and I attacked my keyboard with renewed determination. Crawling home to my folks would be bad enough. Doing it in lime green? *So* not happening.

Tabitha spent about a nanosecond filling out the form and fifteen minutes tapping her feet and humming to Katy Perry's "I Kissed a Girl" drifting over my surround sound.

Meanwhile, I cruised my database for possible matches. I came up with a whopping two—a warlock from Trenton with red hair and a potbelly and a werewolf into Harry Potter role-playing (What? I'm doing the best I can here.).

Tabitha didn't look jazzed about either, but she did agree to check them out. I set up the dates, promised to keep looking and loaded her into a cab bound for a hot new dance club and prospect number one.

I called Mia after that.

"Evie told me you want to lower your standards. Does that mean you're willing to take two orgasms a night instead of three?"

"Actually, I was thinking zero. I'm embarking on a new phase in my life."

"The I'm-never-having-fun-again phase?"

"I'm embracing celibacy."

Yep, zero fun.

"I want you to find me a man who is not into sex in any way, shape or form," she went on. "A guy who doesn't sleep around or look at porn or watch the Victoria's Secret Fashion Show during the Super Bowl halftime. I want a man who'll notice my brains instead of my boobs."

"Your last date pooped out after the first orgasm, didn't he?"

"He couldn't even get it up. I gave him a lap dance, but nothing. I'm tired of being let down. If I have zero expectations, I can't get disappointed, right? I figure I'll just go for the exact opposite of my ideal, that way I'm sure to find *someone*." She sounded so defeated and lonely that my heart hitched.

"We haven't exhausted all of our efforts," I told her. "We can keep looking. We'll eventually find him," I said with more certainty than I felt.

"I'll be too old to enjoy him by then." She seemed to gather her resolve. "No, this is better."

"But is it what you *really* want?"

"I really want a man who can come five times in one night. A man who is faithful and employed, and who always remembers to put the toilet seat down. Know any?"

"One celibate with substance coming right up."

I lined up three dates for Mia—a Sunday school teacher, a city government worker and a pediatric ER nurse named Harmon (no, really). They weren't the most manly men, but they each had a job and very little interest in sex (too moral, too scared of a scandal and too busy). As for faithful, only time would tell on that but the odds were pretty good.

I spent a few minutes thinking about my own love life and the fact that Ty still hadn't said the L word (and probably never would). Irrelevant, I told myself. I didn't need it. I knew and that was good enough. Really.

After that, I followed up on last night's matches and tried not to stake myself.

Sheesh. Didn't anyone have a good time?

"I had a fabulous time," Aurelia Sinclair told me.

"Really?"

"Of course. William is the perfect werewolf. He's strong and virile and bald. Procreation is a given."

"William?"

"The guy down in the lobby. The one in the uniform. He handled my car with perfection. The man definitely knows how to drive."

"That wasn't one of my guests. He was the valet."

"Regardless, I'm forever in your debt."

Okay, so it wasn't a match made in DED heaven, but at this point, a satisfied customer was a satisfied customer. "Would you be willing to put that in writing? I'd love a testimonial for the website."

I got a three-line spiel about how DED was the ultimate hookup service and decided to call it quits on a high note.

I transferred the phones and was just locking up when I felt the prickling on the back of my neck. It was the same creepy feeling I'd had on my way into work. A feeling that turned to full-blown panic when I felt the presence directly behind me.

I know, I know. Megalicious vampire and terror don't exactly go together—unless, of course, I'm the one striking terror in the hearts of innocent villagers. But this *is* New York. You never know what's going to creep out of an alley.

"I don't have any money," I said, fighting to keep my voice even. "And my credit cards are maxed.

And while the sex might be pretty great, I don't even know you and so it's not going to happen."

"You're going to die, bitch," came the deadly promise.

And here I'd thought my night couldn't get any worse.

Seven
❤ ❤ ❤

"I'm going to rip off your head and stuff it down your throat." The deadly voice slid into my ears again and my anxiety eased.

"Nina?" I whirled and found myself facing the tall, svelte blonde who'd been my friend since birth. "Geez, you scared the crap out of me."

"Really?" She shook her head. "I mean, yeah, good. You should be scared, because I'm serious. I'm going to tie you to the balcony and leave you to fry."

I realized in a nanosecond that she meant business. Not because of her tone of voice, but because she was wearing sweats and flip-flops and zero makeup.

"I'm going to truss you up, dump you at the nearest church and let your skin fester until you're nothing but an itchy, oozing mess and then I'm going to—"

"Would you stop with the vivid death threats already?" My gaze met hers. "What's wrong? Why are you dressed like that?"

"I'm being inconspicuous. It's Murder 101—never draw attention to yourself. You have to lay low. Fly under the radar. That way, no one will remember you later in a lineup."

"What are you talking about?"

"You're going down, Marchette." She glared. "You ruined my afterlife."

I remembered Mandy's comment about Nina and the cocoa. "My mother coerced you into going to Mandy's. That's what this is about."

"She coerced Rob and I tagged along. This is about next Friday and her Huntress Club meeting."

"You didn't agree to go, did you?"

"I didn't have a choice. She said I was going to be a part of the family and so I had to meet her friends." Her gaze narrowed and her eyes gleamed a bright, fierce red. "It's all your fault for siccing her on me in the first place. She thinks Rob and I are serious."

"Aren't you?"

"Yes. I mean, no." She shook her head. "I have to break up with him."

"Just because of my mother? Listen, it's only one meeting. You go. You have some refreshments, talk about how great Rob is, and you're home free."

"But that's the problem. Rob isn't great. He has flaws. Major flaws."

"You didn't seem to have any concerns last night in the storage closet."

"I wasn't thinking straight. Now that I am, I see that he's not the vampire for me. Sure, he's got a phenomenal fertility rating. And abs you could pound nails on. And great hands. And he doesn't mind it when I drink the last glass of O+ or misplace the remote or get makeup smudges on the lining of his coffin. Still, he's far from perfect."

I tried to process her words, but my brain stuck on one thing in particular. "Rob sleeps in a coffin?"

A grin played at her lips. "I wouldn't exactly call it sleeping."

"Forget I asked. Let's get back to Rob. What's wrong with him? Maybe we can fix it."

I expected the usual spiel befitting a born male vampire—he's narcissistic and selfish and conceited and money-hungry.

"He's too . . ." She made a face. "*Nice.*"

"No problem. We'll just try to get him to be more considerate and compassionate and—What did you just say?"

She shook her head. "He brings me flowers and he rubs my feet. He even sliced and diced this jerk who kept grabbing my ass when we went to that Nickelback concert last week."

"And the problem is?" Other than murder one, of course.

"He's nice," she said again, "and I'm not. I mean,

come on, I'm so into myself it isn't funny. I'm selfish and conceited and all I really care about is money and sex. I don't deserve a vampire like Rob."

"Trust me, you deserve him. He's every bit as selfish as you are. He's just not showing it. You're in the honeymoon phase."

"But what if we're not? What if he's really a great guy and I'm a bitch?" She shook her head. "He'll get nicer and I'll get bitchier and he'll end up hating me. I can't do that. Better to call it quits right now before we get any more involved. Then we can still be friends. And still have hot, meaningless sex once in a while."

I had a feeling that Nina wasn't half as scared of becoming more of a bitch as she was of changing. Mellowing. Falling in love.

I wasn't going to say that, however. I knew my friend. She was in major denial and the more I pushed, the more likely she was to run the other way. "You're right. You're much too bitchy for my brother. You should break it off now."

She gave me a strange look. "Really?"

I nodded vigorously. "You're beyond bitchy. If there were a Bee-yotch category in the Olympics, you'd win the gold."

"I'm not *that* bad."

"Don't sell yourself short. You're at the top of your game. A master."

"Really?" Instead of looking hopeful, her eyes were bright. I ignored the urge to throw my arms around her and tell her she was the sweetest, most considerate, most wonderful vampire in the world and any male would be lucky to have her.

"You should tell Rob off, pack your stuff, move out and cut all ties," I said instead. Harsh, right? But a matchmaker's gotta do what a matchmaker's gotta do.

She blinked. "You think?"

"Straight up. Then you can go back to boffing busboys and concierge attendants and Rob can find a real vampire who wants to settle down. In fact," I smiled, "I think I might have just the female for him. I signed her up just yesterday. Tall. Brunette—"

"Rob likes blondes," she cut in, fingering a golden tendril that had come loose from her ponytail.

"Rob *liked* blondes. Once you break his heart, he'll go on a mad rampage for brunettes. He'll be dying to go out with my prospect—who, for the record, is also rich and great in bed."

"Don't you think it's a little premature to try hooking him up? We haven't even broken up yet."

"That's true. I mean, he's so stuck on you, he'll probably need time for reality to sink in before he'll even consider another vampire."

"Definitely."

I glanced at my watch. "If I know my brother, he should be back in the saddle in about twenty-four hours. I'll give him a call tomorrow night, provided you go through with it and break up with him tonight."

"The sooner the better," she said, but I could see the doubt in her eyes. She squared her shoulders and turned. "I'm getting this over with right now." She sniffled.

I know, right?

"At the very latest, first thing in the morning," she added as she signaled a cab and flip-flopped over.

"Atta girl," I said as she climbed in.

I gave her a wave as the cab disappeared and said a little prayer that I hadn't just pushed her into making the biggest mistake of her afterlife. With Esther missing and my business spiraling down the toilet, I had enough to worry about.

I spent the next few minutes trying to hail my own cab. When that failed, I disappeared into the alley near DED and closed my eyes. Soon, my heartbeat faded into the steady beat of wings and I flapped my way home.

A quick metamorphosis near the back trash can, and I walked around the front and let myself into the building. Minus a shoe, of course.

There was someone in my apartment.

I'd like to say it was my super-vamp abilities that tipped me off a few seconds later when I reached my floor. Truthfully, though, I was running a quart low. I'd had one measly glass of blood mixed in with the energy drinks. While plenty to start the evening, it wasn't enough to keep me going past midnight.

No, I picked up on the B&E because my door stood partially open and a light shone inside.

I paused in the doorway and debated my options— run for help or bust in and kick some ass.

My gut leaned toward the first, but my inner fashionista kept me rooted to the spot. Everything I owned was in that apartment, including a brand-spanking-new pair of Dior sunglasses and a Marc Jacobs coin purse.

A wave of determination swept through me. I was a born *vampere*. Fearless. Ferocious. And fiercely overprotective of my wardrobe.

I pushed the door open and stepped inside. My gaze scanned the small living room for anything out of the ordinary.

The antique coffee table I'd talked my mother into giving me? *Check.*

My prized collection of *InStyle* stacked on top? *Check.*

Traitorous cat sleeping on my favorite rug? *Check.*

Hunky, blond Swede stretched bare-assed on my sofa? *Check, check.*

I blinked, but he didn't disappear. Still hunky. *Blink, blink.* Still blond. *Blink, blink, blink.* Still naked—

"Vonderful." Hans' thick accent echoed in my ears and distracted me from the impressive package parked against my favorite throw pillow.

My gaze ping-ponged back to his face and his

bright blue eyes. My mom had picked up Hans during a holiday in Sweden. Basically, she'd fallen for his magical hands and he'd fallen for her bank account, and so they'd been a perfect match. He'd gladly given up a poor existence as a shoe cobbler in exchange for a small fortune, food, unlimited spray tan appointments and a personal trainer. He'd also given up his free will and succumbed to my mother's vamp mojo. He now lived in a state of perpetual glam, his own personality whittled away to reflect the man at his most basic form.

In other words, his thoughts read like a testimonial to Swiss Colony.

His name was Hans and he liked cheese. He preferred the smoked cheddar, but on occasion he went a little crazy and indulged in a nut-covered Gouda or a little creamy Havarti. And he went total apeshit over the chive and cream cheese crock spread.

He smiled. "I've been vaiting for you." He pushed to his feet and motioned toward my bedroom.

I glanced at the open doorway. Candles blazed and a pile of pillows waited on the bed.

"I have everyzing ready," he added.

"Ready for what?"

"Massage. We must do massage." Because that's what Hans did. He ate cheese and gave massages, and since I was fresh out of a party tray, he was going for the next best thing.

Another glance at the candles and pillows and my muscles screamed for relief.

"Come." He motioned me into the bedroom, his Johnson bobbing with enthusiasm.

While I have nothing against a naked man stoked at the prospect of putting his hands on me, it just didn't seem right, considering Ty had been here only hours ago. And he'd been naked. And, well, I much preferred him naked to anyone else. That, and my mother would shit a brick if she knew Hans was here.

In case you haven't tuned in, my mother is a tad on the selfish side. And domineering. And since I refused to cooperate and do the Moe's thing, she'd cut me off from any and all amenities—no housekeeping, no massage, no free dry cleaning. I was totally and completely on my own.

Which was exactly the way I liked it. Most of the time. But after worrying all day, I was kinda sorta feeling sorry for myself and, well, he was already here.

I headed for the bedroom. "Would you mind wrapping a towel around your waist?" I asked as I slipped into the bathroom, ditched my clothes and donned a robe.

"I give best massage when I can move freely."

"I get best massage when I'm not distracted," I said as I opened the door. I tossed him an extra large bath sheet. "There's a cheese wheel in it for you if you cooperate."

His eyes glittered. "Cheddar?"

"If you want."

He snatched up the bath sheet, wrapped it around his toned middle and knotted it at his hip. "All eez ready."

Five seconds later, I sank facedown into a mound of pillows. He hit the lights, plunging us into the candlelit darkness. He hummed as he reached for a bottle of scented oil.

The warm liquid trickled between my shoulder blades and for the first time I started to think that maybe, just maybe, Fate wasn't taking a big giant crap right on top of me. Sure, one of my good friends and clients was missing and my mom was an anti-human nut and my best friend in the whole world was about to make the biggest mistake of her afterlife, *and* my happily-ever-after with Ty wasn't exactly the picture-perfect one I'd always dreamt of (he was still made and I was still born and we still had to break the news to my family), but things could be worse.

That's what I told myself as the oil trickled over my skin and Hans rubbed his hands together.

My life wasn't bad. Not even close. I had my friends. I had my family. I had my health. I had a one-of-a-kind pair of Miu Miu silk slippers—

Rrrringgggggg!

The phone echoed and the world cut me off mid–positive reinforcement. I closed my eyes as a wave of *Oh, no* rolled through me.

Would I ever get a friggin' break?

Eight

❤ ❤ ❤

Rrrringggg!

I knew deep in my gut it wasn't Ash calling to tell me that Esther was fine. Or Ty proclaiming his undying love. Or Nina One telling me that she loved Rob and couldn't imagine eternity without him. It was bad news. Fate straining for that final *plopppp.*

I buried my head under a pillow and tried to tune out everything except the feel of the oil pooling on my skin. Ignorance is bliss, right? I would slink away emotionally and hide out for a little while. Maybe indulge in a few fantasies while Hans worked his magic.

I was just about to settle down on a white sand beach and sip a few margaritas when the ringing stopped and the answering machine kicked in.

My mother's stern voice lifted the edge of the

pillow, crawled beneath and smacked me on the side of the head.

"I know Hans is there."

"You do not know that," I murmured into the soft down.

"I do," she said. My head snapped up and the pillow went bye-bye.

I glanced around, but didn't see any surveillance equipment. I eyed Hans, who was busy cracking his knuckles to warm up. Had she bugged him?

"Your brother told me that Mandy sent him over," my mom added as if she could hear the thoughts echoing in my head. "And if he's there, it means he isn't here for my nightly bedtime massage. I haven't missed my nightly in five years, three months and four days, and I don't intend to start now." A hard note crept into her voice. "You have exactly forty-five minutes to get him home or I'm going to call Jonelle Dubois at the club and have her cancel her profile."

Jonelle Dubois was a high-profile born vampire who'd recently lost her significant other to a freak accident involving a Harley, a motorcycle ramp and a misplaced flagpole. Needless to say, she was lonely and in desperate need of a BV father-figure for her thirteen children. Thanks to my mother, I'd landed her profile (and a nice, big fat check, which had paid my Visa for this month and funded the refreshments for last night's soiree).

I gathered the robe to me, slid out from under Hans's hands and headed for the phone.

"I think I'll introduce her to your father's lawyer at tomorrow night's hunt."

I.e. the vamp's version of the Outdoor Channel's *Hunting for Dollars*. We all gathered at my folks' and hunted the *it* person to keep our skills sharp. The prize? Bonus vacation days from Moe's.

"He's nice. Single. His fertility rating isn't all that impressive, but Jonelle has all of the children she wants," my mom went on. "She's looking forward to grandchildren at this point, so I doubt she'll be turned off by—"

"I was about to put Hans in a cab." The words rushed out as I picked up the phone. "I barely got home from work and found him. Just this very second," I added. "I haven't even had a chance to slide off my shoes, much less slip into a robe and stretch out on the bed for what I'm sure would be the massage of my afterlife. Really."

"Lilliana, I don't appreciate you undermining my efforts with Jack's human."

"Her name is Mandy and I wasn't undermining anything. She doesn't like massages," I blurted. "Not if they're given by, um, Swedish people. She's, um, allergic." You try coming up with something better when you're naked and oily and totally stressed.

"Really?"

"Cross my heart."

"Wonderful." My mother cheered immediately. "I'll have Hans serve the drinks at tomorrow night's hunt. That ought to inspire a nasty reaction. Make sure you're on time, dear. I have another plan and I need your help."

No. Not happening. Not this vampire. No way. No how. Nuh-uh.

"Lilliana?"

"Okay," I heard myself squeak.

She's my mother, for Damien's sake. She endured labor and hardship and ungodly cravings (she'd snacked on Attila and a few of his Huns during the third trimester). The least I could do, the very least, was pretend to indulge her wild and crazy plan to prevent my brother and his wife from procreating.

"I'll be there," I vowed.

"Early," she pressed. "Your dad's demonstrating his new right-hand driver. I've seen it in action about a thousand times this past week, so he needs a new audience. Speaking of which, I've invited Remy."

"Great." Remy I could handle. He knew about Ty and so I didn't have to pretend to like him. He would respect my space. We could hide out in the pool house, laugh about old times and have a completely innocent time. No pressure.

"Unfortunately, he can't make it," my mother added. "So I've invited Ivan the OB/GYN."

"Ma—"

"Wear something sexy," she cut in. "No need to put all of our nails in one coffin. A vampire of your caliber should have options, so make sure you go for tight and low cut."

"How about a noose?"

"Lilliana?"

"Tight. Low cut," I grumbled. "Got it." *Not.* I hung up and turned to Hans.

"No massage?" He looked heartbroken.

"Sorry, big boy. You're past your curfew." I headed for the bathroom to trade my robe for some sweats. I wiped off the warm oil and slid into a pink set of Juicy Couture.

Back in the bedroom, I helped him into his clothes—a white T-shirt and matching white slacks—and then ushered him out the door and down the stairs.

"What about my cheese vheel?" he asked as I pushed him down the front walk toward a waiting cab.

"I'll bring it tomorrow night." I fed him and his bag of massage oils into the idling cab, gave the driver the address and watched them pull away from the curb. I was just about to turn and head back inside when I felt the first drop of rain.

It wasn't the cosmic crap I'd expected, but it was close enough, particularly since there wasn't a cloud in the sky.

I glanced up in time to see my upstairs neighbor framed in the window. His eyes were glazed over and I could smell the beer on his breath. He shook his package, stuffed it back into his pants, and disappeared into his apartment and the waiting poker game.

Ugh.

A wave of ickiness swept through me and I hit the stairs at the speed of light. Two seconds later, I was frantically soaping myself under a hot shower. I scrubbed fiercely for the next fifteen minutes and then I did what any super-hot born *vampere* would do after getting pissed on.

No, I didn't go on a killing rampage.

Make that any super-hot born *vampere* with an aversion to violence.

I climbed into bed, and cried like a *bebe*.

"It lives," Max declared when he opened the door of my parents' house early Sunday evening.

Max was my oldest brother and the one who should have been fulfilling my mother's dreams of grandchildren. Unfortunately, he couldn't seem to find a suitable eternity mate. As for unsuitable? He'd become quite the expert. He'd been having a hush-hush affair with a hot-blooded female werewolf who happened to be my father's next door neighbor and arch enemy.

"How's it going with Viola?"

He glared and gave me a shush with his hand. "Could you keep your voice down?"

"You still haven't come clean?"

"There's nothing to come clean about. We broke up."

"What happened?"

"She was getting too clingy." He shrugged. "I had to drop the old ax."

I eyed him. "She broke up with you, didn't she?"

He looked ready to argue, but then he shrugged. "She said I was too overbearing. Can you believe that?" I arched an eyebrow. "Okay, so I'm overbearing. I can't help it. It's in my DNA. Not that it matters now. It's better that we split. We're not exactly the ideal couple. Dad said she poured sulfuric acid on his azalea bushes last week and now he's going to make her pay. He's talking nuclear weapons this time. He found this guy in Trenton who offered to build him a bomb. Speaking of bombs"—he wiggled his eyebrows—"Mom found you a new guy."

I started to turn, but he grabbed my arm. "Cheer up. It's only a few hours."

"Says you. You don't have to try to make small talk with someone you have absolutely nothing in common with."

"So make out instead. That's what I always do." A loud snort carried down the hall, followed by my mother's "Ivan, you have such an interesting laugh."

"Then again," my brother added, "I could stall while you make a run for it."

I was about to give the idea some serious consideration when I heard footsteps. In the blink of an eye, my mother stood next to Max.

"It's about time." She gripped my arm and pulled me inside. The door shut and just like that, I was trapped.

She ushered me down the hall and into the main living room. "Lilliana, I'd like you to meet Ivan. Ivan, this is my daughter."

I smiled. "Hi."

"Hey." The acknowledgment ended with a loud snort.

It was definitely going to be a long and painful night.

"Why don't you two head out to the veranda. It's time to start."

"Where's Rob?" My gaze did a 360 around the room and hope blossomed. "We can't start until everyone's here."

"He canceled," Max said, coming up behind me.

"He what?" Before I could point out that no Marchette had ever canceled when it came to the hunt, my mother herded everyone to the door. A few steps shy, she pulled me to the side.

"I need you to distract the human after the hunt so that I can slip the pill into her drink."

"I'm on it."

I spent the next half hour hiding out in the pool house, listening to Ivan talk about his Ferrari. And his Bentley. And his Hummer.

I have to admit that I'd been initially turned off by the snorting. But it came in very handy. Otherwise,

I would have nodded off five seconds into the conversation.

". . . gets terrible gas mileage, but I don't mind. It's not like I can't afford it." *Snort.*

My head bobbed up at the sound and my watery gaze focused on the source.

He was an all right–looking vampire. Boring as hell, but I'm a firm believer that one female vampire's worst nightmare is another's fantasy come true. "So you like cars?"

"Expensive cars."

"And you're ready to settle down?"

"I've been ready. I just haven't found the right woman. I spend most of my time at classic car auctions when I'm not working. It's a predominantly male hobby, so I don't meet too many women. Just car girls, but most of them are human and so they can't give me what I need."

"What if I told you that I could give you what you need?"

He grinned. "That's why I'm here." He closed his eyes, leaned in for a kiss and . . . *snort.*

I poked him and his eyes snapped open. "Not that."

"But you said—"

"That I could give you what you want, as in help you find it. I'm a matchmaker."

"Your mother said you were a manager at one of the NYC Moe's."

"In my past life." The one where I'd died of extreme boredom and embarrassment. "I own a hookup service in Manhattan. I can help you find that perfect eternity mate."

"You'd do that for me?"

"You and your Visa card. I also take American Express, MasterCard, Diners Club, or you could pay in cash. Cash is always good."

I spent the next ten minutes doing a verbal Q&A with Ivan and keying in the results on my iPhone before the whistle sounded and the hunt officially ended.

I met up with everyone on the veranda just as my father emerged from the surrounding woods, pulling my brother Jack via the whistle around his neck.

"I win again," my father declared.

"Again?" Max trudged up the steps behind them. "That makes twice in the past month."

My father puffed out his chest. "I'm the superior vampire here."

"But you hadn't won in the fifty years prior to that. Twice after a fifty-year dry spell. Something funny's going on—ouch!"

My mother had smacked Max on the back of the head as she came up next to him. "Oh, sorry, dear. My reflexes are still on high alert. Stop being a spoiled sport. Your father won fair and square. And it was well deserved after a seventy-five-year losing streak." My father glared, and my mom added,

"But not for lack of skill. You are a superb hunter and a magnificent father. Which is why you hold back on purpose, so that your children are forced to hone their skills and rise to the challenge."

"Exactly," my father declared. "You're getting lax," my father told Jack. "You didn't even hear me coming."

"I was tired. I haven't been getting much sleep since Mandy and I are trying for a baby."

"I have been keeping him up," she offered, sliding an arm through his. "Come on, honey, let's get you a drink."

Inside, my mother approached an antique cherrywood sideboard and started dishing out drinks. I'd set up an official in-office appointment with Ivan and was just about to guzzle a glass of AB– when my mother snatched me to the side.

"You were supposed to distract her while I slipped the stuff into her glass."

"I was so busy talking to Ivan that I forgot."

"Really?" Her eyes gleamed. "Oh, well. It makes no nevermind. Mission accomplished." She smiled and crossed the room toward my father, who was retelling the story (for the fifth time) of how he'd outsmarted and overpowered Jack.

My gaze swiveled toward Mandy, who stood near the sideboard, a glass of what appeared to be iced tea in her hand.

She lifted the glass and touched her lips and a bolt of panic raced through me.

I reached her in a nanosecond, snatched her glass and downed the contents in one gulp.

"Sorry," I gasped. "It just looked so good and I was really thirsty. I'll get you another one."

One that wasn't spiked with birth control.

The thought struck and I realized what I'd just done. My stomach went queasy and my own ovaries gave a shout of disapproval.

Then again, it's not like I was using them.

As much as I hated to admit it, Ty and I weren't exactly a match made in biological heaven. There would be no babies in our future. No picking out baby furniture or buying teeny, tiny outfits, or framing pics of the ultrasound.

For the record, I've never been one of those sappy vampires who dreams of having a great big baby shower with little pink and blue petit fours and a safety pin corsage. No diaper cake centerpiece. Or pastel-wrapped gifts. I am so *not* a pastel person. I never have been.

Except maybe lavender. I do sort of like lavender.

But I digress. The point is, I've never really fantasized about the baby part. The commitment ceremony, yes. Beyond that? Well, I usually didn't make it past the honeymoon in Aruba.

Still, while I didn't sit around fantasizing about it, it's always been something that I knew I would experience. Sooner or later.

Or so I'd thought.

My chest hitched and my eyes watered. I blinked

frantically. Who needed babies? A great relationship.
A fabulous career. I was set.

Really.

"You should have a soda," I told Mandy as I retrieved a can of Sprite from a small refrigerator
built into the wall. "Tea has too much caffeine." I
popped the lid and poured her a glass.

"What about you?" she asked.

"I think I need something stronger."

As optimistic as I was, I knew my no-*bebes* realization wasn't going down without a chaser.

I grabbed a bottle of vodka and opened up the
hatch.

Nine
❤ ❤ ❤

"She left me," Rob announced when he showed up on my doorstep later that night.

At least I thought it was him.

I blinked away the vodka haze until my gaze focused. His features sharpened and, sure enough, he was standing there, live and in color, and looking as miserable as I felt.

He ran a hand through his short brown hair and grimaced. "Everything was fine early this morning. She came home from work. We had sex. We fed. I did her. We took a shower. She did me. We watched *The View*. I gave it to her. She gave it—"

"I get it." I sipped a cup of Starbucks House Blend and willed the floor to stop trembling. "You. Nina. Sexual Nirvana."

"But when we woke up this afternoon, she was

like this pod chick. Cold. Indifferent. She got mad at me for no reason, so I got mad at her because she got mad at me. Then we got into a big knock-down, drag-out."

"No wonder you weren't at Mom and Dad's."

"She said Mom was a control freak and she wasn't spending another second with her at some stupid hunt."

Forget BFFs. We were definitely twins.

"She said it was over," he went on, "and then she kicked me out."

The news sobered me the way no amount of specialty coffee could. "Oh, Rob. I'm so sorry."

He shook his head. "I just don't know what happened. One minute we were great, the next . . ."

He looked so sad and pathetic and my chest tightened. Guilt rolled through me, followed by a rush of protective instinct. He was my brother, after all.

"I'm sure you didn't do anything."

The statement seemed to snap him out of it. He looked at me as if I'd announced I was going on a no-plasma diet. "Damn straight I didn't do anything."

Rob meet Denial. Denial meet Rob.

"It's all her." He turned and retrieved an Under Armour duffel bag from the hallway. Dropping it inside my door, he pushed past me into my apartment. "She's crazy. She's probably sucked one too many schizophrenics and now it's messing with her brain. That happened to Great-uncle Robert, remember? He was never the same again after he went on a feeding frenzy at that insane asylum."

"But *you've* fed on *her,* right?" I toed his bag out of the way, closed the door and followed him into the living room. "And if she's crazy, then that would make you—"

"Lucky," he cut in, dropping onto the sofa, "that I realized what was happening and took a hike before she contaminated me. I was so outta there."

"But I thought *she* kicked *you* out?"

"You're missing the point."

"That she broke up with you and you don't have a clue as to why?"

"That she broke up with me because she knew I was just a heartbeat away from breaking up with her and she wanted to do it first." He wagged a finger at me. "Don't think I don't know how you females operate. It's all a big game. You get wind that we're getting disinterested and, *bam,* you cut your losses and bail. Then we're left wondering what the hell happened and you get to take credit for dropping the ax." He shrugged. "Not that I give a shit. Let her take the credit. I'm just glad she saved me the trouble and the guilt."

Yeah, I'll bet.

"Hell, I'm happy about it," he went on. "Pumped." He flexed his arms. "Why, this is the best fucking night of my afterlife."

I folded my arms and eyed him. "So what are you doing here?"

"I told you, she kicked me out."

"But it's your apartment. Shouldn't she be the one packing her bags?"

"She's just staying until she finds something she likes. Then she's out and I'm back in. I give it a week, tops."

"Are you kidding me? This is New York. It takes longer than a week to find a parking space."

"I know. That's why it's a good thing I've got a place to stay."

"Where?"

"Here."

My gaze swiveled to the duffel bag and reality hit. *Here.*

Time out.

It's not that I don't love my brother. I do. At the same time, he (like all *mes frères*) can be a royal pain in the ass. He's macho and chauvinistic and conceited and narcissistic and (this is the kicker) even more spoiled than I am. It was hard enough dealing with my own inner brat. I wasn't putting up with anyone else's.

On top of *that,* I was in the honeymoon phase of a new relationship. Ty and I needed our alone time.

Or we would just as soon as his work calmed down enough so that he could actually spend more than a few hours with me.

"You can't stay here," I told him. "Just grow some balls, go home and tell Nina she'll have to go to a hotel."

"I've got balls," he said defensively. "Big ones. Massive."

"Then you won't have any trouble tossing her toward the nearest Hyatt."

"A hotel's so impersonal."

"She works at a hotel."

"Exactly. You wouldn't tell me to sleep at Moe's."

"Hey, there's an idea."

"Very funny."

"It's only fair you should be the one to keep the apartment," I pressed. "It's *your* apartment."

"True, but I can't kick her out on the street."

I wanted to point out that if it had been any other female vampire (and he had a long list of them in his past), he would have kicked her out and slammed the door without so much as a twinge of conscience.

We're talking a born male vampire. Hitler had nothing on 'em.

"I mean," he rushed on, "I *could* kick her out. I *would*. But what if she gets vindictive? I don't want some crazy pulling a *Fatal Attraction*."

At least that's what he said.

But I didn't miss the flicker of hurt in his eyes and the tick in his right jaw. He was upset and doing his best not to show it.

A front that would crumble soon enough, once he passed *I'm the luckiest SOB on earth* and cruised straight into *I suck rocks and it's no wonder she left my sorry ass*.

"A week," I told him. "But then you move back to your own apartment."

"Yeah." He craned his neck, scoped out the surroundings and rubbed his hands together. "So, do you have any blood?" He pushed to his feet. "I'm starved."

"If you're looking for a fresh maiden, I'm afraid I'm all out."

"What about something from the deli?" He started for the kitchen.

I was right on his heels, alarm rattling through me. This was my brother. Marchette flesh and blood. He lived to hypnotize and tantalize and sink his fangs into a sweet, succulent neck. Any neck so long as it was attached to breasts and a vagina. "Since when do you bottle it?"

He hauled open the fridge and ducked his head in. "Bottled blood is as good as any." He pulled a full bottle of imported AB– from the shelf.

"So sayeth a vamp who is totally whipped."

Grabbing a corkscrew, he frowned. "I'm not whipped." He wound the screw into the top and a loud *popppp* followed. "I don't even like Nina."

No, he loved her. He was just too proud to admit it because he thought she didn't love him. But she did. She was just too scared to admit it.

And they said humans were clueless when it came to relationships?

"You should be scourging the countryside for

sweet, succulent virgins," I told him. "At the very least, a semi-decent hottie with great taste in clothes. Unless, of course"—I eyeballed him—"you still have feelings for Nina."

"Are you kidding?" He went for an I-don't-give-a-shit look and failed miserably. "I couldn't care less about her. That virgin thing"—he pointed at me— "I'm on it." Instead of bothering with a glass and a microwave, he gulped the blood cold and headed back to the living room. "First thing tomorrow night," he called over his shoulder.

I followed him. "Why not tonight?"

"It's Sunday," he said, as if that explained everything. He collapsed on the sofa. Bottle in one hand, he reached for my remote and flipped on the TV. "ESPN is running a replay of the Giants versus the Cowboys." He toed off his boots, planted his feet on my coffee table and settled back into the sofa. "I heard it's one helluva game."

"Why don't we go out?" The sooner he started hooking up with new women, the sooner he would realize that Nina was the only woman for him.

That, and the fact that I was feeling pretty crappy. I needed a distraction from the whole Esther situation. Since the office was closed on Sunday, I was on my own for a diversion.

"A brother and sister night," I added. "You know, two siblings doing the town. Kicking up their heels. Having fun."

"Sounds fuckin' A," he murmured, but he'd

already tuned me out. "Maybe tomorrow." He grabbed a throw pillow, leaned back and shoved it under his head. He took another swig of blood.

My gaze went to Killer. "What about you? You up for a walk?" I wiggled my eyebrows. "We could go window-shopping."

Are you kidding me? There's so much estrogen floating around here I'm practically suffocating as it is. He blinked and leapt up onto the couch. Settling next to Rob, he propped his head on my brother's thigh and eyed the TV. *It's about time we had a little testosterone in this place.*

"Fine. Do the male bonding thing." I nailed Killer with a knowing stare. "But if anyone starts a pissing contest, I swear I'm kicking you both out."

I left Rob and Killer in the living room, retreated to my bedroom and spent the next several hours sucking down coffee and Tums and Googling "Mordred Lucius."

Ash had said the ritual site would have special significance for Mordred.

A place he'd been before.

Someplace he felt comfortable.

Powerful.

As odd as his name was, there were actually 108 listed as living in the United States. I went for the only one with a current address in New York (he'd had a driver's license) and continued my search until I'd accumulated twelve past known addresses.

I could only hope he wasn't going for a location

prior to computerized records and Google. He *was* over eight hundred years old.

"I've got twelve possible locations," I told Ash when he answered his cell.

"Who is this?"

"You know who it is."

"Yeah, but I like to hear you say it. You've got a sexy voice."

"Pull your mind out of the gutter."

"Hey, you're the one who called me."

"To relay information, and not the kind that has anything to do with what I'm not wearing. I'm in a relationship. A committed, happy, healthy relationship."

"Sure."

"Do you want to know what I found or not?"

"Not really."

"I found twelve."

"Twelve what?"

"Locations."

"Locations for whom?"

"The warlock. You said he would take Esther someplace he felt powerful, which means it has to be someplace he's been before. I found twelve past addresses for Mordred and I'm thinking one might be the ritual location. I was hoping you could check them out for me."

"I already told you, I can't butt into this. It's out of my jurisdiction and Merle gets very territorial.

He nearly busted a nut because I asked around before handing it over to him."

"What? He's never heard of teamwork?"

"The boundaries between the different divisions of my organization are very distinct. Crossing lines can get you fired in the blink of an eye."

"I'm sorry. I wouldn't want you to lose your job."

"I meant literally. Flames. Smoke. Burning flesh."

"I get the picture." Boy, did I ever.

"If you managed to find a track record for this guy, I'm sure Merle has picked up the trail, as well. Don't worry," he added. "My cousin knows how to handle a rogue warlock."

Ash sounded so confident that I actually believed him. Really. These guys were professionals. They knew what they were doing and I should just sit back and let them do their thing. Esther was in good hands and I had absolutely nothing to worry over.

Life was normal.

Great.

Fan-friggin'-tabulous.

I powered off the computer and peeked into the living room. Rob was on his third bottle of cold blood. Killer had decided to hump my faux fur pillow. And the Giants were getting their asses kicked.

Yep, normal, all right.

Ten

❤ ❤ ❤

I kept up the normal facade for the next two days. But by the time Tuesday night rolled around, I was back to freaking out. Rob was still rooming with me. Killer had ruined all my throw pillows. Ivan had canceled his appointment (and the sizeable check he'd written to DED). And I hadn't heard one word about Esther.

The only thing that had gone right (in theory, at least) was Mia's date with Harmon. They'd played Scrabble and drank hot cocoa and he hadn't even held her hand.

They were in celibate heaven and headed for date number two tonight.

"Are you sure there are no more messages?" I asked Evie as I perched on her desk and rifled through the stack in my hand.

"Just the four from your mother, the two from Mandy, five from Nina Two and one from a guy who wants to sell you Amway." She shoved a few file folders into a kick-ass Marc Jacobs hobo bag and powered off her computer. "Oh, and Tabitha called. She said the guy you fixed her up with last night had blond hair. She doesn't do blonds."

"I know that but they were a perfect personality match."

"Obviously she's more into looks than personality. She said she hopes that prospect number two is more her type."

I had my doubts. He was a redhead, but he did meet the very specific height and weight requirements.

"Did you tell her the third time's a charm and the first two are just warm-up dates?"

Evie nodded. "I also offered her a free dozen donuts and a coupon for Starbucks."

"And?"

"She said she'd rather have the right man." Evie stabbed a button on her computer and the screen went blank. "Don't forget to call that new client—Jonelle So-and-so. We promised we'd call her with details for the first match."

"But I haven't made a match yet."

"Not yet," she smiled, "but the night is young. You have an entire half hour before she expects your phone call." She grabbed her purse. "Gotta run."

"Hot date?"

"I'm playing Bunko with my uncle Harrington."

"How old is he?"

"Too old for Jonelle," she said as if reading my mind. "The woman didn't look a day over thirty in her profile pic."

Make that six hundred and thirty. "She said she likes older men."

"Uncle Harrington isn't an older man. He's an *old* man. Complete with Depends and cataracts and an infatuation with *Wheel of Fortune*." When I didn't look discouraged, she shrugged. "Oh, all right. I'll ask him. But you can't send them dancing. He farts every time he makes a sudden move."

"No dancing," I vowed. I slid her a pencil and notepad. "Write down his phone number and I'll do the rest."

After suckering Evie out of her uncle's digits, I spent the next fifteen minutes convincing Jonelle why an Audrey Hepburn film festival would be the way to go for her first encounter with Harrington Dalton the Third.

Movies are romantic.

There's no need to talk. To touch. To interact in any way, shape or form.

"So why is this the perfect date?" she finally asked me.

"Because there's no pressure. You're relaxed. He's relaxed. It's the recipe for success." And a flatulence-free interlude.

A little more convincing and she finally caved. After that, I checked on Mia's date—they were drinking milkshakes and watching *Seabiscuit*—and then spent a half hour working on a few matches for other various clients.

At least I tried to work, but I kept thinking about Esther and how much she'd wanted to settle down and how she'd entrusted her faith, hope and dreams (and Visa card) with yours truly.

I gave up the matches and pulled out the business card Ash had given me. Punching in the phone number, I settled back in my chair and waited.

"Sorcery and tax evasion," a woman announced after the third ring. "How can I help you?"

"I'm trying to reach Merle Ambrose's office."

"This is it. Merle's the head honcho here, but he's got two assistants who handle the overlapping departments."

"How in the world does sorcery overlap with tax evasion?"

"Sugar, I haven't met a wizard yet who didn't try a wiggle spell on his 1040 every now and then."

"A wiggle spell?"

"You know, a little incantation and some effective animal sacrifice to wiggle out of paying the bottom line. So what are you calling about?"

"A missing warlock."

"That would fall under Mickey's jurisdiction. He's Merle's right hand in sorcery. I'll transfer you."

Fifteen minutes and five Barry Manilow songs later (courtesy of XM's *All Barry All the Time*), I heard a slightly irritated "Yes?"

"Mickey?"

"That's the name they gave me."

"I'm calling about the Mordred Lucius case."

"Do you have any relevant information that might help in solving this case?"

"No. I just wanted an update on how things are going. Esther—the kidnapped vampire—is a close, personal friend of mine."

"I'm afraid I can't help you. We don't give updates. We just collect information."

"I'd like to speak with Mr. Ambrose."

"Do you have any relevant information that might help in solving the case?" he repeated.

"I already said no."

"Then you have no reason to speak with him."

"But—"

Click.

Sonofabitch.

I tried once more and crossed my fingers that I might get someone other than Mickey.

"Mickey here."

Have I mentioned that I'm not exactly the luckiest vampire in the world?

I cleared my throat and took my voice down a notch. "I'd like to speak with Mr. Ambrose."

"Who may I say is calling?"

"Countess Lilliana Guinevere du Marchette." Okay, so the only thing even remotely good about being French royalty is that I could occasionally play the countess card. I tried for my most commanding tone. "I need to speak with him at once. I command thee," I added for effect.

"Would that be about a particular case he's working on?"

"Yes." I cleared my throat. "Correct."

"Do you have any relevant information that might help in solving the case?"

"Not at this time."

"Then I'm afraid I can't—"

"Help me," I cut in, my voice losing the regal tone. "Yeah, yeah. I know the spiel. I just thought you might cut me some slack. My friend is in desperate trouble and—"

Click.

I punched in the number again and went through the motions until I reached Mickey again. "I'm Lil Marchette. I'm calling about the *Mordred Lucius* case." I decided to throw in a little bribery to tip the scales in my favor. "And I'd be more than happy to donate two free matches to anyone who spills their guts about Esther's predicament."

"I don't date, Miss Marchette."

"A man with your charm? I'm shocked."

I could practically see his finger poised on the disconnect button. "Do you have any relevant information that might help in solving this case?" came the preprogrammed voice. "No? Then I'm afraid I can't—"

"Yes," I blurted. "I've got info. Lots of it."

It's one teensy lie. Get over it.

"Hold please," he finally told me after a stunned moment.

Now, that was more like it.

I leaned back in my chair as Barry launched into a lively rendition of "Copacabana." He'd just reached the final chorus when the music ended and a thick British accent echoed in my ear.

"Merle N. Ambrose. How may I be of service?"

My heart gave a double thump and excitement zipped through me. "This is Lil Marchette," I started, my voice dying as two important things registered in my brain: 1) a dial tone blared in my right ear where I held the receiver to my head, and 2) there was a strange tickling on the back of my neck, which indicated that something or someone was standing right behind me.

I bolted to my feet and whirled. The chair tumbled backwards and the edge caught my shin. Pain zipped through me and rattled my teeth.

"What the . . . ?" I scrambled for words. "Who the . . . ? How the . . . ?" *Focus, Lil.* I shook away the vibrating pain and drank in the man standing in front of me.

He was short and pudgy. He wore a red fleece suit and running shoes and reminded me more of Santa Claus than a timeless, all-powerful warlock. His cheeks were rosy and his eyes twinkled. "Merlin?"

"That's Merle N." He held a finger to his lips. "I

like to keep it separate; otherwise, someone's liable to put two and two together. Don't want the SOBs beating down my door, now, do we?"

For a wizard flying below the radar, he was a little off the mark. "It still sounds like *Merlin* when you pronounce it out loud," I pointed out.

"On paper it keeps up the charade well enough. I don't put in too many personal appearances. Knock, knock," he said.

"Excuse me?"

"Not *Excuse me*. You're supposed to say *Who's there?* It's a bloody joke." His eyes twinkled and I fully expected him to belt out a *Ho, ho, ho*. "Don't you like jokes?"

"Yes, but—"

"Then say 'Who's there?' Knock, knock."

I rubbed at my shin. "Okay, I'll bite. Who's there?"

"Dot."

"Dot who?"

"Dot's for me to know and you to find out." He started to laugh. His stomach heaved and shook with the effort. "Wait, wait," he finally managed after several loud, boisterous seconds. "I've got an even better one. Knock, knock."

"Who's there?"

"Ears."

"Ears who?"

"Ears some more knock-knock jokes for you." He roared and I did my best not to roll my eyes. "Isn't that the bloodiest funny thing you've ever heard?"

"A riot." I pulled my chair upright and tried not to look freaked. "So what are you doing here?"

"You called me."

"On the phone," I pointed out.

He shrugged. "I prefer taking my calls in person." The humor fled his expression and his brown eyes hardened. He went from easygoing to formidable in the blink of an eye. I had the sudden feeling that I'd just been hauled into the headmaster's office.

"You have information for me. Is that correct?"

"Yes." Sort of. I launched into the story I'd told Ash, beginning with the matchmaking party and ending with the bloodstained couch.

A puff of smoke and a file folder appeared in his hand. "I know all of that already. It's right here."

"Yeah, well, the more an eyewitness tells a story, the more of a chance she has of recalling something she might have missed in the first place." Or so Ty had once told me.

He leafed through the folder. "Anything new?"

"Maybe next time."

He frowned, his expression darkening, and I glimpsed the legend himself. Awesome. Larger than life. I braced myself, fully expecting him to shout *Abracadabra* and turn me into a toad or a raccoon or something such.

He stared at me a long moment, but nothing happened. Finally, he shook his head.

"What?"

"You're a vampire."

"And?"

"A born vampire."

"*And?*"

"And I've never met such an uneasy born vampire. Most of them are very cheeky and full of themselves. And they're certainly not afraid of me."

"Should they be?"

"Perhaps." He grinned. "I do have a vast and colorful history involving possums." When I arched an eyebrow, he added, "Toads are slimy and I'm allergic to raccoons. Vampires make good possums because they most resemble bats." When I didn't look convinced, he added, "They both hang upside down."

I shrugged. Hey, it made sense.

I quickly noted that I was still upright. Designer shoes. Two legs. Great outfit. My luck was obviously changing, so I decided to go for broke. "What about Mordred? Do you have any idea where he might be?" When he didn't answer, I added, "I Googled him and found a list of past addresses. You might want to check them out—"

"We already have, and we already know where he's taking her. He arrived in Austin last night and rented a car."

I did a quick mental of the list. "That means he's headed for Lonely Fork." It was such a small town, it hadn't even had a mention on Texas Online. "He is, right?" He nodded and relief bubbled through me.

"Mordred lived there about fifty years ago," Merle went on. "Rumor had it that he was this close to getting married, but then he abandoned the chit at the altar and disappeared. The fiancée died several years ago from Alzheimer's. He obviously didn't share his beauty secrets with her."

"Your men will be there waiting for him? For an ambush? A takedown? Whatever you guys do, right?"

"Waiting for him, yes. A takedown? I think not."

"Why not?"

"The sacrifice isn't until next week. There isn't much we can do until then."

What? Anxiety rushed through me, making my heart beat faster. I wanted to jump up, morph into the pink Batmobile and haul ass south to save my friend.

Merlin, on the other hand, didn't look in nearly the same hurry. Rather, he was calm, easygoing. As if Esther's afterlife weren't hanging in the balance.

"He's starving her," I told him. "You know that, don't you?"

"A necessary part of his plan. The ritual is very specific. Each step must be followed to the letter; otherwise, it won't have the expected results."

"But he's *starving* her."

"There's no law on the sorcery books involving cruelty against made vampires, Miss Marchette."

I had a bad feeling about where this was headed, and Merlin's next words confirmed it.

"Until he actually commits the crime, I cannot prosecute him. He must follow through with the ritual. I will be there to deal appropriately with him once he makes the sacrifice."

"What about Esther?"

He shrugged. "It's a small price to pay to eliminate Mordred. She's a made vampire. Expendable. And not my concern."

But she was mine. She was my friend. And she was in this mess because of me.

My stomach heaved and my knees went weak. I sank down into my chair as the truth crystallized. Esther was as good as dead if I didn't do something. Fast.

"Knock, knock," I told Merlin.

"Who's there?"

"Abbott."

"Abbott who?"

"Abbott time you get your butt out of my office so I can get to work."

Obviously, being on the receiving end wasn't nearly as funny. He frowned. "You're a very odd vampire."

Desperate was more like it. "Seriously, I really need you to leave. I've got work to do." If Merlin wasn't going to help Esther, I was going to have to do it myself.

"Do not interfere, Miss Marchette." He nailed me with a piercing stare that made my blood ice cold. "I have been waiting nearly one hundred years for a chance to destroy Mordred. I won't miss the opportunity this time. And I won't be nearly as accommodating should you disturb me again." A wave of his hand and a puff of smoke and Merlin disappeared.

"Nice to meet you, too." I fanned away the smoke and tried to process everything I'd learned.

Merlin had confirmed that Mordred was headed for Lonely Fork. Which meant I merely had to pinpoint the exact location, devise some sort of rescue plan, execute said plan, and save Esther. And all before next Friday.

And why don't you win the lottery while you're at it?

Okay, so I wasn't the most qualified vamp. I wasn't a detective and I had zero experience in dealing with murdering sorcerers.

Still, I *had* done some pretty courageous things in my life. I'd started my own business with nothing but a Visa and a prayer. Even more, I'd stood up to my mother and proclaimed my independence—no more Moe's, no more fix-ups, no more personal maid service. She hadn't listened, obviously (at least when it came to the fix-ups), but the point was, I'd done it. I'd stood up for myself. Embraced a new way of life.

I was strong. Tough. I could do this.

I *would* do this, because I was a good friend.

And friends didn't let friends drive drunk or wear light blue polyester pants or date losers or die at the sharp end of a ritual knife.

Eleven

❤ ❤ ❤

"**Y**ou're going *where*?" Evie's voice drifted over the phone when I called her after a frantic online visit to EverythingsBiggerinTexasbuttheAirfare.com.

"Arizona." I braced myself for a stab of guilt. I was really headed to Austin and then Lonely Fork, but I wasn't going to clue Evie in on my real destination. For her own good, of course. If Ty or my mother realized I'd gone MIA and why, they would start looking for me.

At least I knew my ma would.

Disappointment did the stabbing this time, but I ignored it and concentrated on the situation at hand. A few seconds alone with some ultra-vamp mojo and Evie would be singing like Carrie Underwood. I couldn't risk it. The less she knew, the better.

"I'm flying into Phoenix," I went on, "and then I'll head out to the conference center via cab."

"Have you been drinking?"

Just a glass of O+, but I didn't think that's what she had in mind. "No."

"Snorting coke?"

"Hardly."

"Smoking wacky tobacky?"

"No."

"Riding the monkey?"

"I don't even know what that is."

"Neither do I, but I'm watching *Law & Order: Special Victims Unit* and this guy is talking about riding the monkey. Or maybe it's spanking the monkey." I heard the volume go down on the TV. "So what's with the sudden trip to Arizona of all places? You do know that, other than Scottsdale and a really killer shopping center, the rest of the state is pretty much sand and cacti?"

"Exactly. This is one of those retreats where you get away from everything and focus on how to be a better, more successful businessperson. The more obscure the place, the better, since you're supposed to feel isolated and out of your element. It forces you to grow." Was I great off the cuff, or what? "Besides, I'm not totally roughing it. The retreat is at one of those posh resorts with a full-service spa and a golf course. Not that I'll be getting massages all the time. I'll be busy focusing on how to hook up really diffi-cult clients, complete with prep courses to deal with their little quirks. There's personal hygiene for the smelly ones. Dress tips for the fashionably clueless. Job search tips for the broke losers. You name it. I'm sure to learn loads of important stuff."

Or so I was hoping. While I knew that Mordred was somewhere in or around the small town, I didn't know the exact address where he was staying, or where he was hiding Esther, or where he would make the sacrifice.

At the same time, how hard could it be to find an ancient sorcerer in Lonely Fork? Really. It wasn't like New York or Chicago or L.A. where they had them practically crawling out of the woodwork. We're talking a map dot in the middle of the Bible Belt.

Even more, I was an all-powerful, ultra-sensitive queen of the undead. I could weave my vamp mojo and get anyone (translation, any straight human man or lesbian woman or the swinger who went both ways) to spill their guts in a nanosecond.

I was *so* going to find this guy. And when I did, I was going to make him regret ever crashing my meet and greet and compromising the DED name.

In the meantime . . .

"I need you to keep tabs on Mia. She and Harmon are going for date number three and I want to make sure everything goes okay." Third time was a charm. If all went well, my end of the agreement would be fulfilled with this last date. I.e., my money back guarantee? Fughetaboutit.

"I also need you to follow up with Tabitha and

see how last night's fix-up went. I've got another prospect if she didn't like him." And I was pretty sure she hadn't. While tall, dark, with crazy piercing eyes (as requested), the closest he came to being a warlock was dressing up for Dungeons & Dragons every other Friday for his fantasy video group.

"Where's her file?"

"I've got it with me." I kept all the Other profiles in my own personal stash and doled out info to Evie on a strictly need-to-know basis.

I gave her the name and number for prospect four—a professional bowler/amateur magician from Long Island. He wanted a woman who appreciated his creative side. In other words, one who wouldn't freak when he screwed up the rabbit trick and pulled a sewer rat out of his top hat.

Hey, it was the best I could do on such short notice.

"What about Jonelle Dubois?" Evie asked.

"I've got her file, too. She isn't in as big a hurry, so her next match"—if she ever forgave me for fixing her up with Uncle Harrington—"can wait until I get back. Other than that, I think we're good until the convention ends."

"What about Killer?"

"My brother's house-sitting."

"And Ty? Is he okay with you running off on the spur of the moment?"

"It's business. Besides, we're just dating and semi–living together. It's not like he's given up his place and completely moved in. Or proposed." Or even said the L word.

"Not yet," Evie told me. "Say, why don't you invite him to go with you?"

And risk him stuffing a clove of garlic in my mouth, trussing me up with silver and locking me in my closet? Pass. I already knew what his response would be if I told him I was flying south—namely to stay home and, even more, stay out of it. Not because he was the typical cold, heartless made vampire who didn't give a shit about another made vampire, but because he cared about me and didn't want to see me scared, hurt or dead.

He loved me. Probably.

Yeah, baby. And I've got some incredible beach-front property in Brooklyn to show you.

I ignored the silent dig and focused on my conversation with Evie. "I left him a voice mail telling him we'll get together when I get back."

"How long will you be gone?"

The question was like a vise sliding around my heart and cranking a couple of notches. "Next Friday," I managed after swallowing the lump in my throat. "It'll all be over by then."

"I did it," Nina One declared when I answered my cell an hour later. I'd just walked into my apartment and picked my way through the maze that was now my living room. "Rob's out of here." Her words confirmed the fact that she had no clue Rob had come crawling to me for a place to stay. "Yesterday's news. Gone. Adios."

If only.

I toed a pair of dirty socks that sat near the coffee table. Several empty bottles of blood lay strewn atop my *InStyle* collection. Rob wore a pair of faded black sweatpants and nothing else. He lay stretched out on the couch, his eyes closed, the TV blaring.

"Good for you," I told her as I bypassed the mess and headed for my bedroom.

"So you think I did the right thing?"

"Don't you?"

"Of course. Better to nip it in the bud before things get really complicated. I mean, what was I thinking? No way could I actually settle down right now. I'm in the prime of my afterlife. I like sleeping around and sucking on the cutie of the moment. We were getting way too serious. Your mother made me see that. I'm not ready to pledge myself to one vampire. I don't know if I'll ever be ready."

"Not ready. I totally get it."

"And Rob's not ready either," she rambled on. "Even if he thinks he is."

No kidding. *Rambling*.

"Just weeks ago," the ramble continued, "he was screwing around without a care in the world. Boffing anything with a vagina and a pulse. He doesn't want to be saddled down with a mate and responsibilities and my massive credit card bills."

"I hear ya."

"It's better this way."

"Much better."

"Did he say that?"

"Say what?"

"That it was better not to be saddled with a mate and responsibilities and massive credit card bills?"

"Not in so many words, but I know he's glad you ended it and saved him the trouble of having to do it."

She went silent for several heartbeats. "He wanted to break up?"

"What does it matter? It's over. You don't want to be with him."

"Yeah, but I thought he wanted to be with me. I mean, why wouldn't he want to be with me? I'm one of the hottest vampires out there, right?"

"Absolutely."

"From one of the wealthiest families."

"Definitely."

"With one of the highest fertility ratings."

"You're off the charts."

"So what's his problem? Don't tell me, he's gay."

"He's not gay."

"Then how could he possibly want to break up with *me*?"

"He was probably just blowing off steam, running his mouth, shirking his responsibility. You know how men are." When she didn't say anything, I added, "Stop worrying about it. This is all for the best. You know it. Rob knows it. Let it go. Go out, have fun." *Realize how lost you are without him and come crawling back.*

I know, I know. Nina is a heterosexual born vampire. Immune to my mojo. But cut me some slack. At the moment, my brother's ass was making a permanent indentation in my couch.

"You're right. There's no need to dwell on it. I'm over him. It's finished."

"Exactly. Forget all about Rob."

"Damn straight."

"And his hideous foot massages and spur-of-the-moment gifts like that diamond bracelet from Tiffany's and those cool earrings from BCBG. Talk about lame. And what vampire in her right mind wants a male who brings her breakfast in bed?"

"I kind of miss the breakfast in bed," she said after a long, quiet moment. "And the way he stroked my hair after I finished feeding. And the way he held my hand when we fell asleep. And that cute little way he snores when he's just falling asleep."

My ears perked to the thunderstorm now vibrating the walls of my living room. "*Cute* isn't exactly the adjective I'd use, but suit yourself."

"Oh, it is cute. Sure, it's a little loud, but that's what makes it so endearing. It's bold and powerful and, well, I get tingly all over just thinking about it—"

"Forget Rob," I cut in before she started pinpointing tingle locations and *really* creeping me out. "This dwelling will only make you second-guess yourself and your decision. You aren't second-guessing, are you?"

Pleasepleasepleasepleasepleasepleaseplease—

"Hardly. I'm just saying that it wasn't all bad."

The admission sent a burst of excitement through me and confirmed what I'd known all along—she'd fallen for Rob. What can I say? I had a sixth sense when it came to these things. I was an expert, after all. I made my living by finding and orchestrating love. This was my thing. My bread and butter.

Or, in my case, my AB+ and O−.

"We actually had some pretty good times," she added.

My ears perked. This was it. She was going to admit the truth. Embrace it. *Say* it.

"And?" I gave her a little nudge. *And you were right, Lil. I love him. I love* him. *And thank you for helping me realize the truth. You're the best. You're a master matchmaker. A true professional who knows her business in and out and is destined for major success. A Park Avenue apartment. An overflowing bank account. And the assurance that you will never, ever have to file unemployment or wear a lime green polo shirt for a living.*

"And nothing," Nina said. "It was good. Then it was bad. Now it's over. Time to go."

"But—"

"No, really. I've got to go. I'm meeting Ernesto in five minutes. He's the new bartender downstairs. He makes a mean Mexican Firing Squad." A smile touched her voice. "You wouldn't believe what else he can do with a little lime juice and some tequila. Things should get really interesting."

"Don't you think it's a little premature—"

Click.

Moe's, here I come.

Twelve
♥ ♥ ♥

Time to spill my guts.

Figuratively, that is. Living with Rob isn't that bad. Yet.

I'm talking confession. Laying it all out. Purging my conscience.

While I know being snotty and pretentious is as normal to a born vamp as having fangs and a severe allergy to the sun, I've never really considered myself one of *those*—the elitist, self-involved, I-wouldn't-be-caught-dead-driving-the-same-Ferrari-two-days-in-a-row-or-shopping-at-Wal-Mart types like my ma and all her friends.

Come on. I live in the city. I don't even have a driver's license. As for Wal-Mart . . . All right, so I've never set foot in the big W (city, remember?), but I *have* thought about it (I'm a sap for *anything* retail).

Back to the point—I didn't really think of myself as the normal BV and so flying coach wasn't something that had ever bothered me.

Until I sat down next to Angela Darlene Connolly.

She was a thirty-four-year-old mother of three from Vermont who'd been married half her life. She was president of the Gramercy Elementary PTA, treasurer for the local Little League and she'd won an iPod by selling the most Snickers bars in last year's Tumbling Tots fund-raiser. She didn't drink, smoke or swear.

But man, could she talk.

". . . so I told him, he isn't the only one who needs time for himself. He goes to Colorado twice a year to ski with his fantasy football buddies. He spends every Fourth of July ice fishing in Alaska with his old fraternity brothers. He's been kayaking through the Grand Canyon and hiking in the Appalachians with his softball team. And did I mention Friday night Poker?"

Not yet. But I had a feeling . . .

"Sure, it's fun for him. All he does is deal the cards. I'm the one who spends all day making crab puffs and meatballs and these bite-sized pepperoni pizzas," she rushed on. "And for what? So a bunch of overweight, spoiled men can sit around smoking cigars and stuffing their faces. I don't even like cigars. Why, it takes days just to get the smell out. So I tell him, it's my turn. I deserve a break from the world and a chance to kick up my heels. That's why

I'm here. I'm grabbing my fun while I'm still young enough to enjoy it. My mother-in-law has the kids and Paul's in charge of the house for the next two weeks while I head to Austin to see my sister."

"That's great."

The comment popped out before I could stop it. Dread swam through me as she took the encouragement and launched into a detailed explanation of just how great it was going to be.

"We've got the whole thing planned. We're going to do a little spring cleaning and have a yard sale and hit every flea market we can find. That is, once she's up and around. She had a bladder lift last week and the doctor says she'll have to stay off her feet for another seven days. Until then, I'll be making her meals and cleaning the surgical site and doing bed pan duty."

Party on.

"Do you know there are over fourteen different kinds of bed pans?"

Did I mention that she watches a lot of Discovery Health?

"I didn't know that." Correction, I didn't want to know that.

"Neither did I, but it's true." She proceeded to give a very vivid description (color, size and model number) of the various bed pans—who knew they weren't all round?—that lasted a full thirty minutes.

Yep, you heard me.

Thirty as in three-oh, as in half a freakin' *hour*.

Meanwhile, I contemplated my options. I could a) do the vicious vamp thing and start slicing and dicing or b) stab myself with a fountain pen or c) get the hell outta there.

Forget a. I was wearing a totally cute Iro jacket (dry clean only) and a pair of Twenty8Twelve skinny leg pants in creamy vanilla. As for b, I'd never been much for violence, particularly if it was self-inflicted. I latched onto c and bolted to my feet.

"It was really great talking to you." What? I'm nice. Get over it. "But I have to hit the john ASAP." I crawled over the woman to my left and headed toward the back of the plane before Angela could tell me exactly how much the largest bed pan in existence could hold.

I *so* didn't need that tidbit of info.

I spent ten minutes barricaded in the bathroom, primping and stalling and praying that Angela wasn't a premonition that this trip was going to be one big disaster. Finally, the stewardess pounded on the door to tell me that I would have to return to my seat because we were having some turbulence.

I took one last look in the mirror and forced myself to get a grip. I couldn't hide forever. Even more, maybe I was hiding needlessly. Maybe she'd decided to nap and was now snoring away. Or maybe the rest of the passengers had decided to lynch her and save me the trouble.

Either way, problem solved.

Hopeful, I slid open the door, apologized to the

stewardess for taking so long and marched back down the aisle.

"You're back!" Angela slapped the magazine closed that she'd been looking at and turned her full attention to me. "I was starting to worry."

"I'm fine." I barely ignored the urge to turn and run. Instead, I climbed over the woman on the aisle, sank down in the middle, hands in my lap so that I didn't knock elbows, and braced myself.

Angela shoved her *Good Housekeeping* mag into the front seat pocket and opened her mouth. Before she could get out another word, I whipped my head toward the woman on my left and blurted, "So where are you headed?"

"Back home," the woman replied. She glanced up and her dark brown eyes collided with mine.

Her name was Wanda Wilder and she was a sixty-two-year-old retired nurse. She'd been in New York for her oldest granddaughter's birthday. She'd been married for twenty-two years. Divorced for fourteen. And she'd recently signed herself up on an Internet dating site for seniors.

That's what I'm talking about.

"I'm Lil." I smiled. "I own Dead End Dating. It's a matchmaking service in Manhattan."

"I'm Wanda Wilder. I'm retired now, but I used to work in the ER at St. Mary's Hospital in Austin. I live in Georgetown now. So what brings you to Texas?"

"Business retreat."

"In Austin?"

"Actually, it's a small town about an hour outside of Austin. Maybe you've heard of it. Lonely Fork?"

"Are you kidding?" She waved a hand at me. "My cousin lives there. You staying at The Grande?"

I smiled at the familiar name. "I made a reservation there just yesterday. Is it nice?"

"Nicest place in town. Got a five star rating the last I heard."

Okay, maybe Angela hadn't been a premonition, after all. The trip couldn't be all that bad, not with a fully stocked mini-bar and turn-down service.

"Stayed there myself once when I went to my cousin Ronnie's wedding. He owns the pharmacy in town. Knows everybody who's anybody. If you stop in, be sure to tell him Wanda says hi."

"I'll do that."

She turned and eyeballed the back of the plane. "If you'll excuse me, I think it's my turn to hit the little girls' room. I think I had too much coffee."

"I love coffee," Angela declared as Wanda pushed to her feet and scooted into the aisle. "I grind my own beans. You wouldn't believe what they use to fertilize some of those coffee beans." She started talking again, barely pausing to take a breath. I seriously debated popping the nearest exit hatch and vamping it down to Texas.

Unfortunately, I'd checked my luggage and so I was stuck for the next two hours.

"Beverage service," the stewardess announced several long minutes later. "Coffee? Tea?"

". . . even heard they use mouse feces to lend flavor to some of the different cocoa beans . . ."

"I think I'm going to need something stronger," I told the woman.

"How about an energy drink?"

"Only if it's got a vodka chaser."

"This can't be right," I told the cabdriver. I blinked my blurry eyes just in case I was having a liquor-induced hallucination. It had been over two hours since I'd crawled off the plane, but I was still feeling the aftereffects of coping with coach via cocktail.

Note: I am never, *ever* drinking another Red Bull and vodka. I mean it this time. Cross my heart.

"You said The Grande. This is The Grande."

I eyed the two-story structure. A gravel parking lot butted up to the walkway that ran the length of the building. A bevy of cars and pickup trucks crammed the area, obliterating my view of the bottom floor. But I could see the doors lining the upper walkway. Small air-conditioning units perched in each window. My gaze shifted to the right and a single glass door. The word *Lobby* had been spelled out in vinyl letters on the glass. "But it's supposed to be a five star hotel."

"It is." He pointed to the sign blazing near the side of the road. Underneath *The Grande,* spelled out in pink neon, a caption read *"Rated 5 Stars by the Lonely Fork Gazette."*

"How many hotels are actually in this town?"

"Counting this one?"

"Yes."

"That would be one."

Which meant zero competition when it came to ratings.

He leaned over the back of the seat. "If you want, I could head back up the interstate. I think we passed a Motel 6 about forty-five minutes outside of town. They're not the fanciest place, but they're new. I think they even got those beds that you feed a quarter into so's they'll vibrate."

I shook my head. If I intended to find Mordred, I needed to be right in the thick of things. He was here, which meant I was staying here. Besides, I'd maxed out my Visa to buy the plane ticket and book four nights at the masterpiece sitting in front of me. As queasy as I felt, I could barely stand the cab idling, much less a vibrating bed.

"Suit yourself." He opened the door and climbed out to retrieve my luggage from the trunk.

I handed him two fifties and a DED card.

"What's this?"

"In case you're ever in New York and you get bored doing crossword puzzles every night."

His gaze widened. "How'd you know I like cross-word puzzles?"

Because I'm an ultra-sensitive born vampire who can read your mind. I shrugged. "Lucky guess."

Lose the crosswords, join the local VFW hall and find a girlfriend. I added the silent command as I stared deep into his eyes for a quick second. *And* do not *mention that you live with your mother.*

Grabbing my suitcase, I gathered my courage, made my way around several pickups and a Kia and headed for the lobby entrance.

The inside wasn't much better than the outside. There was a small sitting area in front of the desk. A scarred coffee table sat center stage surrounded by a worn green sofa, a paisley print chair and a brass floor lamp with a dingy shade.

I fought down a big *uh-oh* and tapped the bell on the desk. Three *dinggggs* and an exasperated sigh, and an old man finally hobbled from the back room.

"Don't get your girdle in a twist. I'm acoming." He had snow white hair and watery blue eyes. His name was Elmer Jackson and he'd been running The Grande for nearly forty years. "What can I do you for?"

"I have a reservation. Lil Marchette? Double bed. No smoking. Premium sheets and four goose-down pillows."

"Let me have a look here." He pulled a pair of glasses from his pocket and flipped several pages on a large scheduling book that took up half the counter. "Sure thing. I got you right here, little lady.

Only it's for a double bed, regular sheets and two cotton pillows."

"But that's not what my reservation says." I pulled out the confirmation I'd printed off the Internet. "It offered me a choice of sheets and I distinctly checked premium."

"Ain't got no premium. Ain't got no goose down either."

"Then why does it say so online?"

"Ain't sure. My nephew takes care of the website and I s'pose he thought it sounded good." He grinned. "The boy likes to exaggerate sometimes."

I had half a mind to complain, but I'd sort of fudged myself on some of the fabulous amenities offered by DED. Free gourmet dessert? Krispy Kreme. All you can drink imported beverages? Starbucks House Blend.

"Two pillows will be fine," I murmured.

He smiled, pulled out a form and handed it to me. "Just print your name and address and sign here."

I scribbled my info and handed the slip back to him, along with my Visa for any extra charges.

"You'll like it here," he told me. He took the card, placed it on an ancient-looking credit card machine and rolled the top back and forth. "We ain't as big as some, but the rooms are clean and the plumbing works as good as the day my daddy installed it."

He'd inherited the place from his father and he fully intended to pass it on to his only son when the time came. The only problem was that his son, Elmer the

Third, fully intended to bulldoze the place and turn the spot into a parking lot for a new Piggly Wiggly.

Elmer the Second had never been too fond of chain stores (he bought his vegetables at the farmer's market) and so he wasn't too keen on the idea. I saw that as plain as day in his deep brown eyes. Along with the fact that he'd worried himself into a complete hair loss and an addiction to Tums. The Grande was his baby. His life. Everything.

"Is there a Mrs. Elmer?" I asked, not because I didn't already know the answer—a big, fat no—but because I wasn't in a hurry for another slip like the one with the cabdriver.

Low profile, remember?

"Why, no." Sadness touched his eyes and I saw a young-looking woman wearing a flower print dress. She stood at the stove dishing up cabbage soufflé and humming an old Frank Sinatra song. He'd hated cabbage soufflé, but he'd never told her that. He'd just slipped it under the table to old Sammy the dog.

He'd trade anything for a bite of that soufflé right now.

"She passed right after our son was born," he went on. "I'd say she's been gone about forty years now."

I let loose a low whistle. "That's a long time to be alone. But then, I bet a nice-looking fellow like you has a lot of lady friends."

"Not unless you count Shirlene at the bakery. She gives me free donut holes when I order a half-dozen Boston creme."

"She doesn't count."

"What about Mabel at the diner? She gives me free refills on my coffee."

"Do you talk to each other about anything other than what you're going to order?"

"No."

"Then it doesn't count. I'm talking about lady friends you laugh with, have fun with."

He shrugged. "I guess not. I'm real busy with the hotel anyhow. I ain't got time for socializing."

"That's a shame, because socializing is my business. I'm a matchmaker." He gave me a puzzled look and I added, "I help people find their perfect match."

"Like a date?"

"It starts with a date." I handed him a DED card. When he arched an eyebrow, I added, "I'm in town on business and I'd be happy to help you out while I'm here."

He eyed the card a few more seconds. "Something like this is probably expensive."

Amen.

That's what my practical side wanted to say, but the sentimental sap took over and I heard myself murmur, "I'm running an out-of-towner special right now. The first three prospects are free."

We're talking cabbage soufflé. The man deserved a little happiness before he headed for the retirement home and his ungrateful son turned his hopes and dreams into asphalt.

"I wouldn't mind having someone to take to Bingo," he finally said after a long moment.

"One Bingo player coming up."

I made a mental note to ask around about available seniors while I was looking for Mordred. Might as well kill two weres with one silver bullet.

I spent the next ten minutes quizzing Elmer on his likes and dislikes. When I had enough information, I took the plastic container he handed me and the small silver key.

"Here's your ice bucket and your mini-bar key," he told me.

I perked up immediately. "There's a minibar?"

"Damn straight." He pointed to my left and I turned to see the small refrigerator wedged between an ancient color TV and a magazine rack. An empty pickle jar stuffed with coins and a few bills sat on top. "Just make sure you pay for anything you take out. Candy and sodas are a buck. Beer is two bucks."

"Any Red Bull?" I heard myself ask. I had half of a travel-sized bottle of vodka leftover in my purse. I'd meant to flush it ASAP, but I suddenly had a feeling I was going to need it.

He shook his head. "We don't do any of those fancy drinks, but there's grapefruit juice."

I considered it for a moment before shaking my head. "I'll pass. Which way?"

"Down the hall, out the side door and around toward the left. You're the door right next to the ice machine." I started to turn and he added, "You might need these." He handed me a pair of earplugs. "The machine's a little old and it gets kind of noisy."

"Can't I just have another room?"

" 'Fraid not. We're booked up. There's a rodeo going on in Pflugerville just a little ways from here. They ain't got enough hotels to accommodate everybody, so we get the overflow. Speaking of which, I hope you don't have a car because we got several horses tied up in the parking lot out back. See, the barn area at the rodeo grounds burned down and so all the entrants are responsible for their animals when they're not showing, at least for the next twenty-four hours. The rodeo people are setting up a temporary holding pen that ought to be ready by tomorrow night. Until then, it ain't safe for walking back there, if you know what I mean."

Boy, did I ever. I took another whiff and my nose wrinkled. "Don't power walk in the back parking lot. Got it."

"You're free to use the front sidewalk," Elmer called after me. "Just be sure to watch out for the calves." My horror showed on my face because he chuckled and added, "Don't worry, this place will be back to normal soon enough."

If only he knew.

Thirteen
❤ ❤ ❤

After getting lost twice, spooking a few horses (so *not* a vamp's best friend) and barely missing what I suspected was a pile of calf poop, I stood in the doorway of Room 6C and tamped down the urge to haul ass back to the big city. Pronto.

The room was about the size of my apartment, but that's where the similarity ended. My place oozed class (at least the part I'd been able to afford to decorate). This place oozed, too, but not in a good way.

An ancient queen-sized bed stood center stage with a bright orange comforter. There were two white Formica-topped nightstands and a matching dresser. An orange papier mâché lantern hung in one corner. Orange shag rugs covered the hardwood floor (seriously). And the pièce de résistance? Orange and turquoise polka dot wallpaper.

A sinking feeling settled in the pit of my stomach as my gaze swiveled to the small open doorway that led to the bathroom.

Polka dot towels. Orange bath mat. Turquoise shower curtain. And more wallpaper.

Run!

That's what my super-intuitive vamp instincts told me. Or maybe that was my snotty, pretentious, vamp DNA.

Hello? It's a decent room. One for which you should be ultra-thankful. What about poor Esther? Chances are, she'd kill for a place like this right now.

All right, so *kill* wasn't the perfect word choice for a time like this.

I had a quick mental of her chained in a cellar somewhere (Did they have those in Texas?) or maybe an attic. Yeah, probably an attic. Or a crawl space.

I saw her sprawled on a filthy wooden floor, a pool of blood beneath her. The musty smell of urine and death hung in the air. Rat droppings littered the area surrounding her. Her body lay broken and bleeding and—

I quickly slammed my mind closed to the rest of the visual. I swallowed the sudden lump in my throat and forced my gaze to make another 360.

It *was* sort of retro, and familiar. I'd once had a mini-smock with that exact wallpaper pattern (talk about prime blackmail material). Most of all, the room was completely free of blood and poop. Unless you counted the walkway outside—see calf reference above—but that was only temporary.

Bottom line, the room wouldn't inspire a page in *Modern Interior,* but I could deal.

I put the *Do Not Disturb* sign on the door, locked and bolted it and shoved a chair under the doorknob—just in case the sign didn't speak for itself. I secured the drapes and blinds and grabbed my suitcase.

I changed into a T-shirt and pink lace boy shorts before pulling out one of the eight bottles of blood I'd brought. It took my eyes a second to focus with all the polka dots and realize that there was no microwave. A quick glance in the bathroom, however, and I spotted a one-cup coffeemaker.

A few minutes later, I poured myself a cup of warm blood, kicked off my shoes and settled on the bed. I took a sip, pulled out my cell and checked my voice mail.

"You have eighteen new messages . . ."

Ma. *Delete.*

Ma. *Delete.*

Ma. *Delete.*

Ma. *Delete.*

Ma. *Delete.*

Ma. *Delete.*

Ma. *Delete.*

Ma. *Delete.*

Message number nine was from my brother.

"It's Rob. Mom's looking for you. She sounded really pissed, so I'd call her if I were you. Plus, she said if you didn't call her, she was going to your apartment to look for you. I really don't want her here because I really don't want to explain about Nina. Not because it bothers me talking about it or anything like that. Hell, no. I can say her name all day and it doesn't bother me one bit. I don't give a shit if we ever get back together. And I surely don't give a shit if she's sorry. Though she should be on account of I didn't do a damned thing. You can tell her I said that, too. On second thought, you might hurt her feelings and I wouldn't want to be a bastard. Not because I want her back. Just because, you know, she's got girlfriends and I know how you women talk. Before you know it, I'll have a rep for being an asshole and I won't be able to get a date to save my life."

Sure.

"So call her. And for the record, I wasn't the one who decided to take a piss on your rug." I heard a *purrrrr* and a *meowwww* in the background. "Who knew the little guy had so much in him? Call Mom." *Click.*

The only person I was calling was animal control to report a rabid cat loose in my apartment.

I relished a picture of Killer getting zapped by one of those cattle prods (not that they use those but, hey, a vamp can dream) for an eighth of a second before number ten echoed in my ear.

"It's Max. Mom's looking for you. She said you

were supposed to help her with some plan and you didn't show. I told her I wasn't your babysitter and that she should head over to your apartment if she really wants to talk to you."

Uh-oh.

"Call her," he added. *Click*.

The next seven messages were from my mother. I deleted all of them and moved on to number eighteen.

"It's Evie. I hope the trip went well and you're soaking up the desert sun at this very moment."

I squelched a twinge of guilt for lying to my one and only employee. I know, right? I should turn on the BV I-don't-give-a-shit-about-anyone-but-myself mentality. I tried. Really, I did. But I was starting to suspect that switch had been broken at birth.

"I found someone for Tabitha," she went on. "He owns a dry cleaners in Queens. He fits the description, but he isn't into magic so much as comedy. He does stand-up every Saturday night. Hopefully she likes jokes more than she does hat tricks. Mia called and said they went to a macramé class for date number three and that she made her own handbag. It was celibacy at its finest and she's thrilled."

I wouldn't use "celibacy" and "thrilled" in the same sentence, but then I'm a born vampire: i.e., a sexual dynamo.

Give me an orgasm or give me death!

"Also, Jonelle had a wonderful time with Uncle Harrington and wants to do it again. The only problem is, he couldn't stand her. Said she was all over him and he didn't even get a chance to nap during the movie."

Come again?

"Even after he farted. It seems she likes a strong man who isn't afraid to be himself and she wants to take him to her salsa club on Friday evening. I warned her what might happen, but she's adamant. Help! And speaking of help, your mother called looking for you."

Imagine that.

"Twenty-three times. That's a new record for her. Anyhow, she kept saying something about an ambush and how if she can't do the ambush in the comfort of her own home, then she'll have to do it elsewhere." *Click*.

Uh-oh.

A wave of anxiety rushed through me and I punched in Jack's number. Surely she hadn't decided to go for the poison. Jack would never forgive her. I would never forgive her.

"Where's Mandy?" I blurted the moment I heard my brother's voice.

"Underneath me," my brother replied. "We're about to have sex. We've been about to have sex for the past two hours, but we keep getting interrupted."

"Is mom there?"

"I like a little kink as much as the next vampire, but I draw the line at that."

"I didn't mean in bed with you. I meant, has she been there?"

"Earlier. She would still be here, but Mandy pretended that she got called out on an emergency at the hospital, so Ma finally left. I swear, if I hadn't seen it myself, I wouldn't believe it. I think she's really starting to like Mandy. She was fussing all over her, propping up her feet and even making her a snack."

Oh-no.

"She didn't eat it, did she?" I blurted. "The snack? She didn't eat the snack, did she?"

"She's saving it until later. She wants to work up an appetite first."

"That's wonderful."

"Says you. You're not the one who keeps getting interrupted."

"I'm sorry. Go back to what you were doing, but *do not* let her eat the after-sex snack."

"Why not?"

"Because . . ." *Our mother's a self-absorbed lunatic.*

I wanted to say it. I needed to say it. The thing is, he'd sounded so happy at the thought that our mom was being supportive of Mandy and the whole baby thing.

I couldn't bust his delusional bubble.

"Because eating too soon after sex can cause really bad cramps."

"No way."

"Way. I heard it on Discovery Health."

"Since when do you watch Discovery Health? Since when do you watch any TV?"

"I watch TV."

"*Platinum Weddings* doesn't count."

"Since I deal with all types of clients at Dead End Dating, I figured I'd better beef up my knowledge of humans. I can't hook them up if I don't know what makes them tick." Can I improv or what? "I also saw a show about reproduction. It said if you're trying to up your chances at conception, you should eat only eggs for seventy-two hours following intercourse. Mom didn't make eggs, did she?"

"It's a ham and turkey sub with mayonnaise."

"Well, then, I guess you'll have to throw it out in favor of an omelette."

"That sounds a little far-fetched."

"To you. You're a born vamp with a weird, twisted digestive tract. Humans are different." I heard Mandy's voice in the background, followed by a few muffled words from Jack. "Mandy said she's never heard about the eggs, but she can see how the protein might play into the fertilization of the reproductive egg."

"See?"

"She says we'll give it a try."

"Great."

A moment of silence settled in and relief swamped me until I heard Jack's impatient, "Can I have sex now or are you going to give me another lesson in Human 101?"

"Throw out the sub," I added before pressing the OFF button.

Disaster averted. For now.

But who knew what my ma would try tomorrow? Or the night after?

I had to do something.

"You can't poison Mandy," I told my mother when she picked up the phone on the second ring. "It's not right."

"Excuse me?"

"It's not right because you, um, promised I could help."

"Lilliana? Where are you? You were supposed to meet me this evening to head over to Jack's. Instead, I had to go alone. Your father was busy with his golf lesson and Max couldn't do it. And Rob said you made him promise to watch Killer, which was the only reason he had to stay at that dump you call an apartment."

I let the comment slide and gathered my strength. "I'm on a business trip." I crossed my fingers and gave her my spiel about the Success 101 Retreat and how it was going to make me a more powerful matchmaker.

"Arizona? That's out in the middle of nowhere."

"The idea is to get away from all distraction, relax and focus on your inner power."

"But we're having a crisis here. Your brother and

his human are probably having relations at this very moment."

"But it won't count because she ate the sub."

"She did?"

"I heard it from Jack's very lips. Which means you don't have to worry about it until, say, next Friday."

"Nonsense. Each pill is only effective for twenty-four hours."

"Not when mixed with food."

"That's ridiculous. Where did you hear such nonsense?"

"Ivan," I heard myself blurt. "He heard it from his OB/GYN buddy and told me. That is, when we weren't making out."

My mother latched onto the comment like a dog grabbing her favorite bone. "The two of you made out?"

"No doubt. So you see, the proteins feed the birth control molecules and improve the pill's effectiveness. With a twelve-incher, I'd say she won't be fertilizing an egg for a good couple of weeks."

"I *did* use a double layer of meat to disguise the taste."

"There you go. Now stop worrying about it until I get back." I spent the next few minutes listening to my mother's suggestions for flowers for the commitment ceremony with Ivan.

"We just sucked face, Ma. It's not like he proposed."

"Not yet, but who knows what will happen at the next hunt?"

"About that . . . I don't think I'll be back from the retreat in time."

"But—"

I cut her off with some gurgling noises. "Oops, I think we have a bad connection," I added in between a *grrrr* and a *shhhh*. "Call you later." *Click.*

I downed the rest of my blood and sat there for several minutes listening to the sounds from outside. The animals. The muted voices from the adjoining rooms. The occasional car that passed by. The faint crying of a baby, followed by a woman's soothing *shh*.

A wave of loneliness swept over me.

Crazy, right?

At the same time, I was hundreds of miles from home in a town I couldn't even find on the map. On a mission to save my good friend from torture and death. It made sense that I would feel a little wigged out.

It certainly wasn't because I was, you know, thinking about Ty and the future and worrying over whether he felt the same way about me that I felt about him.

No, I was just feeling a little lost and I needed to hear a familiar voice. That was the only reason I dialed his number. It wasn't because I wanted to hear *his* voice.

"This is Ty. You know the routine . . ." *Beep*.

"It's me. I just wanted to say good morning. I hope your case is going well." I caught the *Love ya* before it could slide past my lips. "Um, good luck."

I spent the next few minutes outlining a plan of action for tomorrow. I'd check out Wanda's cousin over at the pharmacy and ask him about Mordred. I cooked up a story about a wealthy, prominent woman who'd met and fallen in love with Mordred right here in Lonely Fork years ago. They'd gone their separate ways and now she wanted to reconnect with his son (not that Mordred had a son, but he'd lived here over fifty years ago and so it wasn't believable that he wouldn't have aged since then. He would be an old man by now, but a son . . . He would fit the description I'd jotted down to a T).

My gaze snagged on the stats and something niggled at me. He seemed familiar somehow. I hadn't thought so when I'd seen him at the meet and greet. But now, looking at the details on paper . . .

I shook away the crazy sensation and focused on my story. It was my job as matchmaker and perpetuator of happily-ever-after to find the son and introduce him to his father's first love.

Not the perfect alibi, but I could make it work.

I finished, turned off my phone (just in case my ma decided to call me back), killed the light and snuggled down under the covers. I didn't need to worry about Esther or feel sorry for myself. I had a big night tomorrow and I needed some sleep if I wanted to be on top of my game.

Unfortunately, someone else needed ice and so I spent the next half hour listening to the machine groan and grumble just outside my door before I finally unearthed the earplugs and stuffed them in.

Since I'm Super Vamp, I could still hear every little bump and groan anyway. I ended up burying my head under two pillows and humming to myself until I finally nodded off.

The noise followed me, of course, reminding me how far away I was from my apartment (the most I had to put up with there was CNN and the occasional fight from the couple down on two) and Killer and my life.

Even more, it reminded me of Esther and how alone she probably felt.

Not for long. I was here and I was going to find her. Before it was too late.

At least that's what I was telling myself. I just wasn't so sure I actually believed it.

Fourteen

❤ ❤ ❤

"Dinner's at five," Elmer said when I finally managed to pick up the ringing phone on the nightstand. "We get the stuff catered in once a week from the Porky Pig down the street. It's first come, first served and I got a whole mess of bull riders headed inside right now. If you want some, you'd better get down here before these boys eat up everything."

"I don't really do barbecue, but thanks anyway." I listened to Elmer give me the lowdown on the Continental breakfast being served the following morning—Krispy Kreme and orange juice—and gave him a cheerful "Can't wait" before sliding the phone back into place.

Ugh.

My head pounded and my arms and legs ached. I

felt as if I'd spent the day tossing and turning thanks to a loud ice machine and a persistent calf.

Oh, wait. I *had* spent the day tossing and turning and listening to a loud ice machine and a persistent calf.

I buried my head under the pillow and dove straight into LaLa Land. At least, I tried.

Mooooooooooo. The sound reached beneath the surface and hauled me back to consciousness. My eyes snapped open. I fought my way past a pile of blankets and stumbled from the bed. Peeking around the edge of the blinds to make sure the sun had dipped below the horizon, I hauled open the door and scowled.

"Enough!"

The calf looked at me. I looked at the calf. He *mooooooooo*ed and I *grrrrrrrrrrr*ed. Instead of crazy, sleep-deprived woman, I went for bloodthirsty vampire. I snarled and flashed some serious fang.

The animal gave a frightened moan, pranced backward and scrambled down the walkway. Psyched, I turned toward the ice machine.

"You want a piece of me?"

It knocked and shuddered. I tried the snarl-and-flash thing. No luck. I balled my fingers and popped it on the side. Metal groaned and dented. The machine gave a dying sputter and dumped a load of ice on my feet.

"That's what I thought." I shook off the ice,

thanked the Big Vamp Upstairs that I wasn't wearing my Chanel silk slippers and headed back inside my room.

Quiet settled around me, but I was already wide awake. I stared at the ceiling all of five seconds before reaching for my cell.

Evie answered on the second ring and recited this week's DED slogan. "Dead End Dating. Where love is just a profile and several paychecks away."

It's just temporary, all right?

"How's it going?" I asked her.

"I added a new client today."

"The custom deluxe package?"

"The nifty thrifty, but if it's any consolation, I think she'll be easy to match up. She's been married eight times and she's afraid of being alone. I'm betting we hit pay dirt with the first prospect."

"Any messages?"

"The Amway guy called again, and somebody from the newspaper wanting to know if we're running an ad in the local. Nina One called twice."

Already? I glanced at the clock. It was barely sunset. Two phone calls in the fifteen minutes she'd been awake didn't translate into *good*. Unless she was simply excited because she'd realized that Rob was The One and she was ready to pledge her undying love for the rest of eternity.

I smiled and made a mental note to punch in her digits as soon as I hung up.

"Mandy also called," Evie went on. "Your mother

invited her for cocktails and she wanted you to join them at Crazy Jimmy's."

Crazy J's was an exclusive specialty cocktail bar on the Upper West Side that catered to vampires. They featured over fifty different types of Bloody Marys, from the classic to the spicy Bloody Maria and the Sizzling Caesar. Their award-winning specialty? A Bloody Biker made with imported vodka and—you guessed it—a bloody biker. Since my ma had invited Mandy, I was banking they'd branched out and added a Yaztini to the menu.

"What time?"

"They're meeting at eight."

"Call Mandy back and tell her I'll be there."

"But you're in Arizona."

"Did you tell her that?"

"I didn't actually talk to her. She left a message while I was interviewing the thrifty client."

"Great. Call her and tell her I'll be there, but I'm in the mood for something different. Tell her we're meeting at Pollo Loco instead."

"Should I call your mom and inform her about the change?"

"No. Let her go to Crazy Jimmy's." It was a lame trick, and a long shot, but it was all I had at the moment.

"I don't understand," Evie told me.

"Two words. *My. Mother.*"

"Pollo Loco it is."

While Evie had missed the memo that named

Jacqueline Marchette BV of the year, she'd obviously gotten all the others that had spelled out what an overbearing, self-centered, controlling fruitcake my ma could be.

I told Evie thanks, promised I'd bring her plenty of notes from the conference and hit the OFF button.

Punching in Nina One's number, I listened as Jesse McCartney sang an a cappella version of "Leavin'."

Ouch.

Not that it meant anything. She'd probably changed her mind, realized her love and simply hadn't had the time to change the ringtone.

"It's Lil," I told her when her voice mail finally kicked in. "Just returning your call. I'm on my cell."

I pulled out my laptop and spent the next few minutes checking email before I headed for the shower. Then I did hair and makeup, and tried to pump myself up about finding Mordred.

Because I could do this. I *would* do it.

I'd spend the next few hours searching, find Esther, kick some sorcerer ass and be back in the city by this time tomorrow night. I'd boot Rob out on his BV butt, confront Ty about his commitment issues, land a millionaire client who wanted me to match up every employee in his multi-billion-dollar corporation (complete with a big fat bonus for every couple that actually tied the knot) and all would be right with my world.

I didn't do anything half-ass. Even optimism.

After sliding on a pair of Rock & Republic jeans, a

gold BCBG tank and a pair of ultra-cool pink suede strappy sandals, I left the motel room and made a quick stop in the lobby to pick up a diet soda. Elmer was nowhere in sight, but there was a small sign on the front desk that read *Back in Half an Hour*. The evening news drifted from the small room behind the desk and I heard the steady *crrrunch crrrunch* of pork skins.

And I thought scarfing a pint of blood was icky?

I walked outside, spooked another calf and turned left at the end of the drive. A block down, I hooked a right onto Main Street.

Lonely Fork was the quintessential small town. City Hall, a historic-looking building that dated back to the 1800s, sat at the very heart of the town, next to a small, shrub-lined square with several statues paying tribute to the town's founder—Ulysses Gunther Fork.

The primary retail action was located on the main thoroughfare. A variety of businesses lined the two-lane street, everything from the Happy Cow Diner to LuLu's Tanning and Nails. There was a feed store, a children's boutique, a resale shop, a small grocery and even a five & dime.

An early sunset and an extremely overcast sky put me out and about by five-forty—barely twenty minutes before the entire place rolled up the sidewalks.

Not that I knew this initially, of course. I'm from the city that never sleeps. If you need a latte at three in the morning, no sweat. There were twenty-four-hour fitness clubs, delis and dry cleaners. All night dance clubs filled Times Square and even some of the trendiest boutiques stayed open until ten. It was a vamp's wet dream.

Lonely Fork, on the other hand, fell more into the nightmare category.

I found out this little tidbit when I ducked into the nail shop en route to my first stop—the pharmacy— for a quick cosmetics fix. They had my favorite nail polish on sale. Two for four bucks.

Come on. We're talking *four* bucks. I could barely buy an energy drink for that in the city, much less a bottle of Cocoa Crème *and* Pink Passion.

"That'll be forty dollars and thirteen cents," a woman named Dora Lee Strunk told me.

Okay, so I might have kinda sorta gone for more than two shades. It was a sale, after all.

I handed over my Visa Gold (technically Max's plastic, but I fully intended to pay him back just as soon as I saved Esther, pulled my business out of the financial hole and got back on my Jimmy Choos), tamped down on my guilt and shifted my attention to Dora.

Mid-fifties. Divorced three times. She had three grown sons who were all still single and playing the field. Thankfully. She didn't want her boys to make the same mistakes she'd made, and marriage had been the biggest. She'd stopped believing in love after husband number three, but she was still a die-hard believer in lust and so she kept herself up. She touched up her roots once a month and did an oat-meal and honey facial mask each Friday and went to happy hour at the local honky tonk every afternoon.

"You must be that matchmaker," Dora Lee told me as she slid my card through her machine and punched in the amount. "Folks really pay you to help them find someone?"

"The right someone."

"There ain't no such thing."

That's what you think. I sent the silent thought. Unfortunately, she was as straight as my flatironed hair and she simply stared blankly at me.

"We all hook up with duds every now and then," I went on. "That shouldn't scare you off all men."

"Oh, I ain't scared of men, sugar. I like men. I just don't love any of 'em. Not enough to pick up after 'em or scrub their floors or cook their food every night, when they don't appreciate any of it. I did that for my first husband and he never even said thank you. No, he just ran off with this cocktail waitress from the One-Eyed Bunny. It's this bar out on the interstate. I should have learned then, but I went on to marry two more losers who did pretty much the same thing. No more. I'd rather have fun than a wedding ring. But then you probably don't want to hear that on account of it's your business and all. Say, I bet you're here for old Rawley Pickens," she added. "If ever someone needed a matchmaker, it's that one."

My hookup radar kicked on and I couldn't resist an excited, "Really? What makes you say that?"

"That man don't stand a chance of finding a woman on his own. Been widowed forty-eight years now, living at that big old spread outside of town all by his lonesome." She arched one of her perfectly penciled-in brows. "Is that why you're here? Did he hire you?"

I shook my head. "My client is from New York. She lived here at one point a long time ago and met this man with whom she fell madly in love. It didn't work out. He went his way and she went hers. He passed on, but his son is still alive. She wants to connect with him and give him back an old family heirloom his father gave her back when they were high school sweethearts. My sources say he still lives around here. Maybe you've heard of him. Mordred Lucius." I said the name and stared intently for any sign of recognition.

She mentally rifled through her brain before shaking her head. "Can't say that I have."

"If you remember anything, would you mind giving me a call? You can reach me on my cell." I slid her a DED card and a silent *They're not all two-timing losers.*

Futile, I know, but you can't blame a vamp for trying.

"Will do, honey." She handed over my polish and followed me to the door.

"Great customer service," I told her when she opened the door for me.

"Oh, I ain't here to help you out. I'm locking up. It's

closing time." She glanced at the clock, which read
five forty-five. "Or it will be soon enough. I'm bring-
ing the cheese and crackers to Bunko tonight, so's I
need to get to the Cash-n-Carry before it closes." She
motioned to the grocer across the street. The *Open*
sign had already been turned off and I could see a
man pulling plastic sheets down over the produce out
front. "Sam ain't too fond of last minute customers.
Never misses *Wheel of Fortune,* so he shuts down at
six sharp, like everybody else on this street."

"Everybody?"

"All except for the Dairy Freeze, but they're out
near the city limits on account of the kids hang
around and make too much noise."

A bolt of panic went through me and I blurted a
quick, "Thanks." I left the shop, took a sharp look
to the left, then the right (just to make sure no one
was watching) and then did the vamp version of
some serious power walking.

A few seconds later, I pushed through the door of
Abel's Pharmacy.

Ya gotta love the whole preternatural speed thing.

The pharmacy was a throwback to the golden
oldies. A fifties-style soda fountain lined the right
side of the store. There were small round tables with
old-fashioned silver napkin holders and red vinyl
stools. Two ancient-looking men sat at the far end,
nursing cups of coffee and reading the newspaper.
The rest of the store housed several shelves, filled
with everything from notebook paper to Metamucil.

A small glass window at the rear served as the prescription pickup and drop-off. The sweet sugary scent of fresh-baked ice-cream cones filled the air.

I felt a moment of nostalgia—I'd done my fair share of jitterbugging when Elvis had been king and poodle skirts all the rage.

I let loose a sigh and headed for the fountain.

"What can I do you for?" asked the man who stood behind the counter. He had a dark brown comb-over and caramel-colored eyes. A white apron covered a short-sleeved white button-up and black slacks. "The drug counter's closed, but we're still serving sodas. Can I interest you in a root beer float?"

"I don't do dairy very well." Or any other food group. "How about just the root beer?"

"Coming right up."

His name was Ronnie Abel. Wanda's first cousin and the proud father of three college-aged girls. He'd been married thirty years to a local elementary school teacher named Joyce. He'd been married to the pharmacy even longer. His father had suffered a heart attack at a young age and Ronnie had taken over right out of high school. He ran a one man show—from making a mean banana split to dispensing a bottle of Prozac. *And* he knew everybody in town.

"Genevieve Cranberry," Ronnie declared as he set the root beer in front of me.

"Excuse me?"

"That's who you're here working for, at least

that's where I'm putting my money. If anybody needs a professional matchmaker, it's old Genevieve. The woman's got plenty of money on account of Monty—that's her late husband—had one hell of an insurance policy. Since his death was accidental—fell off his tractor during harvest season and ended up getting processed with a batch of corn—old Genevieve got double the money. Had more than enough to pay for her new boobies and a plasma TV. She always thought Monty was too working class for her, so it makes sense that she'd hire some high-falutin' New Yorker to find her a husband."

"I'm not here to match up Genevieve." I gave him the spiel about an old woman longing to meet the son of her very first love. "Maybe you've seen him." I described the man I'd met at the meet and greet. "His name is Mordred Lucius."

He thought for a second before shaking his head. "There's nobody by that name around here." He grabbed a rag and started wiping down the Formica.

"I knew a Lucius fella once," came the old, scratchy voice from the corner.

My gaze swiveled to the two old men. Darwin Jenkins and Ben Richter. Darwin kept sipping his coffee, his gaze trained on the obituaries, while Ben folded his paper and eyed me.

Ben was eighty-seven and he lived for dominoes. He'd been the state champion twice until his eyesight worsened and he started playing double sixes on the tail end of a three. Lost his title and his wife (ovarian cancer) all in the same year. He'd been spending his days at Abel's ever since.

"Knew him when I was a young gun. He used to live at the Bigby spread way back when. Don't know much about his family, but I'm thinking they had money, on account of he never worked. Just showed up one day and leased the house. Stuck-up fella, if I remember correctly. Waltzed around here like he owned the whole town. Even dated the Homecoming Queen. Caused a pretty big stink, too, on account of it was Pastor Hanover's daughter and nobody dated one of the pastor's girls. Caused a beauty of a scandal. Enough to run Lucius out of town. Moved out in the middle of the night and ain't been back since."

"So you haven't seen anyone who looks like him around here recently?"

He adjusted his bifocals. "Cain't see much anymore, but I don't think so."

"How about the pastor's daughter? You think she might have seen him?"

"I doubt it. She don't live around these parts anymore. Ran away a few months after Mordred. Heard tell she settled up in Dallas, but I don't know for sure."

"I heard she joined a cult out in L.A." Darwin glanced up from his paper. "A group of crazies who worship seashells and dance naked on the beach."

"That's just a lot of gossip," Ben told him. "I knew Tara Hanover and she was a good girl. She wouldn't dance naked on no beach. She wouldn't even put a bikini on for Spring Break up at the lake. Wore this blue cover-everything-up one-piece that hung to her ankles."

"That ain't the way I remember it," Darwin started in. "She wore a red one-piece . . ." The back and forth continued and I turned my attention back to Ronnie.

"If you see anyone who fits the description, I would appreciate it if you could give me a call." I slipped him a DED card.

"Will do. And for the record, Tara Hanover ain't dancing naked on some beach. She's in a retirement home outside of Austin with her sister. Golden Acres, I think it is."

"Thanks." It wasn't the address I'd been hoping for, but at least it was a lead. Maybe.

I fought down a wave of disappointment, gathered my determination, downed my soda and bought a new L'Oréal lip plumping gloss on my way out.

I needed a pick-me-up in the worst way.

I hit three more places—the diner, the bakery and the hardware store—before the town closed up shop. I talked to a total of twelve people, but no one had ever heard of Mordred Lucius or seen anyone that fit his description.

I spent the next thirty minutes parked at the Dairy Freeze while I checked out listings for retirement homes in Austin. It seems that Golden Acres wasn't actually in the city. It was in a small suburb called Round Rock. They didn't have a Tara Hanover registered but they did have a Tara McKenzie. I left a message asking her to call me—she was out bowling with the other retirees—and then polished off two diet sodas.

Hyped on caffeine, I decided to check out the old Bigby place and have a look around. I got directions from the clerk at the local Quick Pick—he hadn't seen or heard of Mordred, either, but he had bet twenty bucks that I was in town to hook up the new city councilman.

The Bigby place sat two miles (that would be a thirty second flight via the Batmobile) outside the city limits. I was hoping for a dark, abandoned shell out in the middle of nowhere. The perfect spot to slice and dice an innocent vampire.

Hopelessness washed through me as I stared at the bright yellow house with ivory trim. A swing set sat in the front yard. The smell of cherry pie drifted from the open kitchen window, along with laughter and the latest episode of *Survivor*.

I walked the perimeter of the house. The yard was well kept and the barn had a fresh coat of paint. No signs of a cellar or torture chamber. Rather, the place looked warm and lived in and—shit.

My eyes burned and I blinked frantically. Crying would ruin fifteen minutes of eye makeup and I was already having a bad enough night. Besides, I was a born vampire. I didn't do tears.

Or fear.

An all-important BV fact that I tried my damnedest

to remember a half hour later when I returned to the hotel, to find my door wide open.

I had brains. I had balls. I had *fangs,* for Damien's sake.

Unfortunately, so did the born vampire sitting on the edge of my bed.

The sweet telltale scent of apple cake filled my nostrils a split second before the deep voice slid into my ears.

"I've been waiting for you."

Fifteen

My heart jumped into my throat and my stomach tied itself into a dozen different knots.

I know, right? I was a sexy, irresistible BV with totally fab hair, an impeccable fashion sense and an
unbelievably high orgasm quotient. Finding a male
BV on my bed shouldn't have been anything out of
the ordinary.

It wasn't.

It was finding a *fully clothed* male BV on my bed
that had me wigged out.

He wore a blue and tan western shirt, Wrangler
jeans starched within an inch of their life and a pair of
Tony Lama brown snakeskin cowboy boots. A dark
brown felt cowboy hat sat next to him on the bed.

I caught another whiff of apples and sugar, reaf-
firming that he was, indeed, a born vampire. At the

same time, there was something else in the air. Something sharp and potent that made my nose burn. My eyes watered and I blinked before giving him the once-over. He had blond hair and mesmerizing green eyes. He looked in his thirties, indicating that he'd lost his virginity later than most.

Translation? Socially challenged.

Nix the I-want-to-have-wild-meaningless-monkey-sex agenda that usually motivated most males of my species.

This vampire was here for an entirely different reason.

My survival instincts kicked into high gear and a growl worked its way up my throat.

"Easy." He held up his hands. "I only want to talk."

Talk?

A male vampire?

Now I was *really* freaked.

I growled again and flashed some serious fang.

He shot to his feet, but his gaze remained calm and steady. "Look, I'm not here to hurt you."

"As if."

"I heard there was a matchmaker in town," he added, his voice smooth and enchanting, "and I wanted to see for myself."

Not that I was enchanted, of course. That parlor trick only worked on humans. Socially challenged, all right. Any male BV worth his weight knew the way to a female's heart was to plop down some green.

He didn't pull out his wallet. Instead, he stared at me, his eyes brightening and glowing for a long moment before cooling back to their normal shade. "You're a vampire," he finally declared. "I never expected that."

"Yeah, well, the world is full of surprises. I never expected to find Wyatt Earp breaking and entering my room." I planted my hands on my hips and eyeballed him. "What's the deal?"

"My name is DeWalt Carrigan. I own the Circle C, about five miles outside of town," he said as if the words were supposed to mean something. When I didn't seem clued in, he added, "It's *the* biggest spread in Texas."

"And this impresses me how?" Every born vamp in existence had a successful something or other. My parents ran a printing and copy dynasty. Remy provided security to celebrities and politicians. Nina One's family did hotels. Nina Two? Feminine hygiene products.

You name it, there was a vamp out there raking in the moolah.

Except for the dating game and yours truly.

Not that I was failing miserably. Hardly. I just wasn't cultivating enough to warrant a full-sized rake. No, I was still using one of those handheld gardening babies.

"I've got over twenty thousand acres," DeWalt told me. "I run fifty thousand head of cattle and I'm the largest beef supplier in the country."

My gaze snagged on his boots and I noticed the worn toes and the mud clinging to the hem of his jeans. My nose wrinkled again and I knew it wasn't just mud. Shock bolted through me.

"*You* run cattle? You personally?"

"I've got several hired hands, but I do a fair share of the work myself. Branding. Roundup. Birthing calves."

"Get out of here." Not that I couldn't see a vampire *owning* a cattle ranch. But actually *participating*? Sure, my dad ran the occasional copy for someone, but when it came to restocking the shelves or changing toner cartridges, he definitely outsourced. "Born vampires don't do manual labor."

"We're not all self-centered, holier-than-thou snobs," he told me. I arched an eyebrow and he shrugged. "So we are, but I like working for a living. I know it seems crazy."

"Suicidal."

He nodded. "But it makes me feel good. I feel like I'm actually doing something with my afterlife. Besides, we're not all descended from royalty. There are a few of us so far removed from the family tree that we didn't grow up wealthy and privileged." Another eyebrow arch and he shrugged again. "All right, so we all grew up wealthy and privileged. My family ran sheep in the Naples countryside and I used to sneak off and help the shepherds every night. Now I've got my own cattle to take care of. Purebred Texas Longhorns. They're a hell of a lot bigger, but the principle is the same. It's very lucrative," he added defensively.

"Hey, more power to you. I'm not exactly mainstreaming myself when it comes to vamp careers."

"You're really a *matchmaker*?"

"Vampires need love, too." It was his turn to arch an eyebrow. "Okay, so they need money, a good blood slave and a banging orgasm quotient/fertility rating more than they need love. But I help them find that, too. I'm also an equal opportunity matchmaker. Humans, born vampires, made vampires, weres, demons—you name it. I haven't actually matched up a fairy yet, but I'm keeping my fingers crossed."

"Do you have references?"

"No. My father would bust a nut if I handed out anything that could double as a kill sheet for one of the SOBs. But I do have a badass Flash website complete with testimonials."

He seemed to think. "Success rate?"

"Ninety-eight percent." Give or take ten or twenty.

"Do you think you could match me up?"

No. That's what I should have said because I was already on an all-important mission to find Esther. The clock was ticking.

Then again, I'd done all I could do at this point and I was stuck waiting around for Tara Hanover to call me back.

I certainly had the time to help DeWalt.

"Do you want a date for a specific occasion, a

companion or a bona fide commitment mate?" I asked him.

"A commitment mate. Five, to be exact."

"The last I heard, polygamy was a human thing."

"I'm not a polygamist." He averted his gaze and I had the strange feeling that he was suddenly embarrassed.

I know, I know. BVs didn't do embarrassment. But BVs didn't do roping and branding either, yet DeWalt Carrigan had just blown that theory wide open.

He mumbled something that even my preternatural hearing had difficulty picking up.

I blinked and tried to process the info. "Did you just say you have mad ducks with green tails?"

He cleared his throat and stiffened. After a few uncomfortable moments, his gaze finally met mine. "I said I have bad luck with females."

My geek-o-meter kicked into high gear. I'd helped a geeky vampire once before. His name was Francis and he was the oldest BV in existence.

While this guy didn't look as hopeless as Francis (he did have the whole rugged cowboy thing going on), I'd learned that it wasn't just looks that made a man lame. Francis had been a die-hard scrapbooker.

Nuff said.

"Crochet? Crossword puzzles? Ceramics? Whatever you're into, it can't be that bad."

He bristled. "I don't do any of that candy-ass stuff."

"Of course not. There's nothing candy-ass about putting together an afghan or making a cookie jar. It's therapeutic."

"I'm not a dork."

"Of course you're not."

"No, really. I'm not. I face down bulls and steers every day." He shook his head. "I'm not talking bad luck as in they don't like me. I'm talking bad luck as in they bite the dust. I've buried eight commitment mates already. The first staked herself with a riding staff in a carriage accident about three hundred years ago. Number two had a knock-down drag-out with a shepherd's staff back in the old country. Numbers three through seven all had similar freak accidents. This last one stabbed herself with a pitchfork while cleaning out the barn."

"That's terrible."

"You're telling me." He shrugged. "Nobody could handle a pitchfork like Luella. That's what I liked about her. She could give me a run for my money when it came to working the ranch."

"Children?"

He shook his head and seemed to gather his courage.

I know, right? BVs usually had the biggest balls on the planet. I fought to keep the surprise from showing on my face and kept my sympathetic come-on-and-spill expression firmly in place.

It worked, because he finally muttered, "My fertility rating isn't what it should be. Not that I can't shoot a bull's-eye. No sirree. I've got great aim. It's just that my boys are a little slow to get there and I haven't been with any female long enough for them to make the trip. I figure if I have several mates lined up waiting to jump right in when one kicks the bucket, I won't waste any time climbing back into the saddle. I think five should be enough."

Can you say *Uh-uh, not gonna happen? Not in this eternity or any other?*

Really. I'd be lucky to find one born female vampire in a town the size of a postage stamp. Five was definitely out of the question.

"We might have to reach outside your comfort zone," I heard myself say.

"Austin? Dallas?"

"I was thinking New York. Maybe Chicago. Philadelphia. Miami. If we really want to find several females, we'll have better luck if we hit the major metropolitan cities." And ones where I was semi-connected. My cousin Renee lived in Chicago. Francois in Philadelphia. Mimi in Miami.

And I thought my name sucked rocks?

"You have connections in those places?"

I gave him a get-real smile. "Do I have connections?"

"Do you?" He gave me a pointed stare.

"My database is loaded with hot prospects," I assured him, despite the fact that I wasn't one hundred percent sure I was going to take him on in the first place.

Backup soul mates? It was just so . . . cold and callous and *un*romantic. It went against the happily-ever-after, one-male-and-one-female, till-*never*-do-us-part foundation that supported my steadfast belief in true love.

Then again, *five* meant five times the usual retainer fee, which meant a year's supply of MAC's new Forever Sunrise bronzer and the ability to make good on my money-back guarantee with the handful of clients I'd failed.

"I'm willing to pay extra for your trouble." He pulled out a black leather-bound checkbook and a pen.

I'll do it.

That's what I wanted to say. But I kept thinking about poor Luella and the pitchfork and how if I'd been her, I'd have wanted DeWalt to mourn more than just the fact that I knew my way around a barn. Where was the devotion? The loyalty? The *love*?

The push/pull went on for a few minutes as my closet romantic tried to kick practicality's ass. The battle ended when DeWalt's gaze met mine.

"I need children," he finally said. "I'm my father's only son. You see, I'm not the only one of the Carrigans with slow swimmers. I've got one sister, but she's much younger. She isn't going to commit to anyone for a very long time, and even when she does, there's no guarantee that she'll reproduce. Her orgasm quotient is about as impressive as my fertility rating.

Ouch.

"I'm really the only hope of continuing our line," he added. "I *have* to reproduce."

"I feel your pain, buddy." Boy, did I ever.

I thought of my own mother and the constant fix-ups. The guilt. The nagging. The disappointment.

My heart clenched and I knew right then that I was going to help him. However unromantic and difficult.

"It's going to be expensive. We're talking five times the usual retainer, plus ten percent for expenses and travel." I gave him the amount and waited for the freak-out. Male BV=tightwad from hell.

DeWalt didn't so much as flinch as he wrote the check and handed it to me.

I stuffed the check into my purse, walked over to my briefcase and pulled out a pen and paper. "I'll need as many details about you as possible. Your likes and dislikes. Your background. Your hopes and dreams. The more I know about you, the better. You can start with your name. Address. Bank balance."

After I finished up DeWalt's profile, I gave him a smile and a reassuring "Five commitment mates coming right up," and sent him on his way. Then I pulled out my laptop and did a database search for every available female I had listed. A whopping three scrolled across my screen.

Numero uno?

Jonelle Dubois.

A zing of excitement went through me as I picked up the phone. After sitting through two dates with Evie's uncle Harrington for lack of a better match, Jonelle would jump at the chance to meet a born vamp male. This was going to be too easy.

"Hi, Jonelle. It's Lil. Lil Marchette. The dress rehearsal's over. Time for the main event."

"What are you talking about?"

"I've got the perfect vampire for you. Wealthy. Handsome. His fertility rating isn't off the charts, but you weren't interested in having more children. Although, you haven't ruled it out either," I added. "In fact, a vampire of your breeding owes it to herself to have as many children as she possibly can. It's your duty. Your right."

"But I sort of like Harrington."

Come again?

"I know it was just supposed to be a dress rehearsal, but he's really kind of sweet. He reminds me of my very first blood slave, John Charles. He's nice and he listens when I talk. That's what I've really been missing for the last six hundred years since Pierre got staked by that Italian SOB when we were on holiday in Florence. The company. See, I've realized that I don't really need a mate. It's the companionship I need, and Harrington is more than sufficient for that."

"But he's old. He won't last that long."

"Then I'll find another one. Blood slaves are much easier to come by than eternity mates."

"He's broke," I pointed out, playing every BV card I could think of. "With the exception of a teeny tiny pension, he has nothing."

"I have plenty of my own money."

"He's impotent."

"What did you say the vampire's name was?"

I gave her DeWalt's stats and set up a meeting for the following evening. She would fly down on her private jet, they would have midnight martinis and she'd be back in Connecticut before sunrise.

That was easy enough.

I was just giving myself a mental high five when my cell rang. Nina's number blazed across the display.

"Hey," I said.

"We need to talk."

"I've got plenty of time right now."

"Not on the phone. I . . ." Her voice faded as she seemed to catch herself. "I really think I need to say this in person."

"That important?"

"*The* most important thing ever."

I knew it.

"You and Rob are back together and you're eternally grateful and you want to tell me how fabulous I am. That's it, isn't it?"

"I'd rather not say anything right now. Where are you? Evie said something about Arizona, but she didn't know the name of the hotel."

"I'm staying at The Grande."

"In Phoenix?"

"Give or take a thousand miles."

"What's that supposed to mean?"

Keep your mouth shut. That's what I told myself. But then she added, "Lil? Come on. I need you. This is huge."

"I'm in Texas," I heard myself say. "But you can't tell anyone. Not my mother. Or Ty. Or Ash. Or some old guy dressed like Santa Claus. *Especially* not an old guy dressed like Santa Claus."

"What the hell is going on? Never mind," she said when I started to give her the condensed version. "You can tell me later. My afterlife is complicated enough right now. Give me the address and I'll be there tomorrow night."

"I mean it," I reminded her after I'd given her the info. "You have to keep this to yourself."

"No problem. I'll see you tomorrow."

I hit OFF and did a mental end zone dance because my luck was finally changing. I'd already found the first prospect for DeWalt, which meant I was one step closer to earning the whopping retainer he'd given me. Nina and Rob were getting back together; i.e., he was *so* outta my apartment.

And Esther?

All right, so I wasn't going to run off on a Vegas vacation just yet. Still, things were starting to work out.

I held tight to hope and shifted my attention to

born vamp prospect number two—a female who'd listed a high fertility rating and a massive bank account as her only must-haves.

Dialing her number, I crossed my fingers and sent up a silent *Pu-leazzzz* that she'd settle for one out of two.

Sixteen
♥ ♥ ♥

One minute I was propped up in bed, sipping a cup of blood and surfing my database—just in case I'd missed a viable born female for DeWalt—and the next, I was standing on a picturesque powdery white beach.

It was the ultimate getaway video in the making. The sun shimmered in the pale blue sky. A soft breeze blew in off the water. Palm trees swayed. Somewhere in the far distance, Barry Manilow sang "Copacabana."

Dreams. Go figure.

A yummy tingle swept through me and my knees trembled. I knew even before I heard Ty's deep, mesmerizing voice that he stood directly behind me.

"I've missed you."

And?

That's what I wanted to say, but since we were smack dab in the middle of a fantasy I decided not to pick a fight. This was about distracting myself and destressing and getting completely and totally naked.

Barry sang louder and Ty stared down at me and, well, I couldn't help but move my hips just a little this way and then a little that way. My hands went to the back of my neck and worked the tie on my hot pink snakeskin bikini. The straps loosened, the conch-shell clasp followed, and pretty soon I twirled and tossed it with the finesse of a highly paid hoochie.

His neon blue eyes gleamed. "You're so beautiful."

And?

I shook away the question and concentrated on the heat skimming my skin. My nipples throbbed and the inside of my thighs trembled.

Ty's gaze darkened and smoldered as his eyes caressed my body and noted every sensual reaction. He wanted to touch me, but he didn't.

Not yet.

I reached for the side ties of my bikini bottom.

"Come on, baby," he murmured, his voice raw and raspy. "Give it to me."

Help!

Wait a sec. Where was my *And . . . ?*

The thought struck and I realized that the plea hadn't come from my own insecurity.

"Lil!"

Esther's frantic voice drew me around in time to see her standing several feet away. She was naked, her body bruised and cut. Blood sizzled down her pale skin and pooled at her feet. The red spread wider, eating up the white sand and turning it into murky crimson muck.

I yelled for Ty, but he stood motionless. He wouldn't help. He couldn't.

Not any more than Ash or his brothers or Merlin. They wanted Esther dead so that they could fry Mordred.

I stepped toward her and she started to sink. Deeper. Faster. *No!* I lunged for her, but the sand seemed to suck at me, making my progress slow and tedious. Anxiety bolted through me, followed by a rush of dread as her head disappeared. I moved faster, struggling, praying. I reached her just as her elbow dipped below the surface.

Her fingers strained, grasping for me. I grabbed her, holding on as tight as I could, but it wasn't enough. The red muck yanked at her, pulling her from my grasp. Just like that, she disappeared. Gone.

Dead.

No!

My eyes snapped open to find the laptop next to me on the bed, forgotten, and the empty coffee cup discarded on the floor. The digital clock on the nightstand read ten A.M. A thin strip of burnt orange outlined the blinds.

A nightmare.

That's all it had been. Just a crazy figment of my very stressed, very active imagination.

Air churned from the window unit, blowing across my skin, and I glanced down.

My bare nipples stood at attention, while my blouse lay in a heap next to me. Along with my bra.

Okay, so most of it had been my crazy, stressed imagination.

I forced my legs to move and pushed from the bed. Peeling off my pants, I reached for my suitcase and unearthed an oversized black T-shirt that read *Cowboy Up*. I slid the cotton over my head and Ty's rich scent enveloped me.

A pang of longing rushed from my head to my toes, fading quickly in the fatigue that gripped every inch of my body. My limbs felt sluggish and my muscles ached.

FYI—vampires don't *have* to sleep during the day. We could stay awake if we wanted to, but our body usually rebelled. It needed the deep, rejuvenating sleep of the undead as much as it needed fresh blood.

Otherwise . . .

The word *cranky* didn't even touch it.

I killed the light, crawled back into bed and buried my head beneath the pillow to escape the noise outside. The *clip-clop* of horse hoofs. The steady *mooooo* of the calves. The clang of tools as Elmer tried to fix the ice machine.

Sleep swallowed me again, sucking me down the way the sand had sucked at Esther.

Her frantic *Help!* followed me and I knew deep

down inside that the striptease hadn't been the only part of the nightmare that had been real.

She was dying.

I knew it. I felt it. And despite several centuries of cultivated optimism, I was starting to think that maybe—just maybe—I might not reach her in time.

Barry was singing again.

I covered my ears and tried to drown out the constant drumming. The rocking voice. The cool mix of synthesizers and—

Wait a sec. Forget Barry.

I fought my way through the blackness until recognition dawned and I realized it was Katy Perry. She wailed about hot and cold and yes and no and in and out and—sheesh.

Now, I like Katy as much as the next ultra-trendy, five-hundred-and-holding-year-old vampire, but I was trying to friggin' sleep here.

". . . up then you're down . . ."

I groped for the noise. My hand closed over my cell and I forced my eyes open long enough to kill the sound. My gaze snagged on the caller ID. Guilt spiraled through me and my finger paused on the OFF button. A split second of indecision (and a few *He loves me/He loves me nots*) and I pressed TALK.

"Yeah?" I mumbled.

"Rise and shine," Ty's deep voice echoed in my ear, and my hormones gave a squeal of excitement.

Bad hormones. "Easy for you to say. You didn't

have a stampede outside your window." Not to mention the all-day attempt to fix the ice machine. The spray of gravel as the pickup trucks and animal trailers moved out.

I pushed to my feet and walked over to peek around the blinds. Sure enough, there wasn't a calf in sight. *Back to normal.* Elmer's voice echoed in my head and I realized that the rodeo must have opened their temporary holding pens for the animals.

The last few rays of sun sizzled across one of my fingertips. A wisp of black smoke spiraled up into the air and pain bolted through me. I snatched my hand away. Normal. Sure.

"What are you talking about?" Ty's voice drew me away from the window.

"Nothing." I sank back down on the bed. "It's my neighbors," I heard myself say. "They must have been having a party."

"Funny, but I thought you were the one having the party."

"I'm afraid I don't know what you're talking about." That's what I said. Meanwhile my brain scrambled for a very lengthy and painful death for my not-so-fave brother.

"You're the only one. You could hear the music down the block. Rob is one hell of a host."

Uh-oh.

"He and Nina broke up, so he's at my house mourning the loss."

"Sugar, he didn't mourn the entire time I was there.

He danced a lot. And fell on his ass a few times. And annihilated a few of your lamps. And I even saw him stand on your coffee table and do several AB+ shots. But that was it. No crying. No depression. Nothing." He grew silent for a long moment while his news sent me into a complete mental freak-out.

My coffee table?

My lamps?

Oh, no, he didn't.

"Why don't you tell me what's really going on," Ty finally said.

"I think they're both just really stubborn," I blurted before I lost it and launched into a description of exactly how big an ungrateful, inconsiderate, clueless asshole my brother really was. "She loves him even if he is an ungrateful, inconsiderate, clueless asshole." What? I can't vent? "But she doesn't realize it and he loves her but he doesn't realize it, and neither one of them will say it." *Not unlike someone else I know,* I added silently.

"I'm not talking about Nina and Rob. What's going on with you? Where are you?"

My stomach tied itself into several knots and guilt crept through me. "Didn't you, um, get my message? I'm in Arizona."

"See, that's the funny thing. *I'm* in Arizona and you're nowhere around."

I contemplated the possibility all of five seconds. "You're not in Arizona," I finally told him.

"And neither are you. You lied to me."

"I did not. I mean, technically, you might call it a lie but I'm supposed to be escaping from the world. This retreat is really important to me. I want to get the full experience, so I figured it was better if I kept my actual whereabouts a secret. That way I won't have any distractions."

"This doesn't have to do with Esther, does it?"

"Esther who?"

"I'm serious, Lil. You need to stay out of it. Merlin and his men already have the situation under control."

"By *under control* you mean he's sitting around on his ass, waiting for the ax to drop, while Esther suffers."

"The ritual doesn't call for an ax. It's a knife. An ancient Mayan dagger used to sacrifice victims to the gods."

My stomach pitched. "Whatever. The point is, nobody cares what happens to her."

"They've got rules to follow. That's the way it works."

"That stinks."

"Lil—"

"I mean, it *would* stink if I weren't a self-centered, narcissistic vampire who didn't give a shit about anyone or anything except my fantabulous self. But I am, so it's all good. I could care less and there's no way in the world I would take matters into my own hands," I rushed on, "and look for Esther on my own. Not this vamp."

"Merlin and his men will destroy anyone who tries to stop Mordred from making the sacrifice. They want to put him away for good and this is the only way to do it."

"Which is exactly why I'm staying far, far away from Texas and minding my own self-centered business."

"Yeah."

"Really. Geez, would you look at the time? I'm late for *Dieting Tips to Slim Down Your Overweight Clients*. Can't miss that. Gotta run." I killed the connection before he could ask me any more questions.

And before he could add anything like *Please be careful* or *I miss you* or *I love you*.

If he'd wanted to, that is.

No sooner did I switch my phone to vibrate than the dial-up on the nightstand started to ring. I had to hand it to Ty. He was fast and persistent.

A tiny thrill went through me and I barely resisted the urge to snatch up the phone. Come on. It's not like he was calling to declare his devotion. He was going to chew me a new one.

I knew that and so I was *not* picking up the phone.

Then again, it might not even be Ty. It might be someone with a tip about Mordred. I'd handed out cards to dozens of people. Maybe it was finally paying off.

I snatched up the receiver. "Lil Marchette."

"Meatloaf sandwiches and fried pickles," Elmer said. "Just delivered. You in?"

"Pass."

"Best meatloaf in town," he added.

According to the *Lonely Fork Gazette,* no doubt.

"I'm not really hungry."

"City folk," he murmured. "It just ain't natural living on carrot sticks and whole wheat and all them fancy schmancy protein shakes and such. Gimme real food any day."

And gimme a friggin' break.

"Just so's you know," he went on, "the lobby will be closed tonight. I'm playing Bingo over at the VFW."

My worry faded in a rush of excitement. "You have a date?"

"Does Tallulah Pierce count?"

"That depends on the circumstances. Did you ask her out?"

"Not exactly. I have to pick her up on account of I'm the only one at the VFW who'll let her sight dog ride in the front cab of their pickup. He's old and a little incontinent."

"Aren't we all?"

"That's what I always say. Anyhow, I give her a ride every week to Bingo, so I guess you might consider it a date."

"Do you kiss her good night?"

"I shake her hand and sometimes I scrape poop off her shoe if she steps the wrong way before the dog can stop her."

"That doesn't really qualify her as a love interest."

"Then I guess I'm flying solo."

Not for long. I slid the phone into its cradle and reached for my cell. I entered my password and checked my voice mail. Tonight was the night. I was going to get a break in Esther's case. A witness who'd seen someone fitting Mordred's description. A concerned neighbor who smelled rotting vampire. An innocent bystander who'd heard screams or crying or something.

I held tight to the hope as the first message echoed in my ear.

"I'm at Pollo Loco," Mandy said. "Where are you?" I ignored a spiral of guilt and hit DELETE.

Message two. "I'm at Crazy Jimmy's," my mother said. "Where are you?" *Delete.*

Message three. "I'm still at Pollo Loco. I'm giving you fifteen more minutes. In the meantime, I think I'll have the nachos."

Message four. "I'm still at Crazy Jimmy's and I'm drinking Bloody Marias all by myself. I've tried calling Mandy, but she must be on the phone because it's going straight to voice mail." *Delete.*

Message five. "I know you're up to something—" Ty started. I hit DELETE before he could finish.

Message six. "You're getting in way over your head—" *Delete.*

Message seven. "Stay out of it—" *Delete.*

The end.

So much for helpful tips.

I punched in the number for Golden Acres and asked for Tara.

"Sure, she's here. But she can't come to the phone. She's playing Bridge and she gets real mad when anyone interrupts her. I can have her call you when she's finished."

I'd already gone that route yesterday. "Why don't you just give me directions instead?"

I was through waiting around for a return phone call. I would fly up to Austin and talk to Tara in person.

Not that I had any illusions that it was going to bring me any closer to finding Esther, but I had to *do* something. The waiting for someone to call with a tip and the worry over Esther was driving me nuts.

I walked into the bathroom, peeled off Ty's T-shirt and climbed into a hot shower. I was just rinsing shampoo out of my hair and envisioning a massive break in Esther's case (finding Mordred playing Bridge with Tara while Esther crouched in a nearby closet) when I heard the rattle of the dead bolt and the twist of the doorknob.

What the—

The thought struck just as a hand gripped the shower curtain and ripped it to the side. A scream burst past my lips as I whirled. Shampoo ran in my eyes, but I forced them open anyway, to see Nina One standing on the bathmat.

Her blond hair was pulled back in a ponytail and she had no makeup on. She wore a rumpled Juicy sweat suit and flip-flops (we're talking the plain, plastic kind). I knew right then that something bad had happened.

"What's wrong?"

She started to say something, but when her mouth opened, all that came out was a high-pitched squeak.

"Is it that bad?"

More squeaking and a fierce nod.

"Is it your father? Your mother?"

She shook her head.

"Nina Two?" Panic bolted through me. "Did she get hurt?"

She shook her head. I was definitely biting at the wrong artery, so I decided to switch victims.

"Your dad took away your credit cards?"

Another shake.

"Your credit cards got stolen?"

Another frantic shake.

"They're closing Barneys?"

She shook her head and relief pumped through me for a split second. But then Nina squeaked again and I was back to Guess That Tragedy.

"Your favorite Prada bag bit the dust?" When she

did a frantic side to side, I added, "Come on, Nina. You gotta give me something."

She nodded and seemed to fight for her control. She cleared her throat. Her trembling lips parted and she said in a tense, strained voice the very last thing I ever expected to hear.

"I—I'm pregnant."

Seventeen
❤ ❤ ❤

"You're *what*?" I braced a hand against the tiled wall as my knees went suddenly weak.

She licked her lips. "I'm pregnant."

"Pregnant?"

"Pregnant."

"*Pregnant?*"

"*Pregnant.*" She held up a hand when I opened my mouth. "If you keep saying it, I'm going to heave."

"But I don't understand."

"Pregnant," she repeated, "as in PG. Preggo. Stuffed full of tiny vamp spawn."

"I understand what it means." I grabbed a nearby towel and wiped at my burning eyes. "I just don't understand . . ." I shook my head. "How?"

"He kissed my neck and then I nibbled the skin

over his pulse beat and that made him go nuts. The next thing I knew, I was flat on my back and he was—"

"I don't mean how as in a detailed play-by-play," I cut in, wrapping the towel around me and stuffing the edge under my arm. "I mean *how* as in how could you let this happen? Haven't you ever heard of a condom?"

"Are you kidding? I practically own stock in Trojan. They're great for the occasional human encounter or when I pick up a made vampire. They even worked like a charm when I did that werewolf back in '77. You remember him. The one who taught me how to do the hustle that time at Studio 54."

I shook my head. Anything that involved polyester and a Dorothy Hamill bob I'd much rather forget.

"But condoms are powerless against born vamp sperm," Nina went on. "Those suckers just bit right through it." She shook her head. "I am so screwed."

Born vamp. Pregnant.

The facts echoed in my head and reality struck. "Rob's the father?"

"Nah, it's Brad Pitt. He snuck away and left Angie with the kiddos while we did it on top of the Empire State Building. Of course it's Rob's. That's why I'm so freaked."

"Because you don't love him and the thought of being saddled with his spawn is too much to handle, or because you do love him and you're afraid if you go crawling back now he'll think it's just because of the baby?"

"How did you know?"

"I'm a professional, Nina. Understanding vamp nature is what I do for a living."

"I thought you were a matchmaker."

"I am, but in order to be successful at my job I have to understand the nuts and bolts of the vampire psyche."

"Now I am going to heave." She turned and walked into the bedroom and I followed. "What am I going to do?"

"First you're going to tell me whether or not you love him." Because while I'd obviously hit it on the head, I'd been whacking both sides so I had no clue which nail we were talking about. "You do love him, right?"

"I didn't think so. In fact, I was pretty sure I didn't. But then I'm in the bathroom the night before last and I'm feeling really sick. I'm thinking maybe Ernesto had the flu or something and I just had some really bad Mexican. But then I woke up yesterday and I was still feeling sick. I called Nina Two and she told me to take a pregnancy test. I thought she was crazy, but the more I thought about it . . ." She sniffled again. "I figured I'd take one and put my mind at ease." Her gaze collided with mine. "I took five of them and by the time that fifth plus sign appeared, I knew it was true."

"That you were pregnant."

She shook her head. "That I was pregnant and that I loved Rob. See, I wasn't freaked out about the baby. When I saw that first pink plus sign, I actually felt happy."

"That's great!"

"No, it's not. It's the worst thing ever. I can't be happy about this baby and I can't be in love with its father. Rob and I are over."

"Not if you tell him you're sorry. He'll tell you he's sorry. The two of you will get back together. You'll have a nice commitment ceremony complete with a champagne reception at the Waldorf and an ice sculpture shaped liked Count Chocula. You'll honeymoon in Maui. Then you'll come back and I'll give you a nice big baby shower with one of those fab diaper cakes. You'll have the baby and, bam, you'll live happily ever after." I squelched my own sudden pang of longing and focused on Nina.

She actually looked hopeful, but then her face fell. "That's impossible."

"Which part?"

"All of it. If I tell Rob I'm sorry, he'll think it's because of the baby."

"It is because of the baby."

"Yes, but it isn't *because* of the baby. The baby just helped me realize my feelings for him. I don't love him just because I'm having his baby."

"So tell him that."

"He won't believe me."

"He might."

"And he might spend the next eternity wondering if I didn't just hook up with him because I needed a father for my child. I have to have this baby on my own." Her gaze met mine again. "My dad is going to shit a brick."

I thought of Nina's strict, conservative father (much like my own) and my heart went out to her.

In the born vamp society, procreation was all about family mergers and propagating the species. Love didn't figure in, and so Nina's father would never understand why she refused to name the father.

Unfortunately, the sucker for love that I am, I got it loud and clear.

To make matters worse, Nina's eyes grew bright, and before I knew it, she started to bawl.

What?

Nina was a superficial born vamp who shed a tear only when her bank account slipped below an acceptable level or she missed out on one of the shows during Fashion Week.

Stunned, I stared at her for a few fast, furious heartbeats while my brain raced for something— anything—to make her feel better.

"Look on the bright side. Now you have an excuse to buy a new wardrobe."

"I don't need an excuse for that."

"Oh, yeah." I couldn't think of anything else to say so I kept my mouth shut and did the only thing that felt right. I slid my arms around her.

She stiffened at first because born vampires, even

BFFs, didn't usually get touchy-feely. My arms tightened and she melted against me. The tears came harder and if I weren't such a badass vamp, I might have cried too.

For a reason other than the soap residue still burning my eyes, of course.

"What am I going to do?" she finally asked several huge sobs (me) and a couple of hiccups (her) later. She pulled away and stared at me as if I had all the answers.

I had zero, but she was my BFF and she needed a guiding hand.

"First off"—I sniffled and wiped at my own cheeks—"you're going to stop crying. This can't be good for the baby." I steered her toward the bed. "You're going to lie down and get some rest. Where's your luggage?"

"I don't have any. I was so upset and anxious last night that I left home without even an overnight bag."

Which explained the rumpled sweats and zero makeup.

"I took the red-eye and flew into Austin, but it was too early to buy anything. I just checked myself into the nearest five star hotel and slept until sundown. Then I caught a cab here. I figured we could do some shopping later."

I shook my head. "There are exactly two boutiques in town. One specializes in children's clothes and the other is a resale shop."

The color drained from her face. "I think I need to lie down."

"That's a great idea." I steered her toward the bed. "I've got a few errands to run, but I'll be back soon. You can nap until then."

"Resale?" she asked as if trying to digest the information.

"You can borrow something of mine until tomorrow night. Then we'll do a little shopping in Austin before everything closes. I'm sure they have a mall."

"A *mall*? Now I know I'm going to be sick."

"No, you're not. You're going to calm down, close your eyes and forget about everything but getting some rest."

"But I don't even have a toothbrush."

"I'll pick one up while I'm out. Now in." I motioned her under the covers. "And lie on your left side. That helps the circulation to the baby."

"Since when did you become an expert on pregnant women?"

"Since I spent most of my life living with Jacqueline Marchette." Aka the Queen of Guilt. I'd heard my mother's war stories so many times that I now knew more than I ever wanted to know about bloating and fat ankles and raging hormones.

See, having a baby vamp was pretty much like having a baby human. Same restrictions—no feeding on an alcoholic or a chain smoker or a Starbucks addict. Same recommendations—plenty of rest and exercise and extra nutrition. The only difference? The source of the nutrition. "Did you eat?"

"A half a bottle of AB+ before I left the hotel in Austin." She sniffled. "Maybe I should have a snack."

I grabbed the coffeepot and poured her what was left of my own dinner. "Drink up, lay down and close your eyes."

She nodded, drank every drop from the mug I handed her and then snuggled down under the covers.

"Lil?"

"Yes?"

"Promise you won't tell Rob about the baby."

"I won't tell Rob about the baby." About the fact that she loved him? That little tidbit was fair game.

"Scout's honor?" she asked.

"I was never a Girl Scout."

"You wanted to be."

"*Au contraire*. I wanted to be a Princess Brigitte Little Lady in Waiting (the English translation of a snotty, pretentious French game played by all the servants' daughters back in the old country). I'd been nine and desperate to bond with the other little girls that lived at my family's castle. My mother had been strict about no fraternizing with the humans and so I'd had to content myself with watching from afar.

"I sat in on one tea party, but my mother caught

me and threatened to feed the other little girls to our groundskeeper—he was a werewolf—if they let me join the group." Did my ma have a way with children or what? "She banned them from using the kitchen and they blamed me."

"The bitches," Nina said, closing her eyes and snuggling down into the pillow. "I wanted to be a Little Lady, too," she murmured as she drifted off. A few minutes later, she was sound asleep.

I tucked the covers around Nina (we're talking the mother of my niece/nephew/excuse to throw a super-hot baby shower) and headed into the bathroom to pull myself together. Drying my hair, I pinned it back with a pink rhinestone clip. After a little mascara and some lip plumper, I wiggled my way into a pair of skinny black jeans, pulled on a Cake tie-dye silk cardigan and tank and pushed my feet into a pair of purple Cheyenne satin flats.

By the time I walked out of the hotel room, I rocked physically. It was the mental I was having trouble with.

Everything was just too weird. Esther was missing. Nina was pregnant and she'd forgotten her luggage and she was blubbering worse than me when I watched *The Notebook* on DVD. On top of that, I was staying in a room straight out of an *Austin Powers* movie. *And* I was wearing a ponytail.

While I knew I looked trendy cool, I still couldn't remember the last time I'd just pulled it all back, to hell with hair products or a flatiron. But forty-five minutes on hair seemed so unimportant compared to everything that was happening in my afterlife.

That, or I was suffering from some serious sleep deprivation.

After a few seconds of consideration, I latched onto number two. I already had two strikes against me when it came to unbecoming vamp character (working class and a romantic). No need to add a third (compassionate).

My ma would disown me for sure.

Locking the hotel door behind me, I headed for the back alley. I dodged a few suspicious piles (the animals were gone, but the evidence remained) and found a small secluded spot where I could concentrate.

I tuned out the steady buzz of crickets and the voices from Elmer's TV and tuned into the steady thump of my own heart, from the sound echoing in my ears to the pulse in my chest.

My body began to tingle. The sensation started in my toes, sweeping upward until I felt as if it were vibrating in time to the steady *ba-bom ba-bom*. My arms and legs grew weightless and my vision sharpened. I added a mental *All aboard!* so I didn't forget anything (namely the flats, which had cost me two retainers) and then I hopped on the Batgirl Express.

A few seconds later, I flapped my way over the top of The Grande and headed for Austin.

Eighteen

♥ ♥ ♥

"That's Tara Hanover over there," said the old man who'd met me at the front door of Golden Acres.

Bernie MacDougal. An ancient little man with snow white hair and a hunched back that would have made Quasimodo envious. He wore his pants too short and his glasses too thick. He was this close to breaking the Golden Acres' chess record of 863 straight wins. *If* he won this next game about to take place in five minutes and fifty-three seconds—just as soon as the Bridge Club finished and vacated his lucky table—he was going to win a year's supply of Metamucil. With the way the cafeteria served up mac and cheese every other night, he needed all the help he could get. "She's the one on the right."

My gaze shifted to a large woman wearing an orange muumuu and a pair of black cat's-eye glasses. "The redhead?"

"Your other right," Bernie told me.

My gaze bounced to the other side of the table. Same muumuu, different color. This one was pink and wrapped around a chubby woman with pasty white skin and dyed black hair. She wore a ton of foundation, most of which had settled into her wrinkles, making her look even older than her seventy-eight years. Bright red lipstick rimmed her thin lips and bled slightly at the corners. Red rouge splotched her cheeks and blue shadow hovered over her eyes. Crimson-painted nails gripped a handful of cards. She looked deep in thought.

That, or asleep.

I noted the steady rise and fall of her chest. A faint *grrrrrrr* crossed the distance and slid into my ear.

"Are we gonna finish this or what?" Orange muumuu demanded, and Tara jumped.

"Don't get your girdle twisted, Laverne," she growled. "I'm just concentrating."

Yeah. Sure.

I moved to step forward, but Bernie caught my arm. "No sirree, bub. She gets cranky if anyone bothers her during Bridge. They'll finish up soon enough." He eyed the clock. "It's almost time. I need to run back to my room and get my lucky rabbit's foot. Just have a seat over there." He pointed to a group of chairs. "That, or there's refreshments out in the lobby. You can talk to her when she's done."

"Thanks." I sank onto a nearby folding chair. Pulling out my iPhone, I was about to check the two new voice mails I'd received when Katy started singing.

Every head at the Bridge table swiveled in my direction. A dozen pairs of eyes drilled into me and their owners' thoughts rolled through my brain.

What the hell is her problem?

We don't allow phones in here.

Shut that bitch up, will ya?

And a few more that I really didn't want to think about. Who knew old people could be so violent?

I gave them an apologetic smile and sent a mental *You are not mad. You love me and you love Katy Perry and you don't mind the interruption.*

Unfortunately, the men were well past their sexual prime and so my seductive vamp influence was totally wasted. They scowled and one of them gave me the universal peace symbol. I pushed to my feet and headed for the lobby before someone lit a torch and yelled *Death to the Vampire!*

"I need to ask you something," Rob's voice echoed over the line once I hit TALK. My heartbeat kicked up a notch.

Asking meant he suspected and suspected meant he practically knew. Which meant I wouldn't be *telling* him. No, I would merely be answering—truthfully—whatever question he might pose.

"Okay. Shoot."

"Where's the cat food?"

"Yes, she does love—Excuse me?"

"I can't find any more cans in the cabinet."

"Well, let's think about this. Maybe you can't find any more cans because I'm out. If you want cat food, you'll have to go to the store."

"But there's a rerun of the Dolphins playing Pittsburgh."

"Pause it."

"I can't do that. Pittsburgh is about to score."

"Then make Killer suffer until the touchdown."

"Okay."

"I was being sarcastic. Get off your ass and go get cat food. And while you're at it, pick up some more bottles of blood to replace all the ones you've drank. And a new coffee table. And a pair of lamps. And a Swarovski crystal hair clip."

"What?"

You can't blame a vamp for trying.

"Did I say hair clip? I meant commitment ring."

He went suspiciously silent. "Why would I buy a commitment ring?" he finally asked.

"Not for Nina, that's for sure. Really. I mean, you guys are over, right?"

"Right."

"Which means you should be ready in case, you

know, you find someone else and want to pledge your devotion. You never know when you might fall in love or have a baby vamp or both. In no particular order."

"Are you feeding?"

"I'm fine."

"Because you sound light-headed."

"It's called being a good sister. I'm just concerned for you. I want you to have it all. The old ball and chain. The 8.3 kids (vamp statistics). The au pair and the Lexus mini-van."

"I'd rather have a hot stake driven into my heart."

Little did he know, but that was definitely a possibility. Especially when Nina's father found out she was pregnant and my brother had no intention of making an honest vampire out of her.

"So what exactly happened at my apartment?" I rushed on, eager to change the subject before I gave in to the crying romantic in me and told him what was up.

Not that I would. It was Nina's place to tell him and I had no business butting in. Besides, what if she was right? What if Rob totally flipped out? What if instead of being happy and ready to bleed into the commitment vial, he went AWOL and denied Nina and the baby?

I knew that wasn't the most likely scenario, because family was everything to a born vamp. Still. My brother had never been the most compassionate BV. I'd fallen on a pitchfork in our barn one time and instead of going for help, he'd hopped on a horse and headed for the nearest tavern.

His explanation when my father had cornered him? *It's not like she won't heal, Dad. She's a vampire.*

"Ty said you had a party," I added.

"It was just Max and Jack and a couple of the guys from work. We ordered Chinese, sucked them dry, watched wrestling and then demonstrated a few moves and, well, that was one ugly end table anyway."

I rest my case.

His words registered and my brain snagged on the last part. "I thought you messed up the coffee table."

"That was pretty ugly, too."

"And the lamps?"

"You really ought to get a professional decorator in here, sis."

"As soon as I get home, your ass is out of there."

"What'd I do?"

"Out," I barked, and stabbed the OFF key.

Maybe Nina *was* better off without Rob. Women had babies alone all the time. Sure, they were human women. But vampires could be independent, too. We didn't have to settle for a jerk just because society dictated that procreation was *the* most important thing. That was archaic. Stupid. Ridiculous. And it was high time a brave female stood up and said so.

I thought of my own mother's reaction and sent up a silent *Thank you* that said female was not *moi*.

I was just about to stuff my cell back into my bag when I heard the voice.

"Outta my way, Paris Hilton." A huge woman barreled past me, and if I hadn't had fast reflexes (you gotta love being a vamp) she would have run me over and left me for roadkill.

I glanced up in time to see the dyed black hair and pink tentlike dress swish past me.

"Miss Hanover?" I was right on her heels.

"Once upon a time," she called over her shoulder. "Ain't nobody called me that since 1960."

"My name is Lil Marchette. I'm a matchmaker from Manhattan, here on special assignment." I tried to hand her a DED card, but she waved it away. "I'd really like to ask you some questions."

"I only got two words to spare right now—*crab dip*. Now, I don't expect a skinny thing like you to understand, but a full-figured woman like myself who likes to indulge has to pay a certain price if she overdoes it."

"Come again?"

"You deaf, Slim? I said I need to make a deposit." She pushed through a door marked Heffers and I followed.

I realized all too late that we were in the restroom. She disappeared into the first stall while I backtracked toward the swinging door.

"I'll just wait outside—"

"Go on and ask your questions."

"Excuse me?"

"I might be awhile and there ain't a blasted thing to read in here. You might as well keep me company."

"But—"

"It's now or never, 'cause I got people waiting on me. I ain't got time to play Twenty Questions with some Nicole Richie clone."

I stalled just shy of the door. "I thought you said I looked like Paris Hilton?"

"Paris Hilton. Nicole Richie. Kelly Ripa. Leonardo DiCaprio. Don't think I didn't read that article on celebrity eating disorders in last week's *National Tattler*. Why, one great big breeze and you're liable to blow away."

"Trust me, I do not have an eating disorder." Unless you counted an all-liquid diet.

"Girlie, you're nothing but bones. I could snap you like a chicken."

Such charm and charisma. I could totally see why this woman had been voted Lonely Fork Homecoming Queen.

"So what do you want, Bones? I ain't got all friggin' night."

I gave her the spiel about looking for the son of the high school sweetheart. "I heard you were acquainted with his father. Mordred Lucius?"

"Mordred?" She let loose a low whistle, followed by a few grunts. "Now, there was a hot-looking man."

"So you went out with him?"

"I don't know if I'd call it going out. But we sure as shootin' hooked up a time or two." She chuckled. "Or three."

"What can you tell me about him? What did he like to do? Where did he like to go?"

"All the way." The comment came from the doorway behind me. I turned just as the door swung open and another woman pushed inside. Same pink muumuu. Same black hair. Ditto on the caked-on makeup.

Wait just a friggin' second.

I did a double take. My gaze locked with the woman's and I knew in an instant that she was the real Tara Hanover.

Now Tara Mackenzie. She'd been widowed for twenty years and living in Golden Acres for the past five. She had one daughter and seven grandchildren, and she rarely saw any of them because they were busy with their own lives. Which was why she'd moved in here. Between shopping and Bridge and arguing with her sister, she didn't have time to miss her family.

She'd had a mad bad crush on Mordred Lucius back in the day. She'd given him her virginity in the backseat of his Chevy Impala. She'd meant to give him her heart, too, but he'd disappeared the next day. She'd blamed her father for running him off, but when he didn't come back or make any attempt to contact her, she'd realized that he'd just been using her for sex.

Much the same way her twin sister, Dara, had been using him for sex.

Twins.

The realization hit as Tara barreled past me.

"Jesus," she huffed as she wedged herself into the second stall. "Haven't you ever heard of a Krispy Kreme?"

It wasn't enough I had to deal with one hater. No, I get double the fun.

"I'm not skinny," I heard myself say. "It's called svelte."

"If you say so." Fabric rustled and the toilet groaned as Tara collapsed on top. "Why don't you tell her the truth?" she said to the stall next to her.

"About how Mordred was a hell of a lot more attracted to me than he was to you?"

"About how you jumped his bones every chance you could get. The poor fella didn't stand a chance."

"You're just mad because he kissed me more that night than he did you."

"He did not. You kept jumping in front of me."

Wait a second. "The two of you went out with him at the same time?"

"I wouldn't call it going out." Dara chuckled. "He definitely went in."

"You're shameless," Tara told her sister. "What would Daddy say?"

"What he always said—that you were the good one and I was the bad one. But I think you proved him wrong that night. Horndog."

Tara inhaled sharply. "You know good and well that I didn't go there for that."

"Sure you didn't. Nobody in their right mind went to Miller's Creek unless they were looking to get lucky."

"Miller's Creek?" I asked. "What's that?"

"Only the most romantic spot in town. The water, the moonlight." Tara sighed. "It was breathtaking. Magical."

"It was the local Lover's Lane," Dara added. "Tara showed up one Saturday night when I was there with Mordred."

"I wanted to make sure that she didn't hurt him," Tara offered. "He was a good man."

"He was a sex fanatic and the only reason you showed up was to see why he was so over-the-moon for me. You were jealous and you wanted to see what I had that you didn't."

"You're crazy. We're identical."

"On the outside maybe. But inside, I'm Pamela Anderson and you're Oprah."

"I am not Oprah."

"Yes you are. Though I have to admit you shed the Oprah for a few minutes that night. I swear, I never knew you had it in you."

I got a sharp visual of Tara and Dara, minus the muumuus, crammed into the backseat of Mordred's car.

My stomach heaved and I almost bolted for the nearest sink.

"You didn't . . ." I searched for the words. "I mean, you're sisters, right?"

"We did him," Dara told me, "not each other."

"Would you stop talking like that?" Tara screeched.

"Just telling it like it is."

"No, you're not. You're making it sound filthy and trashy."

"It was filthy and trashy, and I loved every minute of it. So did he."

"He did not."

"Have either of you seen Mordred lately?" I blurted, eager to shift the topic to something that didn't make me want to OD on the nearest package of Tums.

"Not since that night down by the creek. It started out as a date and ended in a threesome on account of Tara showed up. Mordred told her how much he loved her and, bam, a Hanover sandwich."

"He did love me."

"He left the next day."

"He left you, too."

"I didn't love him."

"You're heartless."

"And you wear your heart on your sleeve."

"Bitch."

"Pushover."

O-kay. I backed my way out of the bathroom and then turned to bolt before the shit hit the fan. Literally.

My nose wrinkled as I headed down the hall,

followed by a steady *pop pop pop* and a very loud *splattt!*

A few seconds later, I was winging it back to Lonely Fork. I replayed the conversation with the twins and tried to discern what I'd learned tonight.

They'd had a threesome. He'd had a Chevy Impala. They'd had a threesome. Tara was the good twin. They'd had a threesome. Dara was the bad twin. They'd had a threesome. Both women liked Bridge. They'd had a threesome.

This was so not getting me anywhere.

I needed to change tactics. To think outside the box. To think like a murdering sorcerer hungry for eternal life.

Where would I go if I were this close to slicing and dicing a poor vampire?

A fortified hideout with a ten-foot electric fence and lots of angry Dobermen pinschers. That's the conclusion I came to as I headed to the Quick Pick to buy toiletries for Nina.

If I were about to commit a felony, I would stay deep in hiding until the deed was done. No cruising around town. Or visiting the local library to check out books. Or stopping off at the diner for coffee. Or dropping by the Quick Pick for cigarettes.

My gaze fixed on the man who stood at the counter with a pack of Marlboros in one hand and a forty in the other. He wore starched khakis, a blue button-down shirt and white running shoes.

No. Way.

No. Friggin'. *Way.*

He must have felt my stare because he turned. My disbelief quickly faded in a rush of *I told you so.*

The search was now officially over.

I'd found Mordred.

Nineteen
❤ ❤ ❤

I have to admit, I'd spent so much time thinking about finding Mordred that I hadn't actually thought about what I would do when I caught up to him. Sure, I'd envisioned swooping in, opening up a can of whoop ass and saving Esther. But I'd never broken the scenario down into a step-by-step plan.

Go here. Do this. Kick this. Save that.

Nada.

Hence the great big bolt of *Holy shit* that rushed through me and jacked up my adrenaline until I felt as if my veins would explode.

Do something! That's what my brain screamed. *Wipe the floor with his lying, kidnapping, meet-and-greet-crashing hide.*

But that wouldn't help Esther. She would still be out there. Locked up somewhere. Alone and dying.

The realization had me ducking down behind a Slushee machine while Mordred forked over a twenty and waited for his change. The Slushee machine whirred. The scent of sticky sweet blue bubblegum surrounded me. And I thought smelling like cotton candy was bad? Seconds ticked by, and finally the register gave a loud *dinggg* and spit out several coins into the change dispenser. Man-made soles slapped the tile floor and the bell on the entrance gave a jingle.

I counted to five, swore never to look at a piece of blue bubblegum and then headed for the door.

"Wait a sec," the clerk yelled, and I realized I still clutched a toothbrush in my hand.

"Ssshhhh. I'm gonna pay for it." Just not at that particular moment. I grabbed the door handle. The bell jingled.

"Come back here, punk!"

"I'll be back. I swear." When he reached for his shotgun, I added a mental *You don't want to shoot me because I'm a) trying to save my friend's life and will come back ASAP and pay for the stupid thing and b) a bona fide hottie that you would seriously like to get with.*

Here's the thing about men and hot women . . . even if a guy knows his chances are zilch, he'll still do everything in his power to bend over backward for an impressive pair of boobs. It's a law of nature or something.

Sure enough, his eyes went glassy and the shotgun lowered a few inches.

"Come again," he called after me.

I rest my case.

I flew out the door and hooked a left in the direction I'd seen Mordred take. A plan crystallized as I slid across the concrete toward the side parking lot. Let him lead me to Esther. Then beat the crap out of him.

I peered around the corner of the building in time to see him climb into a small compact car. A blue Kia with tan interior and one of those weird ignition locks that were all the rage with car rental companies. He sat there with the door open and the interior light on while he stuffed his cigarettes on top of the folded visor and put his drink in the cup holder. A sharp, musty scent spiraled through the air and crossed the gravel toward me. My nostrils flared and my heart dropped to my toes.

I zeroed in on the passenger side and the dark stain that covered the seat back. Hunger twisted at my gut. Rewind to a quick mental of Esther slumped in the seat, her afterlife seeping all over the fabric upholstery, and a growl bubbled up my throat.

Okay, so maybe I'd beat the crap out of him first and then force him to lead me to Esther.

With the ripe scent of blood teasing my senses and the dread poking at my stomach, it seemed like one hell of an idea. My vision went red and my thoughts centered solely on the murdering a-hole in front of me. I launched forward.

I made it three steps before a hand gripped my

ponytail and yanked me backward. I hit the pavement with a loud *thwack*. Pain blurred my vision and my eyes watered. Through the fog, I caught a quick glimpse of a man's face looming over me.

I blinked and tried to focus. No, make that two men.

Another blink. Three?

My survival instincts fired to life and my alter ego—big, bad vamp—took the lead, but it was too late. I instantly realized why the SOBs—mere humans, all of them—were able to take out vamps the world over on a regular basis.

A distracted vamp meant a vulnerable one.

"Wait—" I started, only to have a wet rag shoved over my face.

Don't breathe. The command echoed through my brain, but my mouth was already open. The overpowering scent of garlic spiraled inside, burning and twisting down into my lungs. My stomach convulsed. Pain ripped through me, followed by a rush of paralysis that seeped through every muscle.

And then everything went blessedly black.

Forget blacking out.

I'd bitten the dust and gone straight to H-E-L-L, and the proof was right in front of me.

Faded. Brown. Scuffed.

They were the cheapest loafers I'd ever seen.

My watery gaze shifted to the right and a pair that looked even worse than the first. Faded. Brown.

Scuffed. *And* they had a hole in the toe. I caught a glimpse of a dingy white sock and the unmistakable scent of Fritos.

Okay, so *these* were the cheapest loafers I'd ever seen, and I'd definitely hopped a train six feet under. The view was for shit. My head hurt. My body ached. The high-pitched sound of wailing demons filled my ears.

". . . she doing hanging upside down?" The familiar British accent pushed past the wailing demons (aka the distinct ringing caused by the fact that I was hanging upside friggin' down and the blood was rushing to my head) and pulled me back to reality.

"Standard procedure to subdue a vampire suspect," another voice replied. "We followed the textbook on this one, boss. Just like you said. Garlic to subdue her. A shot of sedative. And then we trussed her up and put her into an inverted holding position."

"That's textbook for a were possum," the British voice replied. "And you don't use garlic, it's ether. Textbook for vampires is garlic, sedative and then a continuous chorus of 'Kumbaya.' The overdose of warm fuzzies turns their predator brains to mush. At least while in captivity."

"Dammit, Carl. You said we were doing the right thing," a voice said.

"What do I know? I barely passed Captivity 101."

"Just get her down and sit her on the sofa," said the British accent.

Hands pulled and tugged at me. A few seconds later, I was sitting upright on a burgundy sofa. The blood drained from my head and slowly I started to focus on my surroundings. Impossible at first with a floodlight trained on my face.

"What the—"

"Reposition the light," the British accent snapped. "We don't want her going blind right in front of us."

"Vampires can do that?"

"Dammit, Carl, don't you remember anything from the academy?"

The light shifted. The glare refocused in the vicinity of my knees, and I blinked. This time, I didn't just see white polka dots. Instead, I picked up on my surroundings. Small sitting area tastefully decorated in burgundy and brown. A down comforter covered a king-sized bed to my right. A mini-bar sat against the far wall next to a flat-screen TV.

"W-where are we?" I croaked, my lips cracked and dry. My mouth tasted like old gym socks and garlic bread.

"The Holiday Inn," replied the smooth British accent.

I instantly perked up. "There's a Holiday Inn in Lonely Fork?"

"It's about forty-five minutes on the opposite side of town, on the way to Fredericksburg," Merlin replied. "We don't have to actually stay in town while we wait Mordred out. We just have to be there at the end."

My gaze found him just in time for *the end* (after I'd picked my hope off the floor and resigned myself to plastic furniture and polka dot wallpaper). He wore a purple shirt and slacks. Black loafers with tassels. He still looked like Santa Claus with his rosy cheeks and snow white beard, but a more pimped-out version. "Starting your own rap label?"

Despite his self-professed sense of humor (if he belted out a knock-knock joke I was going to start bleeding from my ears), he didn't look the least bit amused. His eyes glittered like hard chips and my entire body went ice cold.

"What is this?" My gaze zeroed in on the video camera that sat near the blinding light. "The confession booth on *Big Brother*?"

"Training visual. My men watch the tapes so they can focus in on their weak areas and perfect their apprehension techniques." His gaze darkened and his pupils flashed like bolts of lightning. "I told you not to interfere."

"I didn't interfere. I was buying a toothbrush."

"You were following Mordred."

I went for my best laugh. "Says you. You've got no proof that I was following anyone."

"We saw her, boss." The comment came from one of the men standing off to the side, near the video cam. He had brown hair and was dressed classic cop—white button-up shirt, dress slacks, powdered sugar on his collar.

"Yeah," the other man—blond hair, same outfit

but with sprinkles instead of sugar—added. "She was out for blood."

"That shows how much you guys know. Blood makes me squeamish."

"But you're a vampire," Merlin pointed out, looking surprised for the very first time since I'd met him.

"Yeah, well, we all have our flaws." I tugged and pulled at the ropes binding my hands, but oddly enough they didn't snap.

"They're reinforced with silver thread, soaked in garlic and fortified with my own binding spell."

Which totally explained why my fingers and toes felt numb.

A sliver of fear worked its way through me. While I knew it was doubtful that Merlin would off me right here and now (I was a born vamp, after all, and I seriously doubted he wanted to start a civil war between BVs and sorcerers), he did look royally pissed.

On top of that, his backup (Cheap and Cheaper) didn't look like the brightest bulbs in the tanning bed. Anger and ignorance didn't make for good judgment, so I wasn't placing any bets on getting out of this situation in one piece.

Still, I wasn't going down without a fight.

I pasted on my most intimidating expression and sent a silent *You want to untie me right now* to the brunette. My gaze collided with his, but I didn't pick up so much as a name.

I blinked and focused, but . . . *nothing.* "What did you do to me?"

"My men are protected by a privacy spell that keeps them from being susceptible to the vast number of Others who might want to influence their thoughts. You can't crawl into their heads, vampire. They're immune to you."

"My name is Lil, thank you very much, and if you untie me now, I won't call Ash and have him report you." If I couldn't glam my way out, I'd have to try bullshitting.

Merlin chuckled. "Is that so?"

"Take it to the bank."

"I should be scared right now, eh?"

"If getting your ass fired scares you, then yeah, I'd be a little squeamish if I were you."

He chuckled again. "I'm not getting fired, my dear. See, I've broken no super-natural law." He spared a glance at the video camera. "I'm on record with a textbook apprehension."

"For a were possum," I reminded him. I pleaded with the video cam. "This is no way to treat a born vampire. I have rights, you know." Okay, so I didn't have rights so much as I had a zillion relatives who would be out for blood if Merlin harmed one hair on my ultra-fab head.

"The only thing you have is a death wish. I've already called Ash and told him what you're up to."

Uh-oh.

"I haven't, however, called our superior and reported the situation." He smiled then. A cold, callous expression that sent a chill straight through me. "If I do, your demon friend is going to be in a lot of trouble."

"But Ash didn't do anything."

"He investigated a crime scene that was clearly in my jurisdiction, without permission. And he fed you information that should have remained confidential. Both charges are enough to kill his career. He'll be back in hell faster than you can run that smart mouth of yours."

Wow. We're talking fast with a capital F.

"I don't like anyone butting into my business." He nailed me with a stare. His gaze brightened this time, his pupils shimmering like wisps of smoke. My head felt suddenly very heavy. "If you continue to follow Mordred, I will make sure that the death you face is far worse than that of your made vampire friend."

While my sluggish brain couldn't envision an ending that could be worse than getting Ginsued by an evil sorcerer, my gut told me that all-powerful Merlin could come up with something.

I ignored my trembling knees. What? I was in deep doody. I was entitled to a little raw terror.

"I wasn't following Mordred," I told him again. "Seriously. I had no idea he was even here." When Merlin nailed me with another stare, I added, "I mean, I knew he was here in this town because you told me after I Googled him, but I wasn't at the store looking for him. I was making an innocent purchase on behalf of my freaked-out friend."

"She *was* carrying this." Cheap held up the pink Colgate number I'd swiped from the store.

"See? I wasn't lying."

"That proves nothing."

"It proves I wasn't in the store for Mordred."

"Maybe not, but you're in Lonely Fork because of him."

"No." Not entirely. "I have a client here." I thought of Elmer and his eagerness to find a Bingo partner. "In fact, I have several."

"Name one."

"I'm afraid that's confidential information. In other words, none of your beeswax."

It wasn't the smartest thing to say, but I couldn't help myself. I felt physically powerless (and way out of my BV comfort zone) and my mouth was the only thing working at the moment.

He waved a finger at me and I felt a strange tightening around my throat.

"You're not funny," he told me.

"Yeah, well, neither are you," I croaked. "Your knock-knock jokes suck."

He stared at me long and hard for a moment and the tightening continued until I thought my trachea would rupture.

Then as quickly as the sensation started, it ended. His expression eased. The finger fell to his side and relief swamped me.

"If you're merely in town for a client, then I don't

have any reason to keep you here, now, do I? That is, unless you're lying. Are you lying to me, Miss Marchette?"

"Who, me? I never lie." At least not unless I was in an afterlife and death situation with Santa's evil twin. "Just call me Abe."

He didn't look convinced, but he signaled his two henchman anyway. They went to work on the ropes, one at my hands and the other at my feet.

The pressure eased and the silver threaded rope fell away. The feeling quickly returned to my hands. My feet came next and I flexed my ankles. I became quickly aware of the fact that I could actually move the toes on my right foot. A quick glance down, and I knew why.

"Where's my shoe?"

Cheap shrugged. "Must have fallen off when we were getting you into the car."

"Did you pick it up?"

"What am I? A bellboy? My hands were full."

"Don't look at me." Cheaper shrugged. "It was all I could do to keep from dropping you. You're heavy. Not that you're fat," he blurted when my gaze narrowed to dangerous slits, "but you were dead weight at the time."

"A lot of dead weight," Cheap added.

This was not happening. First I'd lost Mordred. Now my shoe. "That was a three hundred dollar pair."

"You spent three hundred dollars on *shoes*?"

"They're special edition Cheyennes. Suede with leather soles. Fur-lined."

"So?"

"So they're *fur-lined*. You just don't leave a shoe like that lying on the sidewalk somewhere."

"I don't know if it fell off on the sidewalk. It could have just as easily fallen off in the alley or the parking lot. We had to drag you a little ways."

My backside throbbed in testimony, and righteous anger bolted through me. "If I weren't so weak, I'd crack your head against that wall."

"I thought you had an aversion to blood."

"I'll make an exception in your case." I flashed him a little fang to prove my point and he stumbled back a few steps.

"Stand down, boys." Merlin held up a hand. "I think you'd better go, Miss Marchette. And I don't just mean back to the motel. Pack your bags and go back to New York."

"I can't do that. I have a client here who's depending on me."

He eyed me a long moment as if searching for something. "Stay, then," he finally said. "But keep your distance from Mordred. No looking for him. No asking around town about him. Leave him alone. Is that clear?" He held up his finger to further his point and I felt the unmistakable tightening around my throat again.

"Crystal," I rasped.

"Good." His hand dropped to his side and he smiled. "Knock, knock," he said as I pushed to my feet.

"Stuff a sock in it." I stumbled past him and yanked open the door. His chuckle followed me out, along with the whisper soft promise, "We'll be watching you."

I limped around the outside of the Holiday Inn, stifled the urge to check myself in and found a dark spot where I could unleash my inner bat.

A few seconds later, I headed back to The Grande minus my shoe and Nina's toothbrush. My head and legs hurt like a sonofabitch. I'd made a useless trip to Austin to be verbally abused by the twins from hell. I'd found Mordred, only to lose him. And I'd had my afterlife threatened. Talk about a shitty night.

But at least one good thing had come out of it— I'd had confirmation that Mordred was, indeed, in town.

And if he was here, so was Esther.

Twenty
♥ ♥ ♥

The flight back to the motel felt more like two hours than two minutes. Merlin had zapped my strength and my entire body felt as if I'd trudged up the Himalayas. The only thing I wanted was to crawl into bed.

Unfortunately, Nina had beat me to it. She was sprawled on top of the comforter. Three empty bottles of blood surrounded her and she was chugging a fourth. The television blazed, sending a sprinkle of shadows across the walls. Her tear-streaked face glistened in the dim light.

I immediately forgot my own misery in the face of hers.

Rob had called and it hadn't gone well. That was the only explanation for the waterworks.

I waited for her to volunteer a little info, but when

she kept her gaze trained on the screen, I knew I was going to have to ask.

Did he call? Did you tell him? Did he get mad?

"What's up?" I heard myself say. Did I cut to the chase or what? I flipped on a nearby lamp and a soft yellow glow pushed back the shadows. Then I kicked off my one remaining flat and said a silent prayer that the mate had found a good home with someone who appreciated it as much as yours truly. Maybe a one-legged fashionista.

"I'm just watching this old black-and-white movie."

"The TV is black-and-white. Every movie looks like that."

"Oh." She sniffled and took another swig of blood. "It's really good. See, there's this woman, Gwen, and she's in love with this guy, Rudolfo, but she thinks he's in love with his dead wife. He's the captain of this pirate ship and she's a nurse he picked up on one of his raids. He's ransoming her, but he doesn't really intend to take the money. He's going to give the money to Gwen so she can fulfill her dream and start her own hospital when she gets back to civilization. See, he's really in love with her and she's in love with him even though she thinks he's a shit for ransoming her. She thinks he's out for revenge because he hates her. See, she couldn't save his baby or his wife years ago during childbirth and so they died."

"And they don't just talk this out and avoid all the drama because . . . ?"

"There wouldn't be a movie if they did that."

"But they might actually be happy—"

"Shush." She waved me silent. "She's about to try to escape while the ransom is being paid."

I tossed my purse onto a nearby chair and was just about to collapse on the edge of the bed when my foot came up against something hard. I bent over to retrieve empty bottle number five.

"How many of these have you had?"

"How many did you bring?"

"Eight."

She glanced at the partially full bottle in her hand. "Seven and a half."

"You drank *seven* bottles of blood? In the last four hours?"

She shrugged. "I couldn't help it. I woke up starved." She took another swig and my gaze hooked on the red heat sliding into her mouth.

I felt like the kid who's ice cream had melted before she'd had a chance to take a bite. "Those bottles were supposed to last me the duration of my trip."

"I'll buy you more."

"There's no place to buy bottled blood in Lonely Fork."

"We'll do takeout."

And what, pray tell, is vamp takeout? Picture a hot Italian stud showing up with a nice pulsing artery for the ordering vamp and a double cheese and pepperoni to replenish his own strength after the fact.

"No takeout either."

She shrugged again. "So go out and feed. What's the big deal?"

The big deal was that I didn't go out and feed. Not since I'd vowed to give up gratuitous sex and hot, ravenous feeding to find my One and Only.

All right, so I'd sworn off the hot, ravenous part even before that. While I knew I wasn't consciously hurting anyone, I still felt a pang of guilt when I sank my fangs into some poor unsuspecting schmuck.

"You're too sensitive," Nina told me. "It's just dinner."

I watched her dab at her eyes. "*I'm* too sensitive?"

She sniffled and grabbed a Kleenex. "I may have overindulged just a teensy bit on the AB+."

I picked up another discarded bottle. "Geez, you think?"

"I'm eating for two now." She seemed to realize what she'd said and the tears started all over again. "I *am* eating for two," she blubbered. "I am so screwed."

"Babies are cute," I heard myself say. Like I knew. "Sweet. Cuddly." When she didn't seem convinced, I added, "Besides, you can find some really hot baby clothes these days." That got her attention. "Gwen Stefani has that entire line that she did for Kingston. And I saw Tom and Katie's baby wearing Baby Chanel in the last *InStyle*."

"Really?"

Not. But it sounded good and it was enough to slow the tears. "And Baby Gucci," I assured her. "You'll have the trendiest baby in New York."

"I will, won't I?" she asked as she handed over what was left in the last bottle of blood. "Maybe it won't be so bad."

"It'll be great. Now come on." I tugged her to her feet.

"Where are we going?"

"You're going to take a shower. It'll help clear your head." I led her into the bathroom and turned on the spray. "Relax and pull yourself together. I'll leave some clean clothes by the sink." I turned to leave while she peeled off her clothes.

"Lil." Her soft voice stopped me just outside the doorway. "Thanks."

Before I could say anything, she stepped into the shower.

I walked back into the bedroom, snatched up a tissue and wiped at my own suddenly misty eyes.

Sympathy tears.

That's what I told myself.

Nina's hormones were raging so mine were obviously joining the protest. I'm a vampire, after all. We lived by the three Nos: 1) no tears, 2) no compassion, 3) no polyester. No way was I crying because I was touched or because I'd had a rotten night or because Esther was still missing or because I'd lost my stupid shoe.

And no friggin' way was I crying because Rudolfo

let Gwen walk away after the ransom drop without ever telling her that he loved her. Sure, he told her about the hospital and that he didn't blame her for his dead wife and son. But he didn't say *the* word.

Because he was a clueless jerk, no doubt.

Well, that and the fact that there was still a good half hour left. The producers were obviously leaving that little tidbit until the very end.

Sure enough, Rudolfo redeemed himself and they all lived happily ever after.

I gushed all of five seconds before my stomach growled. I grabbed a few dollars out of my purse and headed down to the lobby. Elmer had his *Come Back Later* sign posted and the TV turned full blast. I listened to a few questions from *Are You Smarter Than a 5th Grader?* (for the record, I definitely was) as I walked over to the small fridge. I stuffed a few dollars into the pickle jar and pulled out a Mountain Dew. It wasn't anywhere close to a Red Bull and vodka, but I was out of options. A sugar rush would have to do. I listened to a geography question as I guzzled the can and then grabbed another.

By the time I got back to the room, I was wired and seriously considering an appearance on national television. I'd so nailed the question about Yellowstone National Park.

"Hey." Nina was sitting on the bed again. She wore my favorite Armani tee and a pair of yoga pants. She'd pulled her hair into a ponytail and her lips were glossy and slick with MAC Tahitian Sunrise.

"Somebody feels better."

"A shower was just what I needed." She indicated my cell on the nightstand. "Your phone was ringing so I picked it up. Evie said to tell you she fixed up Tabitha with some guy named Miller."

"You mean Milner?" I did a quick rifle through my mental file. "The manorexic English teacher from Queens?"

"Evie said he's not a manorexic. He's just thin because he's a vegan. He's also a fierce advocate for PETA, not that he included that on his profile. Evie just found that out tonight."

"What happened?"

"Tabitha was pressing her to meet Mr. Tall, Dark and Six Foot Two, and Milner met the height requirement. So Evie set up the date and sent them to Jack Hughey's."

"The steak place?"

Nina nodded and dread rolled through me. "It seems this guy Milner tried to rescue Tabitha's rib eye before she could cut into it. They ended up in a fist fight in the parking lot."

Why me?

"Tabitha's fine," Nina went on. "Just a few cuts and bruises, but Milner was so weak from lack of proper nutrition that he couldn't really hold his own. He's got two broken ribs and a broken nose. *And* he had to have stitches because Tabitha stabbed him with her steak knife when he tried to take the meat away from her."

Ouch.

"Evie said she tried to make peace with both of them. She bought Tabitha a membership to the Steak of the Month Club and sent a year's supply of Dietrim to Milner." At my arched eyebrow, she added, "They're the only diet supplement that doesn't experiment on animals. Anyhow. Tabitha's dead-set on talking to you now. Evie told her you were out of town, but that just made her all the more anxious. Evie wants you to call her ASAP."

I was starting to think my night couldn't get any worse, when the faint scent of cherries jubilee and Chanel No. 5 wafted through the air and wrinkled my nose.

Nah.

No way.

Not no, but *hell* no.

Denial raged through my head, followed by a jolt of panic when the *click clack* of expensive high heels thundered in my eardrums. The scent grew stronger and the doorknob trembled. I bolted to my feet, but it was too late. The door opened and there she was. My worst nightmare.

"Ma?"

Twenty-one
❤ ❤ ❤

It was the sedative.

And the lack of sustenance.

And the stress.

All three were screwing with my brain waves and causing hallucinations. That's what I told myself. But no amount of blinking (or praying) could make my mother disappear.

She was real and she was here and I was *so* screwed.

She stood there in the doorway looking as *Vogue* as ever in a gray Stella McCartney shift dress and gray python Christian Louboutins. She carried an alligator bag that matched the eight suitcases stacked behind her and a smile so big and wide that it made my legs shake.

"I came as soon as you called," she declared,

her voice shattering the steady *PleaseGodNo* that echoed over and over in my head.

"But I didn't—"

"No, no, don't apologize for dragging me away from your father. Sure, he's this close to losing it completely and nuking our entire neighborhood with this homemade contraption he's been building, but he'll just have to blow himself up without me. As if a bomb is going to get rid of Viola. I keep telling him werewolves are like cockroaches, but the man is obsessed. I've got Remy keeping tabs on him for me, so I'm all yours. We think it's lovely of you to invite us down to share this experience."

"*We?*"

"Hi, Lil." Mandy picked her way past the luggage and came up next to my mother. "Thanks for inviting me."

"Inviting you?" Cut me some slack. We're talking my worst nightmare here.

"To participate in your retreat," my mother said. "I've always wanted to focus on my inner strengths. Of course, we *vamperes* have both inner and outer strength and I don't really see the difference. But I'm always up for new challenges and experiences."

A pod person. That was the only explanation. In addition to the multitude of Others out there, there were also little green body snatchers.

"I can't wait to get started." She rubbed her hands

together. "It's going to be magnificent." She slid an arm around Mandy's shoulders.

Seriously.

"The three of us together"—she gave Mandy a squeeze—"setting goals and overcoming our weaknesses." She released Mandy with an abruptness that sent her stumbling backward, and eyeballed me. "Speaking of which, you should really work on your attitude, dear. Maybe tone down the pickiness. Otherwise, you'll never find a mate."

Lose the *X-Files*. Jacqueline was definitely present and accounted for.

"When Evie filled us in on all the fun you were having," my mother rushed on, "and how you wanted us to come down and join you on your little retreat, I called Mandy and had her take a few days off at the hospital." She beamed. "And here we are." Her glance traveled around the room. "You're actually staying here?"

"I know it looks bad—" I started, but she cut me off.

"Where's the mini-bar?"

"No mini-bar." Abject horror lit her gaze and I couldn't help myself. "No Jacuzzi. No turn-down service. No concierge. No complimentary bottle of AB– or a nice, comfy coffin with an extra-thick pad." Those last two were only available at the Plaza, which was owned by Nina's father and, therefore, catered to the undead. But hey, I might as well lay it on extra thick, right?

She visibly swallowed and I gave myself a mental high five. This was it. She'd turn and hightail it back to Connecticut.

Or, at the very least, a five star hotel in Austin.

"Oh, well. That simply means fewer distractions." She cleared her throat. "We can devote our full attention to one another."

Talk about a great big fat sack of *No*.

"It's not too bad," Mandy offered. "You should have seen my dorm room back in college. Talk about pathetic."

"I can only imagine," my mother readily agreed.

"Besides," Mandy went on, "the desk clerk was nice and they do have snacks in the lobby."

"Wonderful." My mother turned to Mandy. "Why don't you run down and fetch me some Doritos and a few candy bars?"

"But Mother Marchette, you don't actually eat Doritos and candy bars," Mandy pointed out, and the vein in my mother's right temple started to throb. "Do you?"

"Oh, you'd be surprised what I eat, dear. And please call me Jacqueline. All my friends do."

"I don't really feel comfortable doing that." Mandy shook her head. "You're my elder, after all."

The vein swelled and threatened to explode. "How respectful of you," Jacqueline finally said, her words tight and controlled. "But the snacks aren't for me, dear. If you intend to conceive, you need to keep up your strength."

"I doubt Doritos will do much by way of nutrition." She seemed to think. "Then again, I am on vacation and I could certainly use a snack. They had dinner on the plane, but it was spaghetti and I'm allergic to tomatoes."

"Such a tragedy," my mother said, but I didn't miss the gleam that lit her eyes. I had a bad feeling our *retreat* was now going to include tomato paste facials.

"Be back in a flash." Mandy headed for the lobby.

Meanwhile, I was still trying to process the all-important fact that my mother was here. Now.

"Close your mouth, dear." My mother waved a hand. "You're liable to swallow one of these pesky flies."

"There's a bug zapper in the bathroom," I heard myself say.

"Oh, joy."

Here. Now.

"You need to feed, Lilliana. You're much too pale."

"What are you doing here?" I asked when I finally managed to find my voice.

"Protecting my son. The Yaz attempt at Crazy J's backfired. I think someone is trying to sabotage me."

"What a bitch." I summoned my most shocked/ innocent expression. "So, um, what makes you think that?"

My mother gave me a knowing look. "Someone switched restaurants."

"The traitor."

"Mandy said it was Evie and Evie said it was you."

Busted. "It was me. I switched the restaurants on purpose. But I did it for you, Ma. If Jack had found out, he would have been even more determined to have a human baby, just to spite you."

"Your brother can be quite the rebel."

"You need to come up with something more subtle. Why not just scare her into giving up the baby effort?"

"You mean like flash my fangs and threaten her?" She looked hopeful. "Maybe rip out someone's throat right in front of her?"

"Just tell her how hard it is. Talk to her. Maybe she'll change her mind on her own."

She gave it a moment's consideration and I thought she might actually agree with me. But then she shook her head. "I need a more direct approach." She waved a hand. "What do you think about suffocation?"

"I'd go for something a little more inconspicuous."

"Strangulation?"

"Too hands-on."

"Bullet to the head?"

"Listen, Ma, I know you like a good kill as much as the rest of us vamps"—self excluded—"but Jack would never forgive you. You know that. He's in love with Mandy." She narrowed her gaze. "Or at least he thinks he is."

"You're right," she said after another contemplative moment. "I can't very well shed Mindy's blood and have him hate me for the rest of his afterlife."

"It's Mandy, Ma. Not Mindy."

"Whatever. I'll just have to think of something else. At least I can rest easy for the next week. That fact alone makes all the smiles and horrid enthusiasm doable. They certainly can't reproduce with a thousand miles between them. Not that your brother's sperm isn't up for a lengthy swim. He's a Marchette, after all. But even Marchette sperm would have difficulty crossing several state lines."

I'm as confident in my sexuality as the next modern vampire. I've burned my share of bras (a few off-the-rack babies I'd gotten on sale) and been to over a dozen Passion Parties and I'd even sat through the 9½ *Weeks* DVD seven times in the hope of trying out a certain cherry scene with one hunkilicious bounty hunter. I was totally secure, and I certainly didn't blush when it came to talking sex.

"Though your uncle Richard did manage to impregnate Aunt Denise while she was in Palm Springs and he was in Las Vegas on a business trip a few years ago. Apparently, they'd had intercourse before he'd left and the little buggers managed to survive two solid weeks until Denise had another orgasm and released a viable egg."

But *ewwwwww*.

"How did you find me?" I blurted, eager to dropkick the subject of my family's super spoodge and distract myself from the ickiness creeping through me. My mom's radar shifted past me and homed in on Nina.

I turned in time to see my friend shrug. "I might have left a message on Rob's cell letting him know where to find me in case he realizes he's crazy about me and feels the need to fly down this very second and declare his feelings. Obviously, he hasn't made the revelation." She teared up, which kept me from ripping her a new one.

My mother, on the other hand, wasn't nearly as selfless.

"Rob has a message for you." Jacqueline's gaze collided with Nina's. "He said to tell you that he's giving you the apartment and picking up the rest of his things. He said he'll be completely moved out by the time you get back."

My hopes shot sky high. "He found a new place?"

"I wouldn't call it new. It's ancient. And extremely small. One bedroom. Minute living area. Microscopic kitchen."

"That sounds like my apartment."

She smiled and dread rolled through me. "It'll be just like when you were growing up. Of course, you had your own suite and Rob had his and there was an entire castle between the two of you. And lots of tasteful furniture. And expensive rugs. And several servants." She gave a shiver. "How you manage in that sardine can, without at least a foot masseuse, I'll never know."

My gaze narrowed. That was *my* sardine can.

She waved a hand and rushed on, "Nevertheless, it'll be a wonderful chance for the two of you to re-connect. You can go hunting together. Perhaps scout out potential blood slaves."

"Sounds fab." *Not.*

"You need a positive influence in your afterlife."

"It's Rob, Ma. Last New Year's he got so shit-faced he tried to sink his teeth into the yard sculp-ture of Aphrodite."

"So he'd had a few too many toasts? It was a hol-iday."

I arched an eyebrow. "And the time he tried to hump Dad's life-sized cutout of Tiger Woods?"

"That was the fourth of July. And he thought it was Halle Berry."

"He propositioned Grandma Jolie."

"Groundhog Day. And my mother *is* a beautiful woman."

"This is crazy." I shook my head. "No. Uh-uh. Not happening. He's not crashing at my place per-manently."

"Why ever not?"

"Because . . ." It was time he stopped being an

irresponsible jerk and started owning up to his responsibilities—namely the born female vampire who loved him and the baby that was on the way.

"I might want to prance around in nothing but my thong," I blurted. What can I say? My ma scares the crap out of me. "I can't very well get my naked on with Rob parked on my sofa."

"So you wear a robe. It's a small sacrifice to help a member of your family."

"What am I supposed to do if I meet that perfect vampire and he wants to sleep over? Or move in? How will we all fit?"

"Don't be silly, dear. All vampires are perfect."

"You're missing the point. Say I meet The One. I can't spend eternity with someone if they don't even fit in my apartment."

She nailed me with a stare. "Have you met some-one?"

This was it. My chance to come clean and tell her about Ty and the fact that I'd practically pledged my afterlife to him and he hadn't so much as hinted at the L word.

"Not yet. But you never know. It could happen just like that. One minute I'm single and the next I'm happily attached and giving up half—er, make that a quarter of my closet space."

What? I've got a lot of stuff.

"Rob can come and live at home if that happens," my mother informed me. "In his old room."

Sheesh. Now I'd never get him out of my place.

"Listen, Mom—" I started, only to be interrupted by the sound of metal clunking down the walkway outside.

Three heartbeats later, Elmer wheeled in what looked suspiciously like a mattress.

"Here you are, Mrs. Marchette. My last double roll-away." He tapped the edge. "She's a beaut, ain't she?"

Reality hit me like a cheap shoe right between the eyes. "You're really staying *here*?" I turned to my ma. "In this room?"

"Rodeo lasts through next week," Elmer informed me. "This is the best I could do without a reservation."

My recent kidnapping rolled through my head and hope fired to life. "But there's a Holiday Inn on the interstate going toward Fredericksburg. Complete with mini-bar, down comforter—you name it. Really, Ma, you can't possibly want to stay here."

"Lookee here—" Elmer started, but I silenced him with a mental *Shut up now and I'll do my best to hook you up with DoraLee at the nail salon.*

His mouth snapped closed.

"Just look at this place," I rushed on. "It's totally beneath you. Tasteless. Cheap. You can't be serious."

She cast a look around and I didn't miss the *You said it* in her gaze. To her credit, however, her smile didn't falter. "Lilliana, it doesn't matter where we stay. All that matters is that Millie's here instead of back home humping your brother." My mother smiled. "It'll be delightful."

Delightful meaning about as pleasant as having my skin peeled away inch by inch.

And I thought Esther had it rough?

Twenty-two

I spent the next five minutes stacking my mother's luggage in every available corner while she, Nina and Mandy piled on the bed to talk about "girl stuff."

Angelina's latest comments about Jen.

Jen's *No comment* regarding Angelina's comments.

Brad's comments about Angelina's comments about Jen's no comment.

It seemed my mother had been forced to fly coach since she'd booked at the last minute. Rather than slaughter the woman next to her (who insisted on showing the 389 photos of her newest grandson), my mom had opted for no bloodshed and the latest copy of *Entertainment Weekly*.

Go Ma.

"What do you think, Lil?" Nina tried to draw me into the conversation. "Is Ang a hater or what?"

"I think she's insecure. That reminds me"—I snatched up my phone—"I've got a long list of desperately insecure singles depending on me." I made a mad dash for the bathroom and locked myself in.

Scrolling through numbers, I found Tabitha's home and hit ON.

"I'm so sorry about tonight," I told her the minute her voice mail picked up. I gave her the line about the importance of a few practice dates when traveling the road to happily ever after. "In the meantime, I'm doing everything possible to make the journey short."

With my anxiety raging and the possibility of a refund in my near future, I needed a serious pick-me-up. I punched in DeWalt's number for a quick update on his date with Jonelle.

"She's great."

Relief swamped me. Maybe I didn't totally suck at this matchmaking thing.

"We're seeing each other tomorrow," he went on. "Who's next?"

Okay, so maybe I did suck.

"Another? Sure. No problem. One fertile female BV coming right up."

Since I didn't have one, much less four, waiting in line, the urge to freak hit hard and fast. I counted to ten (the top ten new designers featured in Barneys' upcoming spring collection), which relaxed my muscles and successfully distracted me from the urge to hang myself from the shower rod.

Mia was next on my call list and I instantly regretted punching her digits. She'd gone into withdrawal from lack of sex, slipped with her tattoo needle and put a heart on some guy's testicle. But other than a major lawsuit, her life was just great (bye-bye, regret). She liked Harmon and was still determined to go through with the no-nooky policy. She figured if she made it through one more date (a free Lawrence Welk tribute concert in Central Park) she could handle anything, even a lifetime of boring and sexless.

I didn't have a good-looking nympho waiting in the wings, so I quickly agreed. "Who needs sex when you can have companionship?"

"Exactly," Mia said. "I'm through looking for a needle in a haystack. I'm settling for the hay, and I owe it all to you, Lil."

At least I had one satisfied customer out there.

Still, I found myself Googling Nymphos-R-Us on my phone just to see if maybe there wasn't a local chapter that might provide a surplus of prospects.

Take the money and run, right? I would have except my conscience kept niggling at me and, well, we're talking *Lawrence Welk*. I couldn't just sit by and let anyone endure that kind of torture.

I called Rob next, but his voice mail was full. I sent a text instead

Get. Out. Now!

I toyed with the idea of calling Ty, particularly since he'd left me two voice mails.

A cryptic *Stay out of it* and a resigned *I know you won't stay out of it, so be careful.*

Was this vamp my soul mate or what?

I dialed his number, but hung up after the third ring. Really. What was I going to say? He would just start questioning me and I would have to lie and, well, that was no way to treat a soul mate. Better to let the whole thing blow over. I wouldn't have any reason to lie, and honesty was the best policy. Until then? Avoidance.

My mother gushed, "Margie, you're so witty. I'm so lucky to have you as a daughter-in-law," and I eyeballed the small window near the ceiling. No way was I squeezing my butt through that, but I could totally flap my way out if things got too deep.

I pulled out my new pink nail polish. I was just swiping my baby toe when Nina knocked on the door.

"You can't stay in there forever."

I finished up the toe and moved on to my nails. "I'm not staying in here forever. I'm escaping through the window in a matter of minutes."

"You can't do that. We need you for Truth or Dare."

"Now I'm really out of here."

"I know it's kind of lame, but it was Mandy's suggestion. She thought it would be a great way for us to get to know one another."

"I lived with my mother for four hundred and ninety-nine years. Trust me, I know all I need to."

"Your ma brought two cases of blood."

My stomach gave a traitorous growl. "I'm not hungry."

"It's imported."

My fangs tingled and I swallowed. "N-no thanks."

"Come on. It's girl time."

"It isn't *girl time*. I'm here on business. How am I supposed to concentrate and hone my matchmaking skills with my mother here?"

"It's just a few days. As soon as you find Esther, we all go home."

"Esther?" I went for a laugh. "Esther who?"

"I saw the bloody sofa, remember? I know you. You're like a pit bull. She disappeared on your watch. You're not just going to let it go. Besides, what else would bring you to Texas? And don't give me that crap about finding your inner strength. You can do that at Bloomingdale's like the rest of us."

"She's in trouble." I told her about Mordred and the ritual. I ended with a "I know she's here, but I can't seem to get a solid on her exact location."

"You're thinking about it too much. You need a break. Play some Truth or Dare and have a little fun. Maybe it'll help."

"Getting grilled by my ma hardly qualifies as fun."

"Please." Her voice softened. "You can't leave me out here by myself. I might slip up and start crying and then she'll know."

I debated with my conscience for the next five seconds, capped the polish and hauled open the door. "I'll play Truth or Dare, but if she mentions Spin the Bottle, you're on your own."

She grinned. "You're the best friend a vamp could have."

"Don't remind me."

Barry had finished his opening act and Kid Rock came on as the headlining attraction. The bump and grind melody of "Cowboy" vibrated the air around me and sent a burst of desire pulsing from my knees to my shoulders. My toes sank in the sand. The breeze whispered across my bare skin and made the concho fringe on my bikini tinkle.

Kid kept wailing about the sunshine shining, and every nerve in my body wound tight. Need pulsed through me. I felt sexy. Seductive. *Ready.*

As if on cue, the deep, mesmerizing voice sounded behind me.

"Take off the corset."

"Your wish is my— Wait a sec. A corset?"

I glanced down. Sure enough, the bikini was gone. Instead, I wore a white lace-up, complete with drawstring pantaloons.

The song faded and the wind picked up, whipping at me and plastering the thin material to my skin. I wiggled my toes. Hard, rough wood scraped the bottom of my feet. The floor seemed to tilt and I grasped at the handrail as a wave of seawater welled up over the side and drenched me.

Forget my beach oasis. I was standing at the helm of a pirate ship (à la Rudolfo and Gwen). My heart skipped its next beat as I turned to face my kidnapper.

Okay, so this wasn't so bad.

Ty's blue eyes gleamed with neonlike intensity. His long, dark hair hung loose around his shoulders, framing his handsome face. He was bare-chested, his shoulders broad, his arms ripped. He wore only a pair of tight black pants that left little doubt that he wanted me.

"Kiss me," he commanded, and I stepped forward. My arms slid around his neck and I tilted my head back. I closed my eyes and brushed my lips against his—

"Help!" The cry shattered the whole Stockholm thing I had going on. My eyes snapped open and I twisted around in time to see Esther struggling in the water. Only it wasn't water. It was a thick, sticky crimson that sucked at her.

I tried to jump in, but Ty's arm stole around my waist and jerked me back against his body. He held me immobile while the blood sucked Esther under.

I struggled and the arm clamped tighter.

"Forget about her, dear. You shouldn't be running around, worrying over a lowly made vampire."

Dear?

I twisted, only to find my mother standing behind me. And Nina. And Mandy, who carried a two-headed baby who looked like Eddie Munster and Lawrence Welk.

My eyes snapped open to the dim light of the motel room. I sprawled in the one and only chair. Nina and my mother were piled on the bed, while Mandy snored softly on the roll-away. There wasn't a two-headed baby in sight.

I glanced at the clock. It was five thirty A.M. Still an hour until daybreak. The truth that Mandy shaved her legs only during the summer, Nina had a secret crush on David Hasselhoff, and my ma had once dated Napoleon had obviously been too much excitement for one night. They'd crashed early.

Stretching my sore neck (we're talking one of those plastic upright chairs), I pushed to my feet. My heart chugged like a freight train and my nerves buzzed.

I downed half of one of the bottles that my mother had brought, but it did little to ease the tightening in my stomach.

I could still feel the sea salt on my skin and smell the bloody sea surrounding me. Esther's image alternated with Eddie and Lawrence, and I knew there was no way I was going to fall asleep right now.

I grabbed my purse and my cell and went out for a walk.

At least I intended to walk. To clear my head. To relax.

Before I knew it, I was standing outside the Quick Pick. The store had not opened up yet so Merlin's men were nowhere in sight.

They were keeping an eye on Mordred and he couldn't very well buy cigarettes if the place was closed.

I stood in the parking lot in the exact spot I'd seen Mordred parked. The smell of dried blood still hung in the air and my chest tightened.

The back of my eyes burned and I blinked. I turned and was about to walk the perimeter of the store once again, when I spotted a discarded matchbook.

Kneeling, I dusted off the faded white cardboard and stared at the gold script. *The Waldorf.*

My eyes went blurry again. Crazy, I know. It was a used-up matchbook, for Damien's sake. It wasn't like I'd found a finger or an ear or something equally gross.

Not yet, that is.

Panic rolled through me and I pushed to my feet. I backtracked Mordred's steps to the front door of the store, my eyes peeled for anything else he might have dropped. A receipt. A room key. A map to his present location.

Other than a few cigarette butts and the wrapping from a Slim Jim, I spotted nothing.

I was just about to call it quits and head back to

the motel when a strange awareness shot up my spine. My hands shook and my heart paused. I tried to whirl, but a hand shot out, gripped the back of my neck and hauled me backward.

Here we go again.

Twenty-three

❤ ❤ ❤

"Come on," I blurted as I found myself yanked backward, across the street and into the woods. "The store's closed and Mordred's nowhere in sight. This totally does not count."

"You're an idiot."

"And you're a cheap, fashion clueless goon . . ."

My words stalled as two important points registered in my panicked brain. One, I could still feel my legs (i.e., no sedative poking me in the ass) and two, the familiar voice wasn't anywhere close to what I remembered from my earlier run-in with Cheap and Cheaper.

No, this one was deep. Mesmerizing. And really, *really* pissed.

"I knew you couldn't keep your nose out of it," Ty growled. "I *knew* it."

He whirled me around and my gaze did a quick up and down to make sure it was him.

Black jeans outlined his long, muscular legs. A black leather vest—and nothing but the vest—emphasized his broad shoulders and rock-hard chest. He had his hair pulled back in a ponytail. A black Stetson sat low on his forehead, and I had the crazy urge to yell *Ride 'em, cowgirl* and hop on.

While I was cruising Smut Lane, Ty had already made a detour onto Mad as Hell Boulevard.

He quickly killed the sliver of hope that this was another one of my fantasies. His mouth drew into a thin line. His eyes narrowed into a glare that could cut the average human to the quick.

But I was a vampire. An equal match. A superior one if you bought all the hype my parents had dished out over the years.

I squared my shoulders and summoned my most haughty expression. "Since when did you become my boss?"

"You're sinking into something you don't understand. You have to back off." When I opened my mouth, he held up a hand. "Don't give me that crap about being here on business. I know why you're here. Half of fucking New York knows why you're here."

I started to deny it but my conscience made me clench. "I have a new client. He owns a ranch outside of town. I'm hooking him up with several eternity mates."

"I don't care if you're hooking up the Loch Ness Monster. You need to give this up and go home before you find yourself in even deeper."

"I can't just leave. He's already paid me a full retainer."

That, and Esther needed me.

"It's too late for her," he said, and I knew he'd picked up on my thoughts loud and clear.

"She won't actually die until the ritual. That gives me almost a week to find her." I wanted to beg for his help, but I knew Merlin wouldn't think twice about killing Ty. Like every Other out there, he considered all made vampires expendable. Worthless.

"The only reason Merlin hasn't killed you is because you're born," Ty said, confirming my thoughts. "He would have to explain himself to too many higher-ups. Unless he had proof that you interfered. Then he could justify his actions."

"You mean his warning wasn't just a warning?"

"What do you mean?"

"I sort of ran into Merlin. He warned me to stay away from Mordred. Actually, he did more than warn me. He had a video camera set up." The reality of what had happened crashed down around me and my hands trembled. "He said it was to record the apprehension so his men could use it as a training film. But it wasn't, was it? He wanted a play-by-play of me crossing the line."

And I'd given it to him.

"I know you like Esther." Ty's voice drew me out of the mental ass-kicking I was currently giving myself. "But is that enough to risk your own afterlife?" He shook his head. "For once, stop fighting what you are, Lil, and go with it. Put yourself first."

Easier said than done.

I'd been born with a conscience in addition to my crackerjack fashion sense. I couldn't even feed Killer generic cat food. I sure as hell didn't stand a chance of living an eternity with Esther's death on my conscience.

"Please." Ty's gaze gleamed with emotion and my chest hitched.

"Why are you here?" I heard myself ask.

"To talk some sense into you."

"But *why*?" The question hung between us for several long moments as indecision warred in Ty's gaze.

You know why. The answer finally whispered through my head.

"I want to hear you say it. If you're really committed to this relationship, then stop holding back."

"Ditto."

"What's that supposed to mean?"

"You kept your whereabouts a secret and lied to me. That doesn't say much for commitment."

"That's different."

"Is it?"

Duh. Esther's afterlife was at stake and I'd been lying and withholding for a good cause. Didn't he get that?

Hurt flashed in his gaze.

Obviously not.

Heat crept up my neck and my heart hitched, and like all vampires in denial, I switched from defense to offense. "Let's be honest. My lying isn't the real issue here. It's you—"

"Don't do this," he warned. "It's not the time or the place."

As if I didn't know that.

But I was sick of worrying and wondering and feeling so incredibly helpless. It was time to *do* something. If I couldn't find Esther or reconcile Nina and Rob, I could at least satisfy my own curiosity.

He loves me, he loves me not?

I felt as if I'd spent my entire afterlife standing on the outside. I *was* an outsider. A vampire in a human world. A vampire who sorta, kinda, occasionally thought about what it would be like to be human. I couldn't help myself. I wanted to know what it felt like to bask on a beach and shop during the daytime and eat a chocolate fudge brownie and fall in love.

I wanted to know what it felt like to *be* loved.

And if Ty couldn't give me that, I needed to know.

"You're a commitment-phobe." There. I'd said it. Now the burden of proof was on him.

Come on, I silently begged. *Drop to one knee and tell me how wrong I am. Tell me that you love me and that I'm the only vampire in the world for you.*

His eyes narrowed to tiny slits and the muscle in

his right jaw started a frantic tick. "What did you just say?"

I summoned my courage. "You heard me. I said you're a commitment-phobe."

"*I'm* a commitment-phobe? You won't even introduce me to your mother."

I bristled. "I'm waiting for the right time."

"As in never."

"As in I want to be one hundred percent sure that you're not just using me for a little fun."

"Babe, there's nothing fun about being with you. Trust me, it's work. Hard fucking work."

The urge to smack him was sudden and fierce. At the same time, I feared my hand coming into contact with his handsome face and rough skin and, well, I am a creature of sexual habit. I ignored the thought and focused on my righteous anger. "What is it with you? Why can't you just tell me what you're feeling?"

"I'll do you one better. I'll show you." To prove his point, he dipped his head. His mouth captured mine and his tongue pushed deep.

My hands snaked around his neck and my fingers plunged into the silky thickness of his hair.

What? The man could *kiss.*

He pulled me close, his hands dragging down my spine to cup my ass and fit my pelvis more closely to his. Our bodies melded together for several fast, furious heartbeats before he pulled away.

"That's lust, not love," I heard myself say.

"All that bottled blood is finally getting to you. You're obviously losing it."

Why was it when you said something a guy didn't want to hear, he immediately countered by telling you what a loony bee-yotch you were? "I'm not crazy. I'm realistic. And you're a commitment-phobe," I said again. "P-H-O-B-E."

He shrugged. "I just don't think we need to draw any unnecessary attention to our relationship. The more low-key we keep things, the easier it will be to stay off Logan's radar."

I knew this and I also knew that he felt like he was protecting me. At the same time, I couldn't help but think that maybe, just maybe, he didn't fear Logan so much as he feared himself.

Maybe Logan was just an excuse for the fact that deep down, Ty was no different from every other made vampire out there. Maybe he *was* just interested in sex.

And maybe I *was* a crazy bee-yotch because as much as I knew I should shut my mouth and stop trying to piss him off, I couldn't help myself. "It's you. You're scared to love me."

"I'm not scared."

"Then prove it. Tell me you love me."

"I'm here trying to save your ass. Isn't that enough?"

"Just *say* it."

He eyed me for a long moment. "And if I can't?"

"Then I can't do this anymore."

His expression went dark and thunderous and he looked ready to hit something. Or maybe kiss me again.

I vote for number two.

"Suit yourself," he growled, and then he was gone.

I listened to the flutter of wings and barely resisted the urge to go after him. But I'd made a promise to myself. No more lust over love. No more dead-end relationships. *No more.*

And I wasn't breaking that promise.

If Ty couldn't say the one word I'd waited an eternity to hear, then we had no future together.

I fought back a wave of hot tears and tried to convince myself that I was one lucky vamp. After all, I'd seen his true colors now instead of later and avoided a useless waste of time.

Yay me.

Twenty-four
❤ ❤ ❤

Calling it quits with Ty turned out to be a bad omen of things to come.

As in twelve more rounds of Truth or Dare, eight games of Bunko, ten reruns of *What Not to Wear* and five solid days without so much as a glimpse of Mordred.

Yep, I was *this* close to crawling into a tanning bed and nuking myself. My aunt Sophie had gone that route with a unit she'd bought from QVC and it hadn't been pretty.

Hence the only reason I kept my distance from the Lucky Charm Tanning Salon, Lonely Fork's one and only fake-and-bake mecca.

A nice, clean death via stake I could handle. My folks could still have an open casket. Ty could cry a river and moon over my lifeless, but still perfect bod. I could still wear my favorite French couture. Maybe even a pair of kick-ass stilettos.

But being splattered in a million different pieces with nothing but my last pic (a photo from this past year's Marchette family reunion, where I'd been stuck dancing with my cousin Milton, who'd had his fangs ripped out by an overzealous SOB who'd wanted to make a little side profit by selling them on eBay)?

Pass.

The only pair of Manolos in a store full of Payless? I'd finally convinced my mother that all the Yaz in the world wouldn't keep the inevitable from happening. The only way to prevent Mandy from popping out a human baby was to get her to change her mind about motherhood altogether. Who better to do that than a roomful of women who'd been there, done that?

Enter a dozen members of my mother's Connecticut Huntress Club (half of which, to my utter delight, were now single). One phone call and they'd rushed to my mother's aid in a show of female vamp solidarity. That, and my mother had promised them unlimited refreshments, free pedicures and the chance to win her custom one-of-a-kind Verner Panton rug (to be auctioned off on the last day of the retreat). They had over eighty-eight children between them and plenty of horror stories to scare the cooties out of my trusting sister-in-law.

". . . so I told him, Pierre, you can't drown the

maid in the Jacuzzi. If you want to get rid of her, chop her up and stash her in the crawl space like every other serial killer."

A collective murmur of agreement went through the group of tastefully dressed BVs that filled LuLu's Nails.

My mother had handed over her credit card for a full night of beauty. With the promise of a forty percent gratuity, DoraLee had happily opened up shop and called in every nail tech on staff. Each chair was full. Every nail file buzzed, every footbath bubbled. The place reeked of paraffin wax, nail polish remover, foamy lavender footbath and romance.

Did I mention that I'd invited DeWalt to mix and mingle with the ladies?

He was currently getting matching pedis with Veronique Chatois, a real estate mogul who owned half of Connecticut. Veronique had lost her husband when his plane had crashed in the desert and he hadn't been able to find proper shelter before the sun had turned him into a piece of extra-crispy. She wasn't interested in more kids (Pierre was her youngest and scary enough to turn even a vampire celibate), but she did love to ride horses.

Hey, it was a start.

". . . one minute I'm sitting in the hot tub, relaxing my muscles, and the next I've got a dead body floating next to me. Which wasn't a problem in itself. Georges was always crawling into the hot tub with me and he'd been dead for six hundred years.

But this thing was bloated and bobbing and wearing a plastic shower curtain."

"I always wear Chanel in the hot tub, myself," offered Brigitte Gaston, who sat nearby, her tips being refilled by an overenthusiastic twenty-something (did I mention the forty percent gratuity?).

"Me, too," offered another vamp.

"I prefer Contessa or Bill Blass, myself."

"I didn't know Blass did swimsuits . . ."

"Did he really stuff a body in your crawl space?" The question came from a very pale-looking Mandy. She sat in the far corner, getting her feet pumiced.

The entire room murmured agreement and Mandy turned an even lighter shade.

I gave her a wink and an encouraging smile and she seemed to relax a little.

"You want appliqués?" DoraLee drew my attention as she finished pushing back the cuticles on my pinky. "I've got cowboy hats. Flowers. Or if you're a sports fan, I could do you up with some Dallas Cowboys stars. Or these little spurs."

"Just a clear coat of polish and I'll be good to go." It was ten P.M. and I was late for my nightly stakeout at the Quick Pick.

For lack of a better lead (I'd talked to everybody old enough to remember the sorcerer, namely one ancient-looking biology teacher who'd informed me that the only place he remembered seeing Mordred was in high school detention), I'd been keeping an eye on the convenience store.

Obviously, he wasn't a chain smoker because he hadn't been back. I was counting on the fact that he wanted to keep a low profile (he hadn't aged a day, which wouldn't have been the easiest thing to explain to the few people who remembered him), so I'd ruled out him stopping off for cigarettes during the day.

He'd be back, and when he showed up, I would be there.

And I wouldn't get ambushed this time.

I finished drying my nails and pushed to my feet. I whispered a quick "They're all a bunch of crazy vampires" to Mandy and a "Remember the Chanel booties and the Rebecca Taylor Onesies" to Nina, who was getting a little freaked herself what with all the talk of serial vampires and dead maids and ungrateful daughters who refused to settle down and procreate the species. Guess who? I spared a quick glance at DeWalt, who was having his first threesome (pull your mind out of the gutter, already) with Veronique talking one ear off and Brigitte gabbing in the other, and then am-scrayed on the pretense of making a beverage run.

A few minutes later, I flapped my way into a tree across the street from the Quick Pick and perched on a small branch. My infrared vision did a sweep of the area and came up with zilch. I tamped down my disappointment and settled in to watch.

Two hours crept by and my wings started to get tired. What? I'd been at it five nights straight. I soared to the ground, closed my eyes, focused on my heartbeat and did a quick shift back to megalicious vampire.

I stretched my legs and did a little shake and shimmy to get the kinks out. Much better. I walked a few paces back and forth and was just about to go back undercover when I heard the familiar voice.

"I told you that was her." The comment came from the driver of a navy blue Ford Taurus parked midway up the street.

My ultra–night vision zeroed in on Cheap, who sat behind the wheel, a pair of binoculars glued to his eyes.

"How was I supposed to know?" Cheaper sat in the passenger seat and munched a bag of pretzels. "It could have been any bat."

"How many pink bats do you see flying around here?" Cheap set the binoculars aside, grabbed a small case sitting on the dash and climbed out of the car. His partner followed.

I could morph and get the hell out of there. Now. But the store was closing in less than ten minutes and my ma would kill me if I came back empty-handed.

Making a beeline for the front glass door, I zoomed across the street. They barely made two steps before I reached the store. Inside, I grabbed a six-pack of Red Bull, a few bags of Doritos for Mandy and several boxes of wine.

No, really. An actual *box*.

I dumped everything on the counter, signed my

Visa slip (complete with a tip to cover the tooth-brush I'd swiped during the Mordred sighting) and grabbed my bags. I was just walking out of the store when Merlin's henchmen finally caught up to me.

"Stand down, vampire." The carrying case on the dash turned out to house a sedative gun. "I knew you wouldn't heed Merlin's warning."

"What's that supposed to mean?"

"That you're here looking for Mordred."

"Mordred who?"

"Call Merlin," Cheap told Cheaper. "Tell him she's back and she's interfering again."

"I'm doing no such thing," I told the man as he reached for his cell. I held up my bags. "We're having a little soiree at the nail salon." When he didn't look convinced, I flashed him my newly painted tips.

"That doesn't prove you're not here for Mor-dred."

"If I've got my hands full of Red Bull and Doritos," I pointed out, "how am I supposed to follow a de-mented sorcerer? Pu-lease. We're out in the middle of BFE and I'm wearing three-inch patent leather sling-backs. I'd definitely need a car."

"Not really. It's not that far—" *Whack!* Cheap's hand clamped over Cheaper's mouth and the rest came out like "*mumhumwhamumwhemamum.*"

"What the hell are you doing?" Cheap hissed. "You almost told her the location."

"I didn't tell her he's at—" *Whack!*

"Jesus, Mary and Joseph. You almost did it again. Just keep your mouth shut."

"Listen, fellas, I'd love to stand around and watch you guys play slap and tickle, but I've got a party waiting." I sidestepped them and headed across the street, all the while conscious of the two men behind me.

I strained my ears for the cock of a gun or the slap of footsteps. They'd gotten the jump on me before, but only because I'd been distracted.

That wasn't going to happen again.

"Should we stop her?" Cheaper asked.

"From doing what? Merlin said to take her in if she interferes. So far, we haven't caught her doing anything but spending money."

That's right, boys.

But as pleased as I was to have avoided a massive headache and Merlin's deadly finger, I was doubly upset because Cheaper was right—I hadn't been doing anything but shopping.

Certainly not finding or saving Esther.

And her time was running out.

I dropped off the supplies at the nail salon—Nina was getting rhinestone tips and Mandy was seriously considering retiring her uterus early. Particularly since my mom had decided to break her vow of silence when it came to her precious boys and share a very vivid description of the twenty-nine hours of hell—aka labor—she'd endured to give birth to Jack.

She'd spilled it about the water retention and the

fat ankles and the constant craving for pomegranate juice mixed with deer urine and gypsy blood.

When I got back to NYC, my bro was *so* not living that one down.

"Where have you been?" my mother demanded. "You left hours ago."

"I got lost."

"You've got vampire instincts, dear. That's better than a GPS."

"They were out of wine at the first store, so I had to keep looking until I found some."

"A box?" My mother eyeballed the Zinfandel I'd set on a nearby table.

I grinned. "You wanted to try new things."

"I was thinking more a cucumber face mask as opposed to my usual cinnamon and honey. Speaking of face masks"—she pinned DoraLee with a stare—"have you had any luck with the tomato and dill recipe that I downloaded off the Internet?" She smiled at Mandy. "I just know you'll love it. It's wonderful for your pores."

"But I'm allergic."

"Nonsense." My mother waved her newly done nails. "It only causes a reaction if you consume it. This is an external beauty treatment. It's totally safe."

I listened to my mom cite a few convincing testimonials from various Discovery Health episodes she'd watched on the subject, while the rest of her fellow Hunt Club sisters provided the occasional, "I saw that, too," and "Oh, that's so true."

"I've got a wine cellar," DeWalt announced after tasting the boxed Zinfandel. He held up his glass. "If any of you ladies are interested in something a little more palatable than this cardboard."

Go DeWalt.

A collective murmur went through the place and five minutes later, almost everyone had cleared out.

Did I mention that BVs went for a good Chardonnay as fiercely as a tasty O+?

The only ones left behind were Nina, yours truly and Mandy, who'd promised to stay and try out the new tomato and dill concoction. My excuse? Somebody had to stay and make sure Mandy followed through.

"You're not really going to put that on your face?" I asked her once the place had emptied.

"You aren't really going to make me, are you?" She flashed me a knowing grin before weariness crept across her expression. "I'm actually kind of tired. With my days and nights so mixed up now that I'm off my normal routine, I've been feeling a little out of sorts. And your mom's been running me ragged. Don't get me wrong. I like spending time with her. I think it's good for us to get to know each other so well, but I'm dying to call it a night."

"I'll join you," Nina said.

"No more crying over Rob," I reminded her.

"Rob who?"

"Attagirl."

"You want to try the facial?" DoraLee held up a small plastic mixing bowl filled with red paste.

"I'll take a raincheck. But can I interest you in a suave, sophisticated single who enjoys Bingo and the occasional copy of *Reader's Digest*?"

"I'm not going out with Elmer."

What? I promised him I'd try.

"But my ma might," DoraLee added. "She's in her eighties now. Still has all her teeth and hates tapioca. Likes Bingo."

I smiled. "It's a date."

I parted ways with Nina and Mandy and headed for the Bigby place. Yeah, yeah—been there, done that. But I was out of options since the Quick Pick had closed for the night.

An hour ticked by as I walked the perimeter of the property and kept my eyes peeled for anything unusual. He had to be keeping her somewhere nearby. It was all about power and since he'd spent most of his time here, it only made sense that this would be the site for the ritual.

He'd probably offered up toads and cut the heads off a zillion chickens right there in the living room.

I was just about to peek through the window where the current residents were watching an episode of *Trick My Truck* when my cell phone started singing. I snatched it up, noted my home number and punched the on button.

Play it cool, I told myself. *Drop a few subtle hints about Nina and her condition and let Rob come to the conclusion on his own.*

"Stop being a shit," I told Rob. What? I'd been thinking about Ty constantly since we'd called it quits. I was entitled to a little venting.

"What are you talking about?"

"I know you love Nina. Why can't you just tell her?"

"Hello to you, too."

"I mean it. What is it with male vampires? You feel something, you should say so. We're not friggin' mind readers. It's four letters, for Damien's sake."

"Nina and I split. It's over. I'm going my way and she's going hers."

"So one of you changes direction."

"What if she doesn't want me?"

"What if she does?"

He grew silent for a long moment. "If you called to bitch me out, you can forget it."

"I didn't call you. You called me."

"Oh, yeah. I need clean sheets."

"Why do you need clean sheets? You sleep on the couch."

"Not tonight. I've got a date with the Tanner triplets." I could practically see him rubbing his hands together in anticipation. I could also see the whiskey bottles he'd emptied to build up his courage.

"I figure it's time I moved on and got Nina out of

my system completely," he said, his words slurring just enough to confirm my suspicions.

"You're drunk."

"I am not drunk." Which sounded more like *drrrrunkkk.* "I'm perfectly capable of making a coherent decision"—make that *dee-si-jun*—"and I've decided I want to have sex."

"Rebound sex."

"One is rebound sex. Three is empowering sex."

More like greedy bitch sex. Rob being the greedy bitch, of course.

"The couch won't be nearly big enough for everyone," Rob went on. "We have to use the bedroom."

"Oh, no, you don't. Listen to me and get this through your fogged brain, if you lay one finger on my bed, I'll make sure you regret it."

"How's that? You're not exactly into bloodshed."

"I'll tell Dad that you loaned his chainsaw to Viola."

"That was you."

Oh, yeah. "It's your word against mine. He might believe me and he might not, but he's sure to get really pissed just contemplating the possibility. And you know what that means."

When my dad got mad, he became impossible to work for. He scaled back paychecks and vacation days and generally gave his managers hell.

And Rob would be in his direct line of fire.

"You wouldn't."

"Are you really willing to chance it? Unless, of

course, you don't need the fourteen days—all expenses paid—in Hawaii that he's planning on throwing in as part of his managers' compensation package next month."

"How do you know that?"

"Mom's here and we're now BFFs."

"You're lying."

"See how easy it is for me?"

"Fine, then. I'll just go to a hotel. But it's your loss."

"How's that?"

"You'd have the honor of owning *the* bed that witnessed a triple conquest. Who knows, it might bring you a little luck in the sack."

"You really are a shit." I hit the OFF button and called my oldest brother, Max. After a brief explanation and a "Get over there right now and I'll owe you for the rest of my afterlife," I hung up and fumed.

Rob was a dog. A total player. An inconsiderate one, at that. He wanted to deflower three women at once to prove his inebriated prowess and I was supposed to feel privileged that he chose my bed for the action?

Forget it. He could *conquer* triplets somewhere else.

Like, say, Miller's Creek.

The thought struck as I sat in the motel room just after midnight. Nina and Mandy had already crashed and my mom had yet to return from the wine fest at DeWalt's, so I had the bathroom to myself. I stared at the digital list on my phone of all the things I knew about Mordred.

He'd lived at the Bigby place.

He'd spent *a lot* of time in detention.

He'd dated the Homecoming Queen.

He'd deflowered the Homecoming Queen.

He'd deflowered the Homecoming Queen's sister.

He'd done them both in the backseat of his Chevy Impala while parked at Miller's Creek.

Shit.

Shit, shit, *shit*.

I bolted to my feet, snatched up my purse and headed for the lobby to talk to Elmer.

"Cain't you read?" Elmer grumbled when I rang the bell for the tenth time and he finally emerged from the back room. "It says to *come back later*. That means after I finish watching Tyra Banks. I DVR'd her earlier today. Talk about a pretty gal."

"Sorry, Elmer, but it's an emergency."

"You hurt?" I shook my head and he grumbled, "Then it can wait till my show's over." He started to turn.

"I found you a date."

He stopped in his tracks and a gleam lit his eyes. "DoraLee?"

"Her mother."

He seemed to weigh the news. "Ah, hell, that's close enough. What can I do you for?"

"I need to know how to get to Miller's Creek."

"Ain't much of a creek now on account of the

drought a few years back. Kids even stopped going up there to park and started hanging out at the drive-in." He grinned. "Took my own missus up there way back when. That creek has seen it's fair share of excitement over the years, let me tell you. It was the luckiest spot in town for half the young men around here. Many a boy became king out there." Elmer winked. "If you know what I mean."

My heartbeat shifted into overdrive and desperation swamped me. "That's what I'm counting on."

Twenty-five
❤ ❤ ❤

This can't be right.

I stared at the directions Elmer had written down for me and then back at the barren stretch of earth flanked by a dense forest on three sides. The fourth was a thick wall of rock that shot up at least twenty feet to a flat stretch of land above. I drank in my surroundings once, twice, my senses absorbing everything, from the buzz of crickets to the musty smell of the trees.

According to the paper, I was standing on the bank of Miller's Creek. The top date spot, according to the *Lonely Fork Gazette*.

Maybe ten years ago.

I stretched my imagination and struggled to picture a crystal clear flow of running water, a moonlit sky, a picturesque waterfall trickling over the towering cliff.

Make that fifty years.

I couldn't imagine this shroud of trees and dried-up patch of dirt luring any girl out of her panties, much less two girls at the very same time.

Still . . .

Leaves and twigs crackled beneath my feet as I started to walk. I made several passes around the area, looking for any place where a body might be stashed. A cave. An abandoned well. A freshly dug hole in the ground.

Nothing.

I ran my hand over the rock wall, searching for a hidden lever that might crack it open and reveal a secret room.

While I didn't watch much TV, I'd seen every *Batman* episode. For obvious reasons.

I'd just floated up a few feet to tug on a tree branch when I heard the desperate "Lil?"

My concentration broke and I almost crashed to the ground. My feet hit hard and I leaned over as pain bolted through me.

"Lil?" The voice was stronger now. More desperate.

I whirled and came face-to-face with Nina.

"You scared the crap out of me."

She looked at me as if I'd grown two heads.

"Er, that is, you would have scared the crap out of

me if I weren't such a badass vampire who doesn't scare, period. What are you doing here?"

"I had to talk to someone." A sob punctuated her sentence. "I did it."

"Did what?"

I expected her to say she'd sucked Elmer dry or eaten the tomato facial or something equally awful. We're talking *sobbing*.

"I called Rob to tell him that I love him."

"That's great."

"He didn't answer his phone." Her red-rimmed eyes met mine. "Laura Tanner did."

Oh, no.

"It was the worst moment of my afterlife."

I pulled her into a fierce hug and damned my brother a thousand times as sobs racked her body.

"I love him and he's off screwing the Tanner triplets. He's probably biting them, too."

"I'm sure he wouldn't do that." But the truth was, I wasn't so sure. Rob had fangs and a penis *and* he'd been drunk. The trio made for some stupid decisions. "He loves you. I know he does." At least that much was true. Rob *did* love Nina. He just didn't realize it.

And I wasn't so sure he ever would.

"Come on, let's get out of here. We'll go back to the motel and talk."

She pulled away to stare at me. "But you have to look for Esther."

"Trust me, I'm not having much luck."

"Sure you are," the deep voice rumbled through my head. "I just wouldn't classify it as good luck."

I whirled to find Mordred standing directly behind me.

I swear, everyone was getting the jump on me these days.

He wore the same khakis and blue shirt, only they were streaked with something dark and red. My nostrils flared and hunger gripped me.

"One person's bad luck is another person's good luck. That's what they say, isn't it?"

"Actually, it's one person's trash is another person's treasure, but I guess the concept is the same."

"What's going on?" Nina's tears dried up and she took on a wary stance.

"Why don't you introduce me to your friend?"

"This is Mordred."

"The sonofabitch who stole Esther." She tried to launch into Super Vamp mode, but I caught her hand, my gaze fixed on the gun in Mordred's hand.

It wasn't a normal-looking gun. Rather, it had a large green canister attached to the top. A greenish liquid sloshed in the canister and the familiar scent of garlic prickled my nostrils.

"Don't," I murmured.

"Wise advice." He winked at me. "Unfortunately, you're not half as good at taking advice as you are at dishing it out. You should have listened to Merlin." The surprise must have shown in my eyes because he added, "Yes, I know about your little run-in. In fact,

I witnessed the entire thing. While I have to admit we didn't plan it, it still worked out nicely."

"He's in on this with you, isn't he?"

He didn't answer. He didn't have to.

His eyes danced with a dark, dangerous light. "I still can't believe you bought all that nonsense about fulfilling the ritual. Merlin could stop me right now if he wanted to."

"But he doesn't want to."

He smiled. "I have something he wants." He tapped his head. "I know the secret. The key to a successful ritual. He needs me." When I didn't seem clued in, he added, "Merlin's a powerful sorcerer. The most powerful of our kind, but while he's immortal, he hasn't been able to stop the aging process. The white hair. The wrinkles. He's spent years trying to reverse the process with plain magic, but other than casting a very convincing allusion spell, he can't do anything real. Anything permanent. But I can."

"You're sacrificing Esther for him."

"Hardly." He chuckled, a frightening sound that stalled my heart in my chest. "I went to a lot of trouble to find Esther. I've spent a lot of time working with her, making sure I starve her just enough, making sure she feels just the right amount of pain to fulfill the ritual requirements. I'm not giving her up that easy. She's mine." His gaze narrowed and he aimed the gun. "You're Merlin's sacrifice." He pulled the trigger.

The liquid hit me, dripping into my eyes, my mouth. The scent rushed into my nose and clogged my lungs. I tried to keep ahold of Nina, but she pulled free to cover her face with her hands as he turned the blast on her.

But it was too late.

She stiffened and stumbled backward while my own muscles clenched and jerked. I fell to my knees, my body jerking, fighting before the paralysis gripped me. I hit the dirt face-first. My heart slowed. My eyes closed.

And then I tumbled into a big black pit of nothing.

Never, *ever* drink wine in a box.

That was my first thought when I blinked. My head throbbed and my eyes felt gritty and heavy. I was surely nursing one hellacious hangover thanks to the two glasses I'd downed at the nail salon—

The thoughts skidded to a halt as I became acutely aware of the cold dirt floor beneath me and the ropes binding my hands and feet. The confrontation with Mordred came rushing back in an instant and I glanced at Nina, who lay a few feet away. She was trussed up, too, but she hadn't yet opened her eyes. Which meant the soft crying wasn't coming from her.

My gaze shifted to the right and the vampire that lay stretched out on a bloodstained table, her hands and feet tied at each of the four corners. Esther was naked, her skin raw and bleeding, and my heart hitched. Several strips of flesh had been cut from her legs in various patterns and draped over a long rack that hung on a nearby wall. She trembled, but no sound escaped her dried and cracked lips.

I sniffled and caught my bottom lip. The noise instantly stopped.

What?

I gathered my control and tried to slow my pounding heart. I needed to think. To get a grip and get the hell out of here.

Here looked like the inside of a massive cave and I guessed we were somewhere behind the stone wall that had once been the backdrop for the waterfall. A sliver of light snaked its way around a corner, illuminating a tunnel (the only visible way in or out), and I knew night had faded into day. Judging by the weariness gripping my limbs, I was guessing somewhere around midday.

Ritual day.

The realization struck just as I heard soft footsteps. Mordred appeared, an ancient-looking knife in his hands. He walked over to Esther and lifted one of her eyelids. She flinched and he seemed satisfied that she was conscious enough for what he had in mind.

He went to her right arm and started to cut. A scream ripped through the air and bounced off the walls.

I tugged against the ropes, but it was useless. "Leave her alone," I croaked.

"Jealous, are we?" He finished slicing the skin off her right arm and moved to her left. Once he'd cut a matching piece, he walked over to the rack and draped them both next to the half dozen already on display.

"Don't worry," he said as he turned and headed for me. "You'll get your turn, too." He leaned over me and I braced myself for the pain. Instead, he grabbed a nearby rag and held it over my face.

I bucked once, twice, and then I was out again.

The next time I opened my eyes, the light in the tunnel had faded and the opening yawned pitch black. My throat felt tight and my eyes were watery. Instead of being tied together, my arms were above my head, my hands tied at each corner.

Uh-oh.

I lifted my head and glanced down. Sure enough, I was stretched out on my own table. My clothes were history, but I still had all my skin.

"We didn't want to start the party without you." It was Merlin who spoke this time. "The pain is part of the ritual, so you have to be conscious."

I turned and spotted him as he neared the table. I flashed some fang and growled. "Untie me or I'll rip your head off."

"You and what army?" He chuckled. "Speaking of army, knock, knock."

When I didn't say anything, he lifted the dreaded finger and pinched at the air. My arm tightened painfully, and I gave a loud cry and growled, "Who's there?"

"Tank."

Another pinch and pain ripped through my other arm. "T-tank who?"

"You're welcome." He started laughing then, the sound bouncing off the walls and pounding into my head.

I tugged at my wrist, desperate to get loose and yank his stupid Santa beard.

"You can stop fighting. This was meant to be, Miss Marchette. I knew it the moment I visited your office. You're determined. Persistent. Vibrant." He smiled. "I could feel your life force and I knew then that it was fate. I didn't even have to kidnap you. You followed me willingly. You even gave me the perfect alibi to explain your death."

"The videotape."

He smiled. "I'll tell them that you tried to interfere and I had no choice but to destroy you. With the taped evidence to back up my story, the BV Council won't be able to challenge my actions."

"What about Nina?" I struggled to catch a glimpse of my friend. She still lay in a heap in the corner, oblivious to everything.

"I'll say she got in the way. It won't be nearly as convincing as your death, but I'll have two eyewitnesses to vouch for me."

"Your men aren't here."

"They don't have to be. One spell and they'll say

anything I want them to say. They'll believe it. She got in the way. I had no choice."

"Esther's ready." Mordred's voice drew my attention to the right. He wore a cloak made up of the various strips of Esther's skin. Blood from the fresher pieces drip-dropped down his cheeks. The dagger gleamed in his hand. "One down, one to go."

I was going to die. Really *die*.

The truth hit me hard and fast as the dagger descended.

No seeing my mother or my father or my brothers. No Evie. No Killer.

No Ty.

I'd let him go. How stupid was that? I'd let him walk away. Worse, I'd pushed him away.

The only vampire I'd ever loved.

The only vampire who'd ever loved me.

He did. Even if he hadn't ever said it. I knew it deep down inside, underneath all my insecurities and my crazy romantic notions. I'd fantasized for so long about the perfect vampire that I'd refused to give up my ideal. But vampires aren't perfect.

Fine, so physically they are. But emotionally they're just as messed up as everyone else, me included. Ty had been right. I was every bit the commitment-phobe. That's why I'd put off introducing him to my mother.

Because I wouldn't just be admitting to her that I was giving up a future filled with baby vamps, I'd be admitting it to myself.

That's what I'd really been afraid of.

Committing to Ty and giving up my dream.

But it wasn't the dream that kept me company as the knife sank into my skin. It was Ty. His image in my head. His memory warming my body and blocking out the pain.

"*Sonofabitch*," I ground out through clenched teeth.

Okay, most of the pain.

Hot blood slithered down my calf, drip-dropped onto the floor. Fire swept up my leg as Mordred peeled back the skin.

I clamped my eyes shut and focused on Ty. His handsome face. His toned body. His deep voice.

"Lame, dude. Really lame."

Then again, maybe his voice wasn't that deep.

My eyes popped open and I stared through a fog of pain at the woman who stood behind Mordred.

"Tabitha?"

"Hey, Lil." She gave a finger wave, all party girl bubbly until she turned her attention to Mordred. Her bright blue eyes hardened into hard chips and her smile faded. "It wasn't nice ditching me like that. I've been looking everywhere for you."

Her vivid description of her dream man clicked and I realized she hadn't been looking for a date at all. She'd been looking for Mordred.

And she'd finally hit pay dirt.

Twenty-six
❤ ❤ ❤

"We had a deal," Tabitha reminded Mordred.

While I never would have pegged her for the intimidating sort, she rose to the occasion as she stepped toward the sorcerer.

He backed up.

I had no clue who Tabitha really was, but I knew then that she was one bad bitch.

Merlin lifted his hand to give her the finger, but she nailed him with a stare. "Stay out of this, old man."

His arm fell to his side and stayed there as if some invisible force held him immobile.

"We had a deal, Mordred. I make sure the gods reward you for your sacrifice and you hand over the souls to me. That's the way it's always been between us. Always. But you had to get greedy, didn't you? You wanted to cut me out, make one last sacrifice and gain immortality all by yourself. But it doesn't work that way. The deal calls for a human. A soul. Vampires don't have souls."

Hey.

"You renig," she went on. "I renig."

"I . . ." The words faded into a choked gurgle.

"What's the matter?" She eyed him. "Cat got your tongue?" The moment she said it, his mouth opened. Blood gushed out, followed by something that landed with a *splat* on the floor. "Oh, it's not the cat. It's just me." She leaned over and picked up the bleeding slab. "I've got your tongue." She waved it at him. "And all the rest of you. Ditto for your soul." Her eyes brightened and the walls seemed to vibrate. "Time to go."

Mordred stumbled backward, but it was too late. His fingers started to fall, plopping into the dirt one by one. Then his hands. His arms. He screamed, the sound blending with the rush of wind that seemed to dismember him piece by piece. The ground started to shake then, sucking at the pieces, gobbling them up until all that remained was the sickening skin cloak that lay in a heap on the ground.

"Don't do this," Merlin said when she turned toward him. "The Council won't take my death lightly."

"Oh, I'm not going to kill you. I'm going to warn you. There is no bending the rules. One human sacrifice every one hundred years. You give me the soul and I give you another hundred years looking exactly the way you do now." Her gaze swept him from head to toe. "Doesn't sound so hot, now, does it?" Silence ticked by as she stepped closer to him, until they were nose to nose. "If I were you, I'd turn and run right now."

She blew him a little kiss and he flew backward, slamming into the wall. He scrambled to his feet and ran for his life. "Party on," she called after him.

"Lil." She clucked her tongue as she walked over to me. "You're a mess, girl."

"Who are you?"

"Ixtab," said a deep, familiar voice. Ty's image materialized. He took one look at me and the relief in his eyes turned to something much darker and much more dangerous. "Fuck," he growled as he stared at the raw patch where my skin had been. *"Fuck."* His gaze collided with mine. "I'm sorry."

And I knew he wasn't just talking about my flayed flesh. Warmth seeped through me, chasing away the cold.

I grinned. "You're late."

My reply eased his frown lines and he grinned. His gaze swept the length of me again and his gaze darkened. "You're naked."

"I'd love to stick around for this heartfelt reunion, but I've got a date." Ixtab winked at me. "Evie set me up with a plumber from Brooklyn. We're going salsa dancing."

"Party on," I called after her. "Start talking," I said to Ty.

"Her name is Ixtab."

"And?"

"You know, the ancient Mayan goddess of death. She gathers the souls of victims of suicide, child-birth and sacrifice and takes them to paradise. At least that's what the legend says, but I've got it on good authority that they don't make it past Vegas."

Hey, it made sense.

"Anyhow, she's been keeping Mordred young in return for the souls of his sacrifices. He tried to cheat her this time and she wasn't too happy about it."

I remembered the flying body parts. "Obviously not." I shook my head. Could this night get any stranger?

Right about the time I asked myself that question, I heard the squeal of tires and the slam of several car doors.

Ty heard it, too. "We'd better get you untied." He grabbed the discarded dagger and went to work on the ropes at my feet. Since they were infused with silver and soaked in garlic, he fumbled a few times, but in a matter of seconds, my right foot was free. "It seems Rob called Nina back when he found out that she called him." The bonds on my left foot eased. "When she didn't answer, he got worried and called me." Ty moved around my head and reached for the ropes on my left wrist. "I didn't answer, so he called his brothers, who called your dad, who called Evie, who called Ash." My hand broke free and he moved to the next one. "They were on their way, the last I heard."

"Which ones?"

"All except for Evie. She's holding down the fort back home." The voices grew louder, more discernable, and he cut through the last of the restraints. "They got into town about an hour ago, talked to Elmer, and here they are."

I rubbed at my wrists. "When did you get into town?"

His gaze met and held mine. "Baby, I never left."

I'd like to say that Ty swooped me into his arms at that very second and carried me off into the sunset à la some romantic Taylor Swift song, but hey, we're vampires. No sunsets allowed.

On top of that, I was in so much pain that there was no swooping allowed either.

Instead, he peeled off the dark blue T-shirt he was wearing and helped me into it. I winced and cringed and yelped a few times. Finally the soft cotton slithered over me just as Ash and his brothers barreled through the opening of the tunnel.

Zee and Mo split, one heading for Esther, who was still strapped to a nearby table, and the other going for Nina. Ash rushed over to me, his expression fierce, his eyes glittering with concern. He stopped just shy of touching me, his gaze locking with Ty's. Some silent male thing passed between them, and instead of reaching out he settled for a thorough glance at my leg. "Fucking hell," he muttered. "I'm sorry I got you mixed up with that guy."

"He said he's going to get you fired."

His expression was cold. "We'll see who gets fired." Another sweeping gaze and his attention settled on my face. "Are you really okay?"

"Are you kidding?" I grasped at Ty and let him help me into a sitting position. "Don't get me wrong. I could use a few pain pills right about now. Or maybe a box of wine. But otherwise, I'm fine."

My words drew his attention and he grinned. "I never figured you for a cheap drunk."

"Right now, I'd drink just about anything."

Ty didn't need to hear me twice. He did the swooping then. His strong arms slid under me and he carried me through the tunnel, to the crowd gathered outside.

Ash and his crime scene team descended on the cave while a special medical unit (i.e., a few choice blood donors) whisked Esther away to nurse her back to health. My BFF was awake now and sitting in the back of a nearby cab, a smile on her face. Rob had declared his love in front of the entire crowd, which he'd also demonstrated by flying thousands of miles, and she'd declared hers. I don't think she'd told him about the baby yet, but I knew it was just a matter of time.

Meanwhile, I sat on the hood of DeWalt's black stretch Cadillac, nursed a bottle of blood and explained myself to my parents. Max. Jack and Mandy. The Connecticut Huntress Club. DeWalt. Remy.

Yep, even he showed up.

He looked casual chic in jeans, a pullover Hollister tee and loafers. His blond hair was rumpled, his smile infectious. "Glad to see you're still in one piece."

I glanced down at my now bandaged leg. "Mostly. What are you doing here?"

"I've been babysitting your dad while your mom's been on retreat." He shoved a hand through his hair, which explained the rumpled look. "The man's been trying to buy jet engine fuel for a bomb he's building in his garage. I couldn't let him near an airplane by himself."

"He's really building a bomb?"

"Damn straight I am," my dad said as he walked up to us. "Just wait until I finish. Then we'll see if Viola has balls enough to cut down another one of my bushes."

"Dad, if you launch a nuclear weapon, she'll not only have balls. She'll have a third eye."

Ty paused a few feet away, where he was busy giving a statement to one of the suits Ash had called in. He grinned and I went warm in all the right places.

"I'm definitely going to need a vacation after this," Remy declared.

I nodded. "You and me both."

"Drink up, dear." My mother's voice drew my attention as she came up next to my father. Her narrowed gaze roved me from head to toe. "You still look terrible. And your hair—"

"Mom, I almost lost my afterlife. It's not my proudest hair moment."

"You're telling me." She gave a disdainful shiver. "If this isn't proof enough that you should give up that disastrous business, which almost always seems to land you in trouble, then I don't know what—"

"Ma," I cut in.

"—else to do. However are you going to find a nice male vampire if you're busy running around getting yourself flayed—"

"*Ma.*"

Her gaze collided with mine. "Yes, dear?"

I smiled and motioned Ty over. He reached me in a heartbeat and I took his hand, my fingers twining with his. "I've got somebody I want you to meet."

Epilogue

♥ ♥ ♥

"I forgot to tell you . . ." Evie handed me an envelope. It was a clear, moonlit Friday evening and she was about to call it quits for the night, while I was just getting started matching up New York's sad and single. "Tabitha dropped these off earlier today on her way to meet prospect number twenty-two." I arched an eyebrow and she added, "They're bungeeing near Coney Island."

I pulled out the pair of round-trip tickets to Las Vegas, complete with a voucher for the Mayan Hotel and Casino just around the corner from the Hard Rock. It seemed Ty was right and Tabitha did have ties to Sin City.

She'd spent the past three weeks since the Mordred incident enjoying the long list of dates I'd set up for her as a means of saying thank you for saving my undead hide.

I guess she'd been having so much fun that she felt it was her turn to treat me.

Yeah, baby.

"You're never going to believe where I'm going," I told Nina after I'd punched in her digits.

"Las Vegas."

"Las—How did you know?"

"Because Tabitha sent us tickets, too. Isn't it great? We're all going on vacation together!"

"Who exactly is *we*?"

"You, me, Rob, Jack, Mandy, your mom, your dad—the whole family."

My mom?

My dad?

Everyone?

A rush of pure fear shot through me.

I know, I know. Badass vamp and all that, but we're talking my mother. The vampire who'd endured labor for me. The vamp who'd followed me to Texas to sabotage my youngest brother's attempt at procreation.

The woman was ruthless, and determined.

She'd fixed me up with a total of forty-two eligible BVs since I'd introduced her to Ty. Even news of her coming grandchild and a lavish commitment ceremony (Nina and Rob) hadn't been enough to distract her. She'd simply seen it as a prime opportunity to parade vampires in front of me.

Her family was falling apart right in front of her eyes, at least as far as she was concerned, and she was a vampire intent on holding things together and returning everything to the vamp status quo.

Maybe I'd just skip town tonight. No sense waiting for the whole family. Ty and I could steal away together. I'd get a head start on the gambling. The drinking. By the time my ma showed up, I'd be so inebriated that I wouldn't care if she fixed me up with Elvis's ghost.

"Lil?" Nina's voice drew me back to the present and the all-important fact that I was late. "Are you going to your parents tonight for cocktails?"

"I didn't know my parents were having cocktails." I'd been so busy over the past few days searching for the last two matches for DeWalt, not to mention I'd gone to my first Nymphos-R-Us meeting on Mia's behalf, that I'd barely had time to check my messages, much less return any of them.

At least, that was my story and I was sticking to it.

Was my afterlife back to normal or what?

"Cocktails at eight. Your ma said to be on time because Jack and Mandy are coming and they have some sort of announcement they want to make. Your mom thinks Mandy has finally changed her mind about being a mother."

If only.

But over the past few weeks, I'd figured out that Mandy hadn't been tired on the trip to Texas so much as she'd been pregnant.

I guess now that the festivities for Nina and Rob were over, Jack and Mandy were dropping the bomb. In a matter of hours.

Tonight.

Uh-oh.

Five minutes later, I'd powered off my computer, did a quick mental of all the outfits I was going to shove into my luggage in a fast stop by my apartment and left a message for Ty to meet me at JFK.

It was crazy. Impulsive. And my ma was going to kill me.

But hey, what a way to finally go.

"Where are you off to?" Evie asked as I sailed past her desk and pushed open the glass door.

I smiled. "Sin City, here I come."

Read on for an excerpt from

Here Comes the Vampire

by Kimberly Raye
Published by Ballantine Books

Chapter One

❤ ❤ ❤

I never should have sucked down that last naked virgin.

Shoving my head under the pillow, I prayed for the bed to open up and swallow me whole. No more pounding skull or swirling stomach or aching muscles. And the dreams . . . Sheesh, if I pictured myself humping Elvis in the glass elevators of the Mayan Resort and Casino one more friggin' time, I was going to aim for the nearest stake.

My name? The Countess Lilliana Arrabella Guinevere du Marchette (I think). I'm a five-hundred-year-old (and holding) born vampire. When I'm not lying catatonic, praying to the BMVITS (that's short for Big Momma Vamp in the Sky) to please, please, *please* put me out of my misery, I play head honcho at Dead End Dating, Manhattan's hottest matchmaking service for vampires, weres, Others and even the occasional human. I've got an ultra chic fashion sense, an ever-expanding collection of MAC cosmetics and a fierce bod that's landed me more than my share of super hot boyfriends.

The latest and the crème de la crème? A hot, hunky bounty hunter who wouldn't be caught dead with lamb chop sideburns and a white jumpsuit.

Which made the whole Elvis scenario that much more unnerving, ya know?

Ty Bonner aka Mr. Hot and Hunky, had been the star of each and every one of my fantasies since the day I'd met him. Yes, he was a made vampire, which sort of put a crimp in the whole happily-ever-after thing I'd been cooking up since I was a kid. Unlike born vampires, our made brethren couldn't procreate. Meaning, I wouldn't have to worry about having a little Vlad or baby Morticia with Ty. But hey, I was okay with that. Really. If Brad and Ang could go the adoption route, why not yours truly? Even more, I was about to be an aunt for the first time. I could *so* do the vicarious thing with my future niece or nephew.

At least, that's what I was telling myself.

But that's beside the point. Ty was my leading vampire. When I closed my eyes and gave in to my most erotic thoughts, he was *always* there.

Until last night.

Forcing my eyes open, I stared at the ancient sun stone perched on the nightstand and tried to focus my watery gaze. Not that I could interpret said stone, but I was hoping to catch a glimpse of the digital read-out in the far corner for those guests less skilled in the art of primitive culture.

The Mayan was the newest five star attraction in Sin City, complete with oodles of pricey artifacts in addition to some very real looking reproductions. There were sacrificial altars and stone carvings and drinking vessels and incense burners, and even a small hanging tree located in the center of the casino.

Oh, and did I mention the lost souls?

Seriously.

They were everywhere.

Some nice. Some wicked. Some smelly.

While I couldn't actually see them (I'm a vampire, not the Ghost Whisperer), I could see the proof every time I turned around. We're talking bumps in the night, moving furniture, *eau de* rotting corpse and the occasional Kurt Cobain solo.

I'd received the complimentary stay from none other than Ixtab (affectionately known as Tabitha to all her BFFs), the Mayan Goddess of Death. She was my newest client at DED and had single-handedly saved my fantabulous ass from a demented sorcerer intent on pulling a *Silence of the Lambs*. I'd been so appreciative that I'd hooked her up on about a zillion dates. In return for all the fun she'd been having (she lived to par-tee), she'd hooked me up with an all-expense paid weekend getaway.

Unfortunately, she'd hooked up my entire family,

as well. I'd arrived on Friday, followed by my brothers, their wives, my father, my mother, a dozen members of my mother's Connecticut Huntress Club (that's synonymous for snotty, pretentious, narcissistic female BVs) and Remy Tremaine, chief of the Fairfield Police Department and my mother's latest attempt to find me the perfect born vampire.

Hence my excessive drinking.

I made one more attempt to check the time before giving up the effort and resting my head back against the down pillow. I tried to quiet the Nine Inch Nails drum solo pounding in my head. And that singing . . . Would someone shut that guy *up*?

Yes, it was definitely official. No more naked virgins. Or chocolate martinis. Or whiskey sunrises. Or those funny blue drinks with the cute little umbrellas. No lounging by the pool, soaking up the moon. No more gambling and begging my brothers for extra cash. No more missing Ty, who'd begged off at the last minute to chase bad guys.

I was booked on an evening flight back to New York and my fantabulous life. All the more reason to haul myself up and get moving. I still had to pack and visit the downstairs boutiques.

I pictured the Chanel rhinestone tank I'd spotted when I'd checked in and gathered my resolve.

Several painful moments later, I managed to throw my legs over the side of the bed. I blinked once. Twice. There.

I took a good look at the mess that surrounded me.

The open suitcase, the scattered clothes, the panties hanging from the light fixture—no, wait. That was my bra. My panties were nowhere in sight.

I had a fuzzy memory of the panties coming off in the elevator a split-second before Elvis entered the building, if you know what I mean.

Nah.

Denial rushed through me at the same time that I became acutely aware of the sound of running water and the verse of *Love Me Tender* that drifted from the bathroom.

". . . you have made my life complete and I love you sooooooo . . ."

What the . . . ?

As I pushed to my feet, my gaze snagged on the discarded silk blouse I'd been wearing last night and the round button pinned near the collar. *Here Comes the Bride!* blazed in bright pink letters and my stomach dropped to my knees. A few inches away, a white four-color brochure for the Hunka-Hunka Heartbreak Wedding Chapel lay crumpled on the thick carpet.

". . . all my dreams fullllll-filllled. For my darling, I love you and I always willlllll . . ."

The elevator. The fanged and fabulous Elvis. The missing panties. The button. The brochure.

The pieces started to fit into a weird, twisted puzzle that sent a jolt of dread through me. Anxiety made my legs tremble as I rummaged in my suitcase for my robe.

"Run," a soft voice whispered. "While you still can."

I whirled and found myself staring at the translucent image of a woman standing near the window. She looked to be in her forties with long red hair and a slim build. She wore a blue beaded dress that looked like she'd just been to the prom. Ouch.

"My mother picked the outfit," she said as if reading the horror in my gaze. "It was the only one left on account of Dewey here cut up my clothes after he popped a cap in my ass." She motioned to the apparition standing next to her.

He was tall and lanky with black hair and piercing black eyes. He'd probably been handsome at one point in his life, but now he had a hole in the middle of his forehead, which took off major GQ points.

"Jesus, Mona. Can't you forgive and forget?"

"I'm a ghost, Dewey. That's a little hard to forget."

"You act like it's my fault."

"It *is* your fault. You pulled the trigger."

"You bought the wrong orange juice," he said defensively. "I told her time and time again, buy the extra pulp." He shrugged his narrow shoulders. "It tastes more like the real thing."

"The store was out."

"You should have tried a different store."

"I told you to pay for those anger management classes instead of buying that tool set off of eBay. Then we wouldn't be in this mess."

"Ixtab took pity on us and brought us here instead of sending us down under," Dewey said.

"You mean she took pity on your sorry ass. I don't deserve to go down under. I'm not the one who shot my wife." Mona's gaze met mine. "Ixtab has a weakness for suicide victims. When Dewey, here, turned the gun on himself, she couldn't bring herself to doom him to hell. Something about a final moment of remorse. Now instead of spending my hereafter enjoying myself with free manicures and facials, I have to put up with Dewey, here, following me around." She shook her head. "Run," she said again. "Don't do this to yourself. Don't saddle yourself with one man for the rest of your existence."

"I don't know what you're talking about."

But I had the sinking feeling that I did.

My frantic brain noted a pair of discarded black pants and a Gucci jacket draped over the back of a nearby chair. A *Varooooom, I'm the Groom* sticker had been stuck to the lapel.

"Don't say I didn't warn you," she told me before glancing at her watch. "I'm due for a steam bath right now."

"I hate steam baths."

"So go do something else," she told Dewey.

"By myself?"

"Why me?" she muttered.

The couple disappeared and I became acutely aware of the hard glass dangling between my breasts.

I stared at the small crystal vial filled with a dark crimson liquid and a lump jumped into my throat.

Nuh-uh.

No way.

I didn't . . .

I couldn't . . .

Steam rushed at me as I pushed open the door and stepped into the marbled bathroom. The tile had been arranged in an ancient Mayan pattern, the sink a stone number that would have looked as if it had been plucked from the Mexican jungle if not for the ornate gold fixtures. The shower was one of those open designs with a digital keypad and multiple jets that blasted water from all angles.

Water sluiced over the muscular form of the man standing center stage. He was tall and toned and tanned. And very blond.

A small sound bubbled past my lips. Part cry. Part scream. Part *holy shit*.

He turned then. A pair of vivid green eyes met mine and I found myself staring at Fairfield's finest.

The small vial suspended around his neck confirmed my worst fear even before Remy opened his mouth. "There's my lovely eternity mate."

"But . . . ." I wanted to talk. To tell him he was crazy. To tell him I'd had way too many drinks. To tell him not no, but *hell* no.

Not him.

Not me.

Not *us*.

But suddenly, the only thing I could do was stand there, my heart pounding, my mind racing.

And then the truth weighed down, my legs gave out and I fainted dead-away.